You've Got My Number

You've Got My Number

Angela Barton

Where heroes are like chocolate – irresistible!

Published 2021 by Choc Lit Limited
Penrose House, Crawley Drive, Camberley, Surrey GU15 2AB, UK
www.choc-lit.com

ISBN 978-1-78189-458-3

Foreword

*It's said that life is stranger than fiction and this has proved
to be true on several occasions during my life. There is
a thread that runs through this story that many readers
might find unbelievable, or that it pushes the boundaries
of coincidence; but it happened to my family. All I will
say is that the thread revolves around parrots, and what
the doctor said to my husband some years ago, and the
coincidences that followed, are inspired from real life.*

Acknowledgements

Huge thanks to everyone at Choc Lit Publishing for
all your support, hard work and encouragement.
Special thanks to the Tasting Panel for believing that
You've Got My Number deserved to be published,
particularly those readers who passed the manuscript:
Kim H, Linda G, Claire W, Debbie J, Jenny K, Peggy H,
Joy S, Samantha E, Bianca B, Rosie F, Dimitra E,
Karen M, Margaret M, Cordy S, Vanessa W, Isabel S,
Melissa B, Hannah T, Stephanie H, Jane M, Stacy R,
Elisabeth H, Katie P, Liz R, Susan D, Lizzy D and
Dewi C. Thanks also must go to my editor, whose
talent and sharp eye enabled me to polish my book.

Thank you to the Romantic Novelists' Association and
their New Writers' Scheme. Your feedback, support
and guidance are invaluable to aspiring authors
and your readers' critiques are second to none.
Heartfelt thanks go to Frances, Andy, Gaynor and
Paul, members of my fiction group, Ampersands
and Ellipses. Your positive criticism, optimism and
encouragement helped me with every chapter.

I'd like to also express my gratitude to fellow Choc Lit
authors, Twitter and Facebook friends, and Apricot Plots'
members. I appreciate your support, faith and friendship.

Lastly, to my wonderful family.
You're always so supportive and encouraging.
Thank you. You're my world.

'The least initial deviation from the truth
is multiplied later a thousandfold.'
Aristotle

Chapter One

Daniel Cavanagh sat daydreaming out of a stone mullioned window, looking across the village green. The casement was wide open, allowing the intermittent breeze to flow into the room. The summer heatwave was making it difficult to concentrate on his artwork and a dull ache throbbed at his left temple. Rubbing the side of his head in small circles to ease the discomfort, he squinted through the heat haze that shimmered in the air above the stone ledge of his window. Absent-mindedly, he watched half a dozen red ants scuttling in circles, each one resembling an indecisive ink dot.

At the far end of the green he could see The Royal Oak, decorated with hanging baskets and their wooden benches slowly filling with customers. Daniel's stomach rumbled. He glanced at his watch and scratched a dried paint spot off the number six. It was five o'clock and he'd missed lunch, which would explain his hunger.

Standing up, he whisked red paint from his brush in a jar of fresh water, causing the clear liquid to blush. Then, tapping the brush three times on the rim, he laid it on the table. As he left his studio, he reached for an old paint-stained towel and wiped his hands as he made his way down the enormous carpeted staircase. It curved in a wide semi-circle as if embracing the large crystal chandelier that hung from the double height ceiling. After crossing the hall's parquet flooring, he pushed open the kitchen door.

His kitchen was large but homely, with cupboards of oak. An Aga took pride of place in a brick alcove and his mother's paintings hung on pale pistachio coloured walls. To one side of the room stood a large wooden table with eight chairs. Daniel threw the towel onto an old church pew, disturbing his two spaniels, Goya and Gogh. They had been curled nose to tail, but were now stretching and yawning.

'Sorry, girls, I lost track of time again,' said Daniel.

He walked towards the fridge and opened it. Both dogs padded over to him and sat at his feet, looking hopeful. They cocked their heads to one side.

'That look won't swing it.' He laughed. 'Walk first. Then food.'

He rubbed a tomato against his T-shirt and was buttering a slice of bread when the telephone interrupted him. Putting the knife down, he nestled the receiver into his shoulder and tilted his head to secure it there before continuing to make his sandwich.

'Hello.'

'Hiya, it's me.'

Daniel immediately recognised the familiar voice of his twin sister, Denise. 'Hi, Den. How are you?'

'Could be better. This morning I was sitting in casualty waiting for a raisin to be removed from up Sam's nose. And don't you dare laugh.'

'I'm not. Is asking how it got there a silly question?'

'Apparently, to a four-year-old it made perfect sense to see how far up it could go.'

'Is he okay? Did they get it out?'

'That's where it got embarrassing. We were assessed by a triage nurse and asked to wait to see a doctor. No sooner had she left than Sam sneezed and the raisin flew out of his nose and onto my lap. Before I knew what he was doing, he'd picked it up and eaten it. I dragged him out of there pretty damn quickly. I had to escape before the doctor turned up to see a giggling child chewing on the dangerous obstruction.'

Daniel laughed as he placed two slices of ham on the

buttered bread. 'I suppose you could call that Sam's *raison d'être*.'

'Oh, that's terrible.'

'Sorry, I couldn't resist.'

'Anyway, I was ringing to find out if you'd thought of a date for your exhibition yet? I need to give my workaholic husband plenty of notice to book the time off.'

Daniel sighed. 'I don't know, Den. It'll be some months yet. I'm still at the making lists stage. I've got some canvasses to finish and I haven't found a caterer. Then I've got the invitations to design and get to the printers. It's looking like November, I'm afraid. Trouble is it'll be winter and I don't really want a hundred or more people trudging mud inside.'

'Why don't you hire a marquee?'

'A glorified tent? You've got to be kidding. People will freeze to death.'

'No they won't. A marquee has more than one layer to it and is incredibly weatherproof and insulated. We went to a ball in one a couple of years ago for Simon's company Christmas do, and they had huge heaters. There was snow outside and we were all as warm as toast wearing strappy ball gowns inside.'

'You didn't tell me my brother-in-law was a cross-dresser.'

Denise giggled. 'The women, you idiot.'

Daniel took a few moments to mull this over while he cut his sandwich in half. He sat down at the table and his dogs curled themselves around his feet. 'It sounds like it could be an option. I could whitewash the back dining room, the one with the patio doors leading out into the garden. That room could be the gallery, and the marquee could be just outside the doors for the food and drink.'

'And dancing.'

'At an art exhibition?'

'Do you want the guests to look at your work, have a bite

to eat and disappear somewhere else to party? You should hire a DJ and install a dance floor inside the marquee. Honestly, it'll make all the difference. In fact, why don't you combine our birthday in December with your exhibition? You can decorate the house all Christmassy and make it a party as well as an art exhibition. Friends and family will be coming anyway, so why not make it a birthday to remember?'

Daniel raised his eyebrows as he sat in front of his untouched sandwich. 'For a sister, you come up with some pretty good ideas, you know? Okay that's the date solved, the seventh of December it is. Thanks, Den. I don't suppose you're looking for a personal assistant's post, are you? I could do with you to help me with the rest of my list. In fact, the rest of my life!'

'Sorry, Picasso, my hours are full of two small boys. Why don't you ask in The Royal Oak for some catering advice? Anyway, I'll let you get on. Think about the marquee.'

'I will. Great to hear from you. Say hello to Simon and the boys for me. Bye.'

Daniel lived alone at The Rookery, a large, impressive building adorned with turrets, mullioned arched windows and built in ten acres of manicured grounds. Six years previously, the papers had reported on the tragic motorway accident that killed his parents. His father, Robert Cavanagh, had been a renowned architect and his death alongside that of his wife, Helen, had made front-page news.

At the time of the accident, Daniel had been travelling the world; or running away from his guilt, depending on whose viewpoint you listened to. He was struggling to settle somewhere permanently because he blamed himself for a firework accident that resulted in his best friend's loss of sight in one eye. His incessant travelling assuaged his anxiety and eased his fitful nights, so that eventually what was meant to have been a few months travelling had turned into three years away from home as he'd tried to outrun his demons.

His sketchbook had been his treasured possession. He was passionate about capturing the essence of each country and the spirit of the people on paper. He painted whenever he stayed long enough in one place, encapsulating a look of wonderment, a fearful frown or a euphoric grin with swift movements of his well-chewed pencil. These pictorial memories were then wrapped and shipped back home to be stored at The Rookery by his parents.

Following his parents' death, Daniel's guilt had become more potent when mixed with grief. He refused to see anyone except his twin sister for weeks. Denise lived on the outskirts of London with her husband Simon and one young son at the time, a nephew Daniel had never seen due to his travelling. During his sister's frequent visits, they'd spent hours sifting through old photographs, smiling as they remembered happier times and wiping away tears at the cruel reality of the present. She'd helped him organise personal papers and choose sentimental keepsakes. Their father's study had been full of drawings and plans of buildings that would now never be built. Creations aborted and rolled up into cardboard tubes before being given the chance of existence in some burgeoning metropolis in the world.

They'd walked for miles across the surrounding fields, each sharing their guilt and sadness as freely as they'd shared their mother's womb thirty-two years earlier. As family ties beckoned, Denise's visits had grown less frequent. To help fill the seemingly endless evenings, Daniel painted and drank his father's collection of whiskey and port. If he wasn't daubing a canvas with dark, melancholic pigments, he was staring at the television in an alcoholic stupor. It was usually during these long evenings when Daniel thought about his parents and his estranged best friend, Sean, most vividly. He tormented himself with unresolved guilt while watching the pulsing orange embers in the hearth collapse into grey ash. He blamed his absence for his parents' death and his wrong decision for Sean's loss of sight.

It was on one particularly tormented evening, several months following his parents' accident, when the number three took on a greater significance in Daniel's life. As he sat alone listening to the grandfather clock's unremitting ticking, he became fixated on that particular number. Two accidents. Didn't bad things happen in threes?

As he'd stood up to go to bed, he'd stopped at the library door. His eyes had lingered on the light switch as he pondered a theory. Perhaps if he switched it three times, it would prevent the third disaster from happening.

OFF.

ON.

OFF.

Having said goodbye to Denise, Daniel picked up his sandwich and bit deeply into the soft bread, groaning with pleasure while he chewed. Goya and Gogh stared at him, licking their lips and checking the floor for any dropped crumbs. He stretched in his chair and ran his fingers vigorously backwards and forwards through his hair.

'Okay. How about that walk I promised you?'

With the dogs on leads, Daniel opened the front door. He turned to close it before checking that it was locked. He tried the door a second time. It was still locked. Doubt tormented him, forcing him to try the door for a third time. Immediately the anxiety disappeared and he relaxed.

Since his parents' death, six warm summers had diluted

the colour of Daniel's demons, almost as if the sun had bleached them. But an underlying anxiety persisted. On most days he still felt the need to turn light switches on or off three times and still made three repetitions of several everyday actions. He always checked three times that The Rookery was properly locked and still found himself picking up the third newspaper from a pile in Jackson's Store or choosing a trolley from the third stacked line at the supermarket. It wasn't an obsession that stood out in a crowd. Only he knew of his little idiosyncrasies, and although he knew these foibles weren't common, he was thankful that they gave him some order in an unpredictable world.

He walked beneath the canopy of trees in his front garden, out of a set of iron gates and on to the cricket pitch opposite The Rookery. Although it was nearly five thirty, the sun's heat felt good on his face and eased the ache in his temple. Insects droned overhead, drawing his eyes skyward. White contrails sliced through the sky like a giant game of noughts and crosses. Daniel inhaled deeply, relaxing his shoulders before letting his dogs off their leads, grinning as they tore off across a jigsaw of parched and cracked turf.

Chapter Two

Tess Fenton was scraping parsnips in the kitchen. She pursed her lips while considering her closest friend's question. 'I can't remember,' she told Holly.

'You're kidding me!'

'I'm not. I'm being serious.'

'Take a wild guess.'

'Maybe a couple of months.'

Sitting on the worktop, Holly stopped swinging her legs and leaned forwards, her mouth agape. 'Months?'

'It's not compulsory, you know.'

'Maybe not – if you're eighty!'

Tess chuckled as she patted her friend's legs by way of asking her to move them. Holly bent her knees so that they touched her chin, giving Tess room to retrieve a serrated knife from the drawer.

'Admit it, Tess, it's not normal. You're both still in your twenties, only been dating for a couple of years and already you can't remember when you last had sex.'

'Okay, yes! I admit things have changed over the past year.' Tess top and tailed the sweet-smelling parsnips, blinking each time the knife hit the chopping board. 'Blake drinks too much. He's lazy. He's been using pretentious words since he's been promoted and he chats online with *Star Trek* forums. Hardly grounds for ending things but... we've both changed since we met.'

'Wow.'

'Well, you did ask.'

'I didn't mean to upset you. I was only teasing.'

Tess stopped chopping and rested her hands on the worktop. 'But that's just it, don't you see? I'm not upset. It's as if we're two jigsaw pieces and every so often I have to chip pieces off myself to fit into our relationship. You can only adjust so many times before you're not being true to yourself.' She shrugged, took a roasting tin out of the oven and tentatively peeled open the steaming foil parcel with her fingertips.

'Have you talked to him about it? He may not realise how you feel. Can't you explain that your relationship isn't healthy?'

'Healthy?' Tess leaned backwards to let the billowing steam escape from the foil. 'I'd say there's more life in this half-cooked bird.' She poked the chicken and watched the oily blood ooze down its pale skin, then turned to look at her friend. 'I think it's time to face facts and end things with Blake. I want to change my job and bake for a living and find someone that fits my original jigsaw shape. It's time for a new start.'

In the hallway, Blake was resting his forehead against the kitchen door surround, inhaling the bittersweet tang of waxed pine. Sliding down the wall, he sat on his heels. What was the old adage? Eavesdroppers seldom hear anything good about themselves.

A few minutes earlier, he'd let himself in to Tess's cottage. Despite the frustrations of a hot day with a high pollen count and having run out of cigarettes, the smell of roast chicken when he'd entered had lifted his mood. As he'd removed his imitation brogues, he'd heard the soft mutterings of Tess and Holly. It was only when his name was mentioned that he crept towards the narrow gap left by the open kitchen door.

Oblivious now to their conversation, Blake held his head in his hands and was hyperventilating as quietly as he could. Tess was going to leave him. His face felt hot. Pins and needles prickled his fingertips and his eyes stung. He was horrified at the thought that he might cry. God, he hadn't cried since... since Spock died in *The Wrath of Khan*.

He needed a plan.

And quickly.

Several days later, Tess closed her eyes and faced the warm slice of sunlight that cut across hers and Blake's table in a local coffee house. She concentrated on the kaleidoscope of colours behind her eyelids, caused by the hot June sun flickering through a canopy of leaves on the high street. They'd timed it perfectly, pouncing on the still warm tan leather armchairs just as the previous occupants had vacated them. Blake had been talking into his mobile for the past five minutes, so with her elbows on the table, Tess rested her cheeks on her clenched fists that stretched her mouth into an imitation smile.

Turning away from the comforting beam of sunlight, she distractedly pulled apart the remnants of her mozzarella and tomato panini. The nutty smell of coffee and sweet aroma of melted cheese hung in the air amidst the general hubbub of conversation and clattering of crockery. She didn't know why she'd agreed to meet Blake during her precious lunch hour, especially now that she'd admitted to herself and Holly that things had changed between the two of them. It wasn't just that they were monotonously coasting through their relationship, it felt like their viewpoints and horizons had shifted over time, each diverging in different directions like tectonic plates.

Tess scrutinised her boyfriend over the rim of her coffee cup. Admittedly he was still attractive despite the extra weight his desk job and excessive drinking had added. She watched him lean backwards in his chair, one hand clutching his mobile to his ear and his other hand supporting the back of his neck. His generous stomach revealed a button ready to burst free from his shirt. Tess smiled to herself, amused that she had a lot in common with that button; they were both at a loose end and letting the pressure get to them.

Despite the fact that she was sitting with her boyfriend, Tess saw Blake's eyes linger on the tight black skirt that looked vacuum-packed onto the pert buttocks of their waitress. The girl's hips banged against an adjacent table as she moved backwards and forwards, cleaning the surface in circular movements. He seemed mesmerised and unblinking as he stammered into his phone.

'Yes, yes I'm still here. I was distracted by—'

Tess noted that at least he had the manners to shift uncomfortably when they exchanged glances. She didn't feel jealous. Perhaps, disappointed.

'Great,' said Blake into his mobile. 'If you can navigate your way around that obstacle, I'll shout you a bottle to celebrate. Affirmative.'

Affirmative? Tess nearly spluttered her coffee on the table. Wasn't that what Mr Spock said instead of a simple, *yes*? She lowered her latte and tried to sound interested. 'Big business deal?'

Blake laid his mobile on the table. 'Halcott Manor's coming on to the market at long last. It's a huge pile in the Vale of Belvoir and I've been sweet-talking the owners for months. Have you any idea how much commission I'd make if I sold that place? I could say goodbye to my overdraft for starters and then I'd book a ticket to Amsterdam for Kent's stag weekend in November. Now Henderson's Agency has got wind of it. Parasites. I'd better ring Kent at the office to see if he can head them off somehow.'

Tess's shoulders sank as Blake picked up his mobile again and called the office. She watched him lick a finger and stab at the remaining crumbs on his plate, before nibbling them off his crusted fingertip. He crunched them between his front teeth. She was sick of hearing about Kent's stag weekend. It wasn't that she minded him going away; it was more the fact that for the past two years he'd made excuses whenever she'd suggested that they should go on holiday. Nor did she think for one minute that Blake was looking forward to perusing the clog collections in the markets of Amsterdam or choosing the latest hue in tulip bulbs. She knew his idea of heaven would be smoking dodgy cigarettes and looking at even dodgier women sitting in red-fringed window parlours wearing next to nothing.

She sipped her coffee and watched Blake probe his teeth with his tongue. She noticed that the loose shirt button was now missing and a hairy white mound of flesh was protruding through the gap. She thought the escaping bulge of skin resembled a forgotten marshmallow that had become lost under a bed and was now covered in carpet fibres. She shuddered involuntarily.

Blake snapped his mobile shut. 'He's not picking up. You cold, Tezza? The air con is a bit much, isn't it?'

'I'm fine.'

'You shivered.'

'Did I?'

'Want another coffee?'

Tess shook her head, wondering why a small golden crumb nestling in the corner of his mouth irritated her so much. Perhaps it was her fault, she thought. Maybe she was just too critical. Wasn't he working hard at the estate agency? Didn't he call her this morning and invite her to lunch? Nevertheless. She'd had enough for the moment.

'No, thanks,' she said. 'I think I'll make a move.' Reaching under her chair, she grabbed her handbag. 'I'm heading back to work.'

'Already? What about lunch?'

'Lunch? It's been more like a telephone meeting. Why did you invite me here if you don't have time to talk?'

'I'm sorry.' He held up his hands as if surrendering. 'I know you're fed up and things aren't very exciting at the moment, but I promise things will get better soon. I wish you could be pleased that I've got this promotion. I'm trying to show you that I can work hard. For us.'

'I know. And I am proud of you. You've done well.'

'By chasing commissions, I'm laying the foundations for our future. Isn't that what you want?'

Tess sighed and leaned back against her chair. 'I don't know.'

'What do you mean, you don't know?'

'Nothing. I don't know. I need to get back to work.'

'Tezza wait.' He reached across the table and looked into her eyes. 'Tell me we're going to be okay.'

She shrugged her shoulders and opened her mouth to speak, but no words came. Where could she start? Their relationship had faded in the same way a vibrant painting would lose its colour if left in sunlight. Gradually and unnoticed. Diminished through lack of care and attention. And now he was asking her to explain this in the short time they had left of her lunch hour.

'Now's not the time, Blake. I'll be late.'

'Well, don't say that I didn't ask. I'm not a mind reader, you know?'

'I'm just saying that we don't have time for a *where's our relationship going* conversation.'

'I'm not asking for a deep and meaningful speech. Just that we're okay.'

'Would you settle for, just okay?'

'I can't talk to you when you're like this.' He leaned back and folded his arms.

'Like what?'

'Like you're determined to see the worst in everything I say.'

She sat forwards and whispered. 'You may not have noticed, but the reason it's gone quiet in here is because everyone's listening to us. I'm not sharing my private life with strangers any longer.'

Blake made a point of looking around the room. Exasperated, Tess stood up and grabbed her cardigan from the back of her chair. 'I'm going back to work. That way neither of us will say anything we might regret. Bye.'

'Tess?'

'What?'

He shrugged, sheepishly. 'I don't have any cash. It's the end of the month. I'm a bit short.'

'You and me both, Blake. You and me both.'

Tess didn't give him chance to answer. She hurried out of the air-conditioned coffee shop and into the sticky heat of the day. She didn't look up or wave as she passed him sitting in the window seat. Her lips were pursed into a straight thin line and tears stung her eyes. Thanks to his loud self-important voice and obvious appreciation for their waitress's tight skirt, they'd been the comic entertainment for lunchtime diners.

Marching back to work, her stride slowed as realisation dawned. She'd fallen out of love with him. It was as simple as that. It wasn't his increased BMI. It was him. His being. The part of him that made him who he was, and, more importantly, who he would become. Suddenly everything became clear. She didn't want to meet him in her lunch hour or have his photograph looking back at her every time she opened her purse. She'd had enough. She resolved to finish with him before the end of the month.

That gave her six days!

Chapter Three

The front façade of The Blue Olive was mock Tudor in design and a large bay window reflected the street scene in the afternoon sunshine. A triangular roof gable flaunted exposed beams that were sunk into white rendering. A rainbow of pastas in an assortment of shapes sat alongside olives, ciabatta loaves and freshly made pizzas. It all made a mouth-watering window display that lured many customers in through its doorway.

Tess and Holly had worked at the Italian delicatessen for several years and had been best friends for more than twenty. They never ceased to find it amusing that their friendship had begun by the offering of a cheesy Wotsit!

Tess pushed the shop door open and held up a starfish of fingers to her colleague, Margaret, who was serving at the till. 'Five minutes.'

Once inside the staff room she saw Holly rinsing her cup at the sink.

'Hi. How was Captain Kirk?' asked Holly.

'On another planet. Loud, embarrassing and still calling me Tezza no matter how many times I say I hate it. It makes me sound like a football coach.'

'You haven't changed your mind, then?'

'No. It's just made me more determined to take control of my life. Will you come back for some dinner after work? I'd already invited him and I don't think I could bear another evening with just the two of us. I promise you'll get double portions of dessert!'

After work, Tess locked the door of The Blue Olive and linked arms with Holly. They walked away from the hustle and bustle of Maddox Square, towards Tess's old Mini Mayfair. The afternoon had been slow and boring, but the realisation that her relationship was nearing its end had punctuated Tess's thoughts like a newsflash interrupting mundane programmes.

Although it was early evening, the lack of breeze and the high buildings swathed in reflective glass, seemed to make the heat more oppressive than earlier in the day. They reached her little cream car that was as old as she was, but not wearing quite so well. Its edges were tinged with rust and a few dents on the bodywork lay testimony to the occasional scrapes it had been involved in over the years.

'Phew! It's like a sauna in here,' said Holly, winding down the window and gasping out of it for added drama.

Tess pulled out of her parking space, clicked on the radio and within seconds, the breeze cooled their flushed faces. In between singing along to the music, they discussed Doug the deliveryman, whom Holly had a serious crush on, and her flatmate who was addicted to cleaning.

'Honestly, she polishes tins before recycling them and sponges the vacuum cleaner before putting it back in the cupboard.'

Tess laughed as she negotiated a roundabout. 'I've no sympathy with you. I've asked you to come and live with me and help out with the rent. The only thing we'll be polishing off this evening is a bottle of cold Sauvignon blanc and a box of Quality Street.'

'Now that's my kind of housework. I just wished you didn't live so far away from town.'

An easy silence followed as Tess drove and Holly gazed out of the window. As they left the city outskirts behind, the scenery became greener. Shops and offices gave way to villages and countryside. Children ran along the pavement clutching melting ice-lollies and families struck up barbecues, making the most of the long hot summer's evening. The sweet smell of melting tarmac filled the car as Holly leaned out of the window to watch a hot air balloon pass silently over a golf course.

Thirty minutes later, Tess's car rattled to a standstill outside Rose Cottage, in the village of Halston. The rent was comfortably affordable because most people didn't want a morning commute in rush hour into the city of Nottingham. But Tess didn't mind. For her, living in Halston was like living in a painting. A narrow winding road curled around the village green, where grasses and wild flowers were given free rein to do as they pleased. By day, cows lolled and grazed on the common land, hemmed in by a small electric fence that crackled its warning at passers-by.

The grass of the cricket pitch had been manicured to a smooth velvet finish, where birds dotted its lawn looking like bored fielders. The embattled clock tower of St Mary's Church rose above Halston's homes, protecting the eternally sleeping villagers beneath their headstones. At the heart of the green stood The Royal Oak, a village pub that swelled with the laughter of friends and family as they shared news and embellished stories.

Tess had only moved out of her flat in town three months earlier, but she thought that renting this tiny cottage was the best decision she had made in a long while. Around the gooseberry coloured front door grew a sinewy lemon rose bush that exuded a heavenly aroma. The cottage was small, but Tess loved it.

It had just gone six and having unpegged and folded towels from the washing line, they both agreed that this next hour was to be a Blake-free zone. Tess had talked all afternoon about their relationship and was now sick of the subject.

Soon they were criss-crossing the village green, dodging drying cowpats.

'This is disgusting,' Holly shrieked, as she sidestepped another pile of dung and disturbed a flurry of bluebottles.

'You're in the country now. Smell the flowers, listen to the birds and look at the beautiful scenery.'

'Thank you, David Attenborough. I'll remind you of that when we're cleaning our shoes later.'

They were still laughing when they reached the benches in the front garden of The Royal Oak. Holly went inside to order their drinks, while Tess sat down at a bench in the shade of a tree's canopy. A gentle breeze was blowing and shadows were growing longer. She raised her chin and breathed in the perfume of the blossoming trees.

Something caught Tess's attention as she gazed across the green towards the cricket pitch. A shaft of sunlight momentarily penetrated the leaves and blinded her for a second, making her squint. Meanwhile, Holly walked slowly towards the bench, balancing two glasses of Pimm's, crammed with fruit and chinking with ice.

Holly carefully placed the drinks on the table and pushed one towards Tess. 'What're you looking at?' She sat down and followed the direction of Tess's gaze.

A man was walking across the cricket pitch with two dogs running close by. Dressed in a white T-shirt and dark jeans, the man repeatedly bent to pick up a stick for one of his dogs. Each time he threw the stick, he'd push his dark hair away from his face and occasionally his T-shirt would lift to reveal a taut stomach. Pimm's momentarily forgotten, they stared transfixed.

'I wish I had a dog,' said Tess.

'Dogs?'

'Just one.'

'Are you serious? Adonis is striding across Halston cricket pitch and you're looking at his dogs?' Holly shook her head. 'Tell me he's your neighbour and he's single.'

Tess took a sip of her drink then fished out a slice of cucumber from her glass. 'I've seen him once before coming out of Jackson's Store.' She slowly turned the slice between her fingers, biting the dark green ring of peel while leaving a fleshy star-shaped slice.

'And?'

'And nothing. I don't know who he is. I suppose he must be local if he shops at Jackson's and walks his dogs here.'

Every now and then Holly would swivel in her seat to look at the man and his dogs. They watched him laugh when one of his dogs lay panting on the grass, refusing to fetch the stick. He crouched, sitting on his heels and patted his exhausted spaniel.

Tess laughed. 'You're incorrigible.' She watched her friend who was leaning on her elbows and resting her chin on her cupped palms. Holly had a pretty face with delicate features and blue eyes. Her blonde highlighted hair wasn't the yellowy-blonde hair that looked disastrous after a cheap lean-over-the-bath session at home. Holly spent a fortune every six weeks on professional highlights and a trim off her shoulder length bob. Her style was only let down by the fact that she rarely left herself enough time to blow-dry her hair. So there she sat, looking dreamily at the man and his dogs, with sections of her hair sticking out while others curled under.

'Don't look. Sit still. Oh my God, he's coming this way.' Holly smoothed her hair and sat upright.

Twenty seconds passed. They sat, heads bowed, pretending to drink.

'Where is he?' whispered Holly.

'By the boundary line.'

'Where is he now?'

'Shhh!'

They both sucked on their straws, eyes lowered. Two

spaniels ran past their bench followed shortly by their owner. As he strode past them, they both looked up.

'Lovely evening.' He smiled, looking directly at Tess.

She felt a rush of blood to her face. 'Yes.'

He walked on.

'Yes?' squeaked Holly, mimicking her friend when he was out of earshot. 'All you can say is, "yes"?'

Tess didn't answer. She turned and watched the man's back view stride away. She noticed the valley of the line of his spine under his T-shirt, made by the muscles on his back rising up on either side. She watched his hair move in the breeze. Something inexplicable had happened in that split second they'd met each other's glance. She couldn't think of a single witty thing to say to Holly. She just sat gazing in his direction, watching as he walked away across the village green.

Chapter Four

It was the last day of June and Tess hadn't seen Blake for several days. She'd invited him for dinner that evening in order to explain why she wanted to end their relationship. She knew it was a strange way to end things but she also thought that after two years together, Blake deserved more than a text to say goodbye. For goodness' sake, weren't there parties for celebrating divorce and greeting cards from the dog or the cat these days? Surely she could cook Blake a *you're dumped* meal and add a little explanation into the pot.

Tess had blown caution and finance to the wind with a huge shop at Sainsbury's. She'd bought an ocean of seafood, a bottle of wine, a date and walnut loaf, blackberries the size of fifty pence pieces and dark organic chocolate. She was going to cook his favourite meal of seafood linguine and blackberry and apple crumble. It didn't stretch her culinary skills, but once, when they'd played a game of What If, he'd chosen this meal to be his last request meal. It somehow seemed appropriate.

Tess had been descaling fish and peeling prawns for ten minutes before she realised that she'd left the linguine in the staff room.

'Damn.'

She held her forehead in frustration. She could hardly ask Blake to pick up his *you're dumped* ingredients himself, so she didn't have a choice. She'd have to drive a couple of miles to Jackson's Store in the next village and as it was now nearly six o'clock already, she'd have to get a move on before the shop closed. Tess hurriedly covered the prawns with a food net, washed her hands and grabbed her handbag from the kitchen table.

Soon she was driving along the narrow winding country roads, her mind awash with thoughts of how to finish with Blake. Perhaps she should explain in the *Star Trek* terminology he was familiar with. 'I need space, this is the final frontier.'

Tess slowed her car down to a walking pace, enabling a large delivery van to edge past her on the other side of the narrow twisting lane. Driving closer to the lane's hedges, she cringed as twigs squeaked along her car's windows and paintwork. In her rear-view mirror she saw a black Land Rover Defender pull up behind her as the delivery van manoeuvred his way past them. She peered into her rear-view mirror again to look at the driver. He looked vaguely familiar.

Catching sight of her face in the mirror, she stared in horror. Her reflection was crusty and peeling, reminding her of Marlow in *The Singing Detective*. How could she have suddenly developed psoriasis of such monstrous proportions? On closer inspection, and to her great relief, she recognised fish scales.

The road was now clear and a quick beep from the Land Rover behind only gave her a few seconds to brush the scales off her face. She slipped the gear stick into first, pressed her foot on the accelerator and continued on to the store.

Indicating left, she turned into the small parking area outside Jackson's. She was looking in her handbag, hunting for a mint, when the Land Rover pulled alongside her. It towered above her Mini, its paintwork gleaming like melted tar in the bright sunshine. She was still searching through her messy bag when the Defender door slammed shut on the driver's side. Tess looked up and saw two dogs rubbing dribble against the inside of the rear window. Recognising them, her heartbeat quickened.

Then she saw him. He walked so close to the front of her bonnet that she could almost see his eyelashes. Tess breathed deeply and looked back at the two furry faces that were panting in much the same way that she was.

What should she do now? She needed pasta. Should she wait until he'd left? Surely she couldn't come face-to-face with him without her make-up on and smelling of prawns? But it was getting late and she had to prepare the crumble before Blake arrived. She had no option. She'd just have to dodge him in the aisles. Her heart was hammering. She opened the car door, climbed out and walked towards the shop. Tess hesitated. Her hand rested on the flaking paintwork before she took a deep breath and pushed open the door.

A smell of spices filled the air. She couldn't see him but there were only five small aisles so he couldn't be far away. It was a small intimate shop and she was beginning to waver again and think about hiding in the car until he'd left. Walking alongside shelving that displayed loaves, rolls and cakes, Tess's eyes scanned ahead. The pasta wasn't on this aisle so there wouldn't be a quick getaway. Turning into the next aisle, she stopped. He was sitting on his heels studying a dog food label, with two pints of semi-skimmed milk tucked under one arm.

Tess rocked on her feet, not knowing whether to back away, or take a step closer. Slowly, almost tiptoeing, she moved forwards. He was now six feet away and thankfully still engrossed in the ingredients on the can. Carefully, she passed behind him, holding an in-breath. She almost brushed against his arm. His hair was tousled as if he'd just got out of bed and, on closer inspection, she noticed that his clothes were splattered and smeared with paint. Perhaps he'd been decorating. She passed behind him but didn't dare look back.

Around the next aisle she spotted sauce mixes and dried

pasta. Having quickly snatched up a packet of linguine, she took it straight to the till. With a bit of luck she'd be out of there before he needed to pay. Tess placed the packet on the counter.

'Hello, is that all?' asked Mr Jackson.

'Hi. Yes, thanks.'

'Have you settled in?'

'What? Oh yes, thank you. Just cooking?'

'Anything special?'

'Seafood linguine. I'm in a bit of a rush actually.' Tess discreetly turned to see if the man with the dogs was in sight. Thankfully he wasn't.

'You youngsters are always in a rush. Do you need a mobile top up?'

'Just the pasta, thanks.'

'Stamps?'

'Not today.'

'How about a lottery ticket? Might be your lucky day.'

'Believe me, it isn't. Just the pasta, please.'

'Okay. That'll be one pound, ten pence, please.'

Tess lifted her bag onto the counter and felt for her purse. 'Won't be a sec. My purse is here somewhere.' She searched manically through her cavernous handbag. Hot with embarrassment, she emptied the detritus of her bag bit by bit onto the counter. A packet of tissues, a lipstick, a mobile phone, a set of keys, a half-eaten Kit Kat, several out of date receipts, a packet of painkillers, three biros and some mints. No purse.

'I'm really sorry. I must have left my purse at home. Can I bring in the money tomorrow?'

Mr Jackson leaned forwards, sniffed and furrowed his brow. He opened his mouth to say something, but was interrupted.

'Here, my treat.'

A paint-splattered hand placed a two pound coin on the counter. In front of them all lay the contents of her bag looking like a car boot sale. She knew without looking that the deep voice and tanned hand belonged to *him*. By now her face was on fire with shame as she piled everything back into her bag. She couldn't ignore him, so she quickly glanced at him. Yes – he was gorgeous.

She looked away. 'I couldn't possibly, but thank you. I'm sure Mr Jackson wouldn't mind if I called in tomorrow with the money.' She gave the storeowner a wide-eyed look, trying to convey an urgent telepathic message to him. His mind obviously wasn't receiving the signal, so she smiled through gritted teeth, daring him to say no with her glare.

Mr Jackson was oblivious to her embarrassment. His pale eyes were scrutinising her face. 'I'm closing in ten minutes and I need to cash up and make the till balance. Could you owe this gentleman instead?'

Accepting defeat and wanting to escape this unbearable embarrassment as soon as possible, she accepted the coin without looking up again. 'Thank you very much. I'll get it back to you.'

'Please, don't worry. I'm happy to help.'

Tess held out her hand for the change, picked up the pasta, said a very quick goodbye to the two men then hurried out of the store.

Turning on the ignition, she reversed and sped home leaving a whirlwind of dust in the car park. She stopped outside Rose Cottage, turned off the engine and took a deep breath. What must she have looked like? As if to clarify her thoughts, Tess pulled down the mirror behind her sun visor and studied her reflection. As she peered at the crusty fish scales decorating her cheeks, the Black Land Rover roared past her car.

She groaned in despair.

Chapter Five

Blake shook hands with the glamorous owner of the house he had just valued. 'Thanks for showing me around. I'll get a letter in the post to you confirming my valuation.'

The woman seemed reluctant to release his hand. 'I'm in most days.'

Blake smirked, used to lonely housewives flirting with him. 'I'll see what I can do.'

The woman held his gaze while slowly closing her front door. He turned and walked down the garden path. Still got the old Snipes' charm, he thought. He sneezed then muttered to himself as he opened the door. Sitting in the driver's seat, he sniffed deeply.

'Bloody pollen.' He opened the two front windows, loosened his tie and stretched across the passenger seat for his cigarettes.

Blake was twenty-nine and had an air about him that swayed between self-confidence and arrogance. His cropped hair was fair and despite needing to lose a few pounds, he was an attractive man who made many a female vendor fall over their words in a fluster. He'd been working at Price and Finkle Estate Agency for nine years, having joined them after leaving college. He had slowly worked his way up the corporate ladder, from general dogsbody to associate director. A position he wished would impress Tess more than it seemed to.

Home was a small modern mews house in the centre of town and although he'd tried numerous times to persuade Tess to move in with him, she'd stubbornly decided to rent a tiny cottage out in the sticks, instead. You could dress it up all you liked by calling it Rose Cottage, he thought, but the fact was that the air smelt of cow shit and the village green was dotted with the stuff. To add insult to injury, the fields of floating pollen and exploding seeds made his hay fever worse. Tess called it nature's loveliness. He called it nature's slovenliness. Surely in his late twenties he should be at the peak of fitness and health? Instead, he usually felt drained and drowsy by coughing in the city or sneezing in the countryside.

An off-the-cuff remark by a colleague who'd mentioned smoking, coughing and cancer in one shocking sentence, had forced him to book a doctor's appointment that evening, after work. His constant fatigue had been affecting his job and he had made several silly mistakes recently. It hadn't helped his clients' confidence in him when he'd posted house descriptions and valuation confirmation letters to the wrong addresses. That very morning, one couple had taken their business elsewhere after they'd received a letter describing their newly renovated barn conversion as, '*tired and in need of extensive upgrading*'. He'd been in trouble at work for his mistake and knew it was time to visit his doctor.

But it wasn't only his health that Blake had on his mind. He'd felt uneasy since eavesdropping on Tess and Holly's conversation the previous week. His attempt to show her just how witty and professional he was, had backfired miserably in the local coffee shop. He'd tried to make her feel possessive with his talk of Amsterdam. He'd tried to make her laugh at silly remarks that would have had her giggling last year. He'd tried to make her see that he possessed sharp business acumen while on the telephone to the office. But nothing had worked. She'd stormed off and although he'd gone round to eat that same night, she'd been distant and her friend Holly had played gooseberry.

They hadn't seen each other for the past few days and

had only communicated through a couple of stilted phone conversations. Tess had continued to make excuses not to see him and it had surprised him just how much he'd missed her. He was beginning to wonder if she had dumped him without saying as much but to his great relief, Tess had phoned him that morning to invite him round for some seafood linguine. Surely that was a good sign? After all, you don't go to the trouble of cooking dinner for someone you want to finish with, do you? Let alone choose to cook their favourite meal.

Later that day, Blake stood outside the doctor's surgery sighing with a huge sense of relief. He was suffering from asthma, not the unmentionable – not the dreaded C word. In fact, the appointment also had an additional benefit. Tess knew that he'd been suffering with a persistent cough and she'd urged him to see someone about it. Unwittingly, she had set up the backdrop for his iniquitous lie. A deceit that he hoped he wouldn't have to carry out, but one that he would willingly go ahead with if it prevented her from ending their relationship.

Tess replaced the receiver and sighed. She had rushed for nothing. Blake had called to tell her that he'd been delayed due to an appointment and he wouldn't get to Halston until later. She looked across at the neatly laid table, anxiety gnawing away in the pit of her stomach. She'd hoped that by eight o'clock they'd have finished their dinner and would be hugging goodbye and promising to keep in touch on Facebook. No dramas. No tears. Just two adults shaking hands and heading off in opposite directions. Fat chance!

She reluctantly put the raw seafood in the fridge and covered over the other ingredients on the worktop. It was nearly half past six and he wasn't arriving for another hour.

Weary from the heat, she picked up the packet of pasta and laid the cool plastic packaging against her forehead. She felt sick with nerves about telling Blake they were over and confused that the man in the shop had unsettled her in some way. Tess could feel the throb of a headache threatening and decided to relax and switch off for half an hour with a glass of Australian wine and an Australian soap. Damn Blake. He couldn't even turn up on time to be dumped!

Tess threw the packet of linguine down onto the worktop in frustration. A jar of rosemary fell from the spice rack and sprinkled its contents onto a parcel that had been sitting next to the kettle. Tess began to clear up the herbs and caught sight of the brown paper package while holding a palm full of rosemary. She had forgotten about the parcel that the postman had entrusted to her to deliver to Mrs Campbell across the road. Her elderly neighbour had been out when he'd knocked on her door that morning on his round. That was it then. There'd be no *Neighbours* watched on television now. Instead she'd have to muster the energy to actually visit one.

Tess crossed the road carrying the parcel. She'd only spoken to her neighbour half a dozen times since moving to Rose Cottage in March, but she was a sweet old lady. The gravel on Mrs Campbell's path crunched with each footstep, making Tess grimace at the thought of it scuffing her heels. Seconds after knocking, she could see a shadow shuffling towards her through the stained glass window in the front door.

'Hello, Mrs Campbell. The postman asked me to pass this on to you.'

'Tess dear, do come in.'

Tess followed the old lady's stooped frame down the hall and into her lounge. The room boasted velour upholstery, swirly-patterned carpets, a caged budgie in the corner and lots of dusty knick-knacks. A grandfather clock chimed half past the hour in one corner and the room smelt of old biscuits and mothballs. Tess handed her the package.

'Thank you. You're very kind. How did you know it was my birthday? Do sit down.'

'I'm sorry. I didn't know. The postman gave it to me. Happy birthday, though.'

'What, dear? I must be getting old, Tess dear. I don't hear so well.'

'I said happy birthday and I don't know what the present is,' said Tess, loudly.

'Oh, I see. It's a surprise, is it? What a thoughtful girl you are.'

Tess closed her eyes for a couple of seconds and took a deep breath. She was fond of Mrs Campbell and had found out through their conversations that she was a widow in her late eighties and walked slowly with stooped shoulders due to osteoporosis and arthritis. She thought she'd better change the subject to avoid further confusion. 'How's Chippy?' Tess shouted, pointing towards the birdcage.

'He's a good boy. Aren't you, Chippy? Look! I've got another birthday present.' Mrs Campbell waved the parcel at her green and yellow budgerigar. She turned back to Tess. 'Would you like a cup of tea?'

Tess really wasn't in the mood for chatting right now. With so much on her mind, it was taking all her energy to make small talk with a smile.

'Thank you, but I've got dinner in the oven and it's nearly ready,' she fibbed. 'I just wanted to pass on the parcel. I'm sorry I've got to dash, but we'll catch up soon.'

'Of course. Thank you again, my dear.'

Tess stood up and followed Mrs Campbell down the hallway.

'Do you know I've had five visitors today, including you?'

'That's lovely. Birthdays should be spent with family.'

'Oh, the visitors weren't family. My children live down south, but they did send me a lovely camera for my birthday. You just press a button, apparently. It's my first dignified one.'

'Digital. Lucky you.'

Mrs Campbell smiled to reveal crooked beige teeth. Her lips were wrinkled with lines that splayed upwards and outwards, like a child's drawing of the sun's rays. Her cerise lipstick had worn off her lips but still lurked in the ridges of her deep wrinkles. 'Neighbours have been popping in. Isn't it funny how everyone batons down the hatches in winter and you never see a soul? Then the days get longer and warmer and they all come out.'

Tess waited while Mrs Campbell reached the front door and turned to continue talking. 'Mrs Pringle from next to the church hall called in with some flowers, and Daniel, our local artist, picked me up at lunch time in his enormous car and took me for a sherry at The Royal Oak. Lovely boy, but always covered in paint splashes. How we chuckled when he tried to heave my old bones up into that high seat. Always says hello when he passes with his dogs.'

Tess was suddenly very interested in this new conversation. Paint. Big car. Dogs. 'Daniel, you say?'

'Yes. Did I say he was an artist?'

'You did. Does Daniel have dark hair? Is he tall and tanned?'

'Oh, you've met him then?'

'Sort of.' Tess was impatient to find out as much as she could about him. 'Does he live in the village?'

'He lives at—'

The telephone rang in the hallway.

'That'll be my daughter phoning to wish me a happy birthday. It's cheaper after six, you know?' The old lady

31

opened the front door. 'Please excuse me. I must dash. Bye bye.'

'But… yes, of course. Bye.'

Tess stepped out of the door. It closed promptly behind her and she watched Mrs Campbell's shadow hobble to the telephone. She could kick herself. Why hadn't she accepted a cup of tea? She could have learnt so much more about the handsome villager.

'Daniel. Daniel,' she repeated out loud, walking back across the road. She liked the name.

Back at home, she sent a text to Holly.

Guess wot? I know his name. x

Within a minute a reply beeped. Whose name? Do I look like bloody Mystic Meg? x

Dog walking man. x

Her mobile rang in seconds, as Tess knew it would.

'How do you know? Have you spoken to him? What's his name?'

'Daniel.'

Holly started singing Elton John's song and Tess joined in, '*I can see the red tail lights, heeeaaading for Spain.*'

'Tell me everything,' begged Holly.

'It's not exciting. I took a parcel over to Mrs Campbell's and I asked her. Can you believe she was about to tell me where he lived when her telephone rang? Oh, and I saw him this evening at Jackson's too.' Tess didn't think there was any need to elaborate about her disastrous shopping trip.

'No way! Did you speak to him?'

'I was in a bit of a rush. Apparently, he's an artist.'

'Does he paint nudes? I'd sit for free.'

Tess laughed. 'I don't know. Don't you think I've made a good start by finding out his name and what he does?'

'I suppose, but please try and find out if he's single then you could introduce us.'

Tess's smile faded. Who had her daydreams been kidding? It was unlikely that he was single and she had to face facts, she hadn't made a good first impression.

'Tess?'

'Sorry, I was miles away.' She tried to sound cheerful but felt like she'd just been turned down for a part as a leading lady. Tess forced a laugh. 'Must dash. Blake will be here soon. I'm doing *it* tonight.'

'God, I'd forgotten. Do you say good luck on such occasions?'

'I suppose so. I'll need it. I can't see him taking it too well.'

'No, me neither. Will you ring me when he's left?'

'I will. Just think, Holly, tonight will be the last night he walks out of Rose Cottage.'

Chapter Six

Blake dried himself after stepping out of the shower and fastened his jeans with some difficulty. He breathed in audibly ignoring the roll of flesh above his waistband. He slipped a T-shirt over his head, scrutinised his face in the mirror and tugged at a long hair protruding from his nose. Hooking his forefinger into a tub of hair wax, he extracted a white blob before rubbing it between his palms and through his hair. Tonight he'd be attentive. He'd shaved, cut his toenails and bought Tess some flowers from the local garage. She wouldn't be able to resist his romantic advances. It had been a while.

Within minutes Blake had slammed the front door behind him and locked it. Inside the car, he adjusted his rear-view mirror, straightened the bunch of chrysanthemums and reached for his cigarettes. He lit one, inhaled and threw the box back into the glove compartment.

He listened to his playlist and smoked three cigarettes on his way across town, surprised at the slither of anxiety that was creeping down his spine the closer he got to Halston. The past week had been difficult and doubts about this evening were eroding his confidence. Yes, Tess was bored with her job at the deli and yes, they'd been arguing with each other recently. But didn't relationships ebb and flow depending on external stresses? Surely it would be a little melodramatic to throw in the towel for no real reason? In the future she'd be far better off with him. After all, he was now an associate director with his own house. He'd get his finances sorted and maybe she would finally see sense and move in with him. Hopefully he wouldn't have to lie about his health; it would be unforgivable. But he was thinking of Tess's well being. He was thinking of her.

Blake turned right into Halston and flicked his cigarette butt out of the window. He felt unaccustomedly nervous as he looked across the garden towards the front door of Rose Cottage. His chest wheezed and he tried to calm his heart rate down. Relax, he told himself, subconsciously rubbing the plaster in the crook of his arm where the nurse had taken blood. Why would Tess invite you round to cook your favourite meal, if she didn't still love you? Forget about lying. It won't be necessary. He breathed out, placed his new inhaler between his lips, pressed and took a deep breath. He waited ten seconds before exhaling, just as the nurse had shown him.

Blake let himself in. A mouth-watering aroma of seafood filled the hallway and Emily Sande was singing in the background. All appeared calm, which soothed his mood considerably. He hung his jacket on a hook at the bottom of the stairs and walked purposefully down the hall clutching the bunch of flowers. Inside the kitchen, he saw Tess carving a date and walnut loaf.

Tess had heard him come in and had quickly put down her second glass of wine and picked up the carving knife to look busy. The time had come when she had to explain that she no longer loved her boyfriend. She jumped when Blake came up behind her and wrapped his arms around her waist, presenting her with purple blooms.

'Hello, gorgeous. The food smells lovely. These are for you.'

'Thank you.'

'Have you had a good day?'

'Busy.'

'You feel tense.'

'I'm okay. Just a bit tired.'

'Well relax,' said Blake. 'We've got all evening to enjoy ourselves.'

He pulled aside her hair and nuzzled his lips against her neck. The smell of stale nicotine on his breath was repulsive. Tess's grimace was directed towards the spice rack, so went unnoticed by Blake. She turned with a swift movement out of his reach and opened the fridge door. Knowing that he would be driving back home a single man, she offered him a soft drink.

'Can I get you a glass of elderberry juice?'

'Are you serious?' He laughed. 'Have you got any Chardonnay?' He sauntered to the hob, dipped his finger in a pan and tasted the simmering sauce.

Tess managed to stop herself from moaning about not having washed his hands. What was wrong with her? Why couldn't he do anything right in her eyes? He seemed to be in a good mood. He'd bought her flowers and was being attentive. Tess chewed her lip. It didn't alter the fact that she'd fallen out of love though, did it?

She busied herself by warming two plates under running hot water and carrying the bread to the table. After drying the plates she dished up the food and sprinkled it with chopped parsley.

'It's ready.'

She turned towards the table where Blake had already taken his place. She sat down opposite him and they began to eat. Half an hour passed amicably enough. They talked about work, the state of the housing market and the heat wave. Blake told a few corny jokes and moved on to holidays.

'Samantha from the office has just got back from Marbella. The photos look amazing. You should see the yachts, the bars and the clubs. We should go, you know? We could do with a holiday.'

'But for the last two years you've said we can't afford one.'

'Well, we can't at the moment. But with the extra money from my promotion and the money we'd save if you moved in with me—'

Tess interrupted him. 'Blake, we need to talk.'

'We are.'

'No, I mean talk seriously. About us.'

'Don't you want to go away?'

'I'd love a holiday as much as the next person, but you have an overdraft and I have to budget carefully on a shop assistant's wage. It's time to face facts. Not just financially, Blake, but in other ways too.'

Blake stopped chewing. 'What facts?'

'About how difficult things are at the moment.'

'Don't worry about us,' said Blake, wafting his hand in the air as if batting away an irritating insect. 'We'll be fine. Every relationship has their ups and downs, so why should we be any different?'

'I need to say something. You know how much you mean to me, don't you? We've shared a lot together, but—'

'I love you too, Tezza.'

'That's not what I'm saying, Blake. Please listen and try and understand. It's difficult.'

'Have some more wine.' Blake picked up the bottle to top up her glass, but Tess laid her hand across the rim to prevent him.

'No, I've had enough—'

Blake poured some wine onto the back of her hand. 'Shit, sorry.'

'Leave it. It's okay,' she snapped.

Blake used their two linen serviettes to mop up the spilt wine. Tess got up and walked to the kitchen sink where she rinsed her hand under the tap.

'Blake, I've been dreading saying this because we've spent many happy times together and you'll always be a good friend, but—'

'Did I mention that I went to see the doctor this evening?'

Tess turned from the kitchen sink to face him. 'Oh! That's what your appointment was?'

'Yeh. I took your advice and finally got round to it.'

'You went about your cough?'

He nodded.

'I'm glad. What did they say?'

Blake pulled a face. 'It doesn't look good.'

'What doesn't?'

'My cough.'

'What do you mean?'

'The doctor told me…'

'What?'

'He said he thought it could be serious.'

Tess crossed the kitchen floor and stood in front of him. 'What did he mean by that?'

'Serious. You know.'

'No, I don't.'

'Bad news.'

Tess could see that Blake was now pale and perspiring.

'You know. The C word.'

'I don't believe you.'

'He told me it probably was.'

'He couldn't have. Doctors don't guess.'

'He said he could hear something on my lungs and could tell by my cough. I should get the results from the blood test next week.' He rolled up his sleeve to reveal the pink fabric plaster stuck on the inside of his arm.

Tess was incredulous. 'Why have you waited an hour to tell me this? A doctor can't go making rash statements like that. It's unethical.'

'He says it can't be bronchitis. I don't have a fever and I've had the cough for too long.'

Tess stood open-mouthed in the middle of the kitchen, bewildered. She didn't know what to say. She held her hand against her head and stared at Blake. A couple of minutes ago, she was braced to finish with him. Now he was sitting in front of her, calmly informing her that the likelihood was that he had cancer. Blake usually panicked at the thought of losing his hair wax. He was a hypochondriac who worried about every blister, mole or hangnail. Now here he was, putting on a brave face within a couple of hours of being told he was likely to be seriously ill. My God, hadn't he been telling her silly jokes?

'You've been laughing and telling stupid jokes. Is this another sick joke?'

'Tess!'

'But I don't understand. Why didn't you say something when you came in?'

'I was trying to stay positive. I suppose I've been in denial for the past few hours.'

'This is crazy.' Tess raked her fingers up through her hair and stood there for a few seconds with her head in her hands. This wasn't supposed to happen. This didn't happen during the rehearsals in her head. Her shock turned to anger.

'It's immoral. A doctor should be struck off for guessing like that. I think you should put in a formal complaint. When my grandmother was diagnosed, she had numerous tests and scans before being told the results. She was exhausted, had no appetite and lost a lot of weight.' She stared at Blake. 'You still manage to work every day, you enjoy your food and haven't lost any weight.'

'What are you saying?' he asked.

'I'm saying, don't think the worst. Don't believe an unprofessional doctor. Wait for the results to come back.

And I'm serious about changing your doctor because yours is out of order. I've a good mind to go over there tomorrow and complain. Who did you see?'

Blake's head buzzed with panic. Shit. He'd only bloody well gone and done it. His lie was exposed, laid bare like an oozing, infected wound. He'd known she was about to end their relationship. It was obvious from the word, *but*. You are special, *but*. We'll always be friends, *but*. What choice had he been given? He couldn't have let her say the words. He'd imagined her falling into his arms and professing her undying love and loyalty after he'd told her about being ill. Instead, she was standing in front of him with her arms folded, scrutinising him. He felt like she could see right through him. He couldn't tell her his doctor's name. He was stuck. What could he do? Cough. He could pretend to cough. It would buy more time. He spluttered into the serviettes in his hands and, luckily, his forced cough irritated his throat enabling him to cough more convincingly.

Tess stood in the middle of the kitchen at a complete loss as to what to do. Blake was coughing into the wine-soaked serviettes, but her feet wouldn't move to help him. She watched the scene in front of her as if she was watching a television drama. The credits would roll in a minute. They would be sitting at the table, calmly discussing their separation. If what he said were true, it would complicate things. She wasn't happy and didn't love him any more. Not in the way she believed love should be. But how could she finish with him tonight? She couldn't possibly be that callous. She was sure that his doctor had been unscrupulous by diagnosing without tests, but for now, she would have to put her plans on hold.

Chapter Seven

The following day was Tess's day off from the deli. Her mobile rang while she was daydreaming, making her jump. The screen read *Holly*. She'd been dodging her friend's calls all morning but she couldn't hide forever.

'Hello.'

'About bloody time!' said Holly. 'I must have phoned you six times and left loads of messages. I can't believe you didn't call me after you dumped Blake last night. You said you would and I've been dying to know how he took it. Tess?'

'I didn't do it.'

'I can't believe you chickened out. I knew he'd give you the big doe eyes and I knew you'd fall for it. I bet he looked like that cat in *Shrek*, you know, just before it attacked the ogre with his claws.'

'He's sick.'

'You didn't fall for that old story, did you? He's always complaining of something. He's probably picked up a bug. Never mind, you can do it another time.'

'The doctor thinks he's got cancer.'

There was a pause. 'Sorry?'

'They think it's cancer.'

'I guess we're not talking star signs here?'

'He went to the doctor yesterday about his cough.'

'I don't understand. He went yesterday?'

'Yes.'

'There must be a mistake, then. GPs don't diagnose cancer. Patients get referred to onc... to people who specialise in that specific field of medicine. They're referred to the hospital where they do tests on samples under a microscope? Has he had an X-ray? He's a bit of a hypochondriac; perhaps he's second guessing the doctor.'

'That thought had crossed my mind. I hope he's just got the wrong end of the stick.'

'Do you think he's capable of making it up?'

'Why would he? He has his little faults and irritations, like we all do, but Blake wouldn't lie about his health. He wouldn't do such an evil thing. I'm going to try and find out more.'

'I hope it's a mistake and I'm really sorry if I'm sounding unsympathetic. It's just weird to be diagnosed without a biopsy or X-ray, that's all.'

Tess sighed. 'I know. I feel so guilty for not a hundred per cent believing him. It's all such a mess.'

'He doesn't know you were thinking of breaking up, does he?'

'No.'

'Just bide your time then. You say he has more tests so be there for him until you know for sure. I'll feel awful if he's really sick, but for now, you don't have to feel like you're backed into a corner. There are always options. Just think of breaking up with him as being postponed, not cancelled.'

Tess mulled over her friend's sensible advice. If he *was* sick and the blood results backed up the doctor's initial thoughts, she'd stay with him until he was given the all-clear. Huge advances had been made with cancer cures. Many people recovered nowadays. Just because the passion had gone and he could be irritating, it didn't mean that they weren't still friends.

'You're right. I'm not trapped in this relationship for life. As you say, I'll wait and see if he's mistaken before I think again about ending things.'

'Can I do anything to help?'

'You already have, thank you. I feel better for just talking to you.'

Chapter Eight

Clouds and drizzle competed with each other for the first few weeks of July. Denise was collecting breakfast dishes from the kitchen table and looking for jobs to occupy her mind. She hummed along to a song on the radio while tidying up after her young sons, Sam and Peter. If she didn't hum, she would cry. Every so often, her voice would falter when her thoughts returned to the torment that was on her mind. Minutes earlier, she'd waved goodbye to her sons as they'd run outside to a neighbour's car, their shirts already escaping from their shorts. One of her friends had offered to take Sam and Peter to the church hall for one of the activity days that were running throughout the long summer holidays.

Denise cleared her throat when she heard her husband, Simon, coming downstairs. He walked into the kitchen, a V-shaped frown between his eyes while adjusting his tie. His face softened when he saw her and drew her into his arms. He held her tightly, kissing the top of her head and letting his lips linger there.

'Do you want me to stay, darling? I'll cancel everything,' he said.

'No, I'll be fine. You go to work.'

'Why don't you ring the doctor now?'

'He said to wait two weeks. There's nothing he can do until the results come through.'

'I'll call you straight after my meeting.'

Denise could feel his hot breath as he spoke into her hair. She felt safe in his arms. He stood back and reached for her hands, holding them both.

'Take it easy, I love you.' He kissed her softly on her forehead, his face drawn with worry.

'You too. I'll be fine. See you later.'

She waved him goodbye, blowing kisses as he walked down the path to his car. Her smile faded when she closed the front door.

Balancing two cereal bowls, spoons and mugs, Denise dodged toy cars on the floor and placed the items in the sink. If she made a list, she could keep herself busy all day. If she didn't stop, she might not think about it too much. She glanced up and looked out of the window. The trees swayed in the gentle breeze as greenfinches and blue tits pecked at the seeds that the boys had topped up yesterday evening.

She thought back over the last week and wondered how her life had been turned upside down so abruptly. It was as if something had picked up her ordered life and scattered it on the floor. Perhaps she was worrying needlessly, after all—

Denise froze.

She gripped the edge of the sink. Another bird had settled on the fence. She instantly felt the hairs on her arms stand up. She held her breath, her hand moving slowly to her mouth. This bird reminded her of the doctor's prophetic words; words that made this moment, terrifying. Despite her body shaking, her thoughts wandered back to the idyllic family day out the previous week, where it had all begun.

'Come on, slow coach. We're nearly there.' Denise was panting as she spoke.

Sam was lagging behind. With his head bowed, he pushed his chubby hands onto his bare scuffed knees with each laborious step he had taken up Parliament Hill. Simon was a little way ahead with their elder son, Peter. It was a Sunday afternoon on a warm sunny blue-skied day and the melody of an ice cream van tinkled up the hill.

Denise was always happiest when surrounded by her

family. That day, they'd been exploring Hampstead Heath. Living close by meant that over the years they'd already discovered most of its wonderful secrets. Hidden glens, ponds obscured by leafy willows, crooked trees for small boys to climb and, best of all, the stunning expansive views from the top of Parliament Hill. The boys loved visiting the adventure playground and watching the entertainers, clowns, puppets and magicians. Fairs visited on summer bank holidays and Simon took them fishing on the calm lakes. When each summer was almost over and the hint of autumn floated in the breeze, they'd pick a basket of blackberries to freeze and cook throughout the winter months. It was a wonderful place to people-watch, fly kites, share picnics or just to wander and talk.

An excited yell from the top of the hill drew Denise's attention upwards. She shielded her eyes and laughed when she saw Simon and Peter waving their arms above their heads, having reached the summit. She stopped and waited until Sam caught up.

'Mummy, can we have an ice cream when we go back down?'

'Of course, but let's play king of the castle and sit on the top of the hill first.'

'Can we sit on our favourite bench?'

'If it's free we can.'

Denise had held out her hand to her youngest son, which he grasped.

'Mummy?'

'Yes, darling?'

'Can I have a piggyback?'

She chuckled. 'Mummy is very old and doesn't have your young legs. I can't carry a little boy as well.'

'I'm not little. I'm four.'

'Compared to Mummy and Daddy, you're little.'

'And Peter?'

'Yes, and Peter.'

'Mummy?'

Denise was panting. 'Yes'

'How old are you?'

'Hmm, well you shouldn't really ask a lady how old she is, but because I know you can keep a secret, I'm thirty-two.'

'Mummy?'

'Yes, Sam.'

'If you're thirty-two and Uncle Daniel is your twin, then he is thirty-two too!' Sam giggled and repeated, 'Thirty-two too, two too.'

'That's right. There are no flies on you, are there?'

Sam had looked at his arms and bent double to survey his legs. 'No.'

'No, it means… never mind. Look, we've made it.'

Simon had an arm draped around his elder son's shoulders.

'Hello, you two,' said Denise.

'Beat you,' Peter teased.

'Mum is very old and has thirty-two legs,' said Sam. 'No, I mean her legs are thirty-two and old, so I had to stay with her.'

Simon laughed and kissed her cheek. 'Sexiest old legs I've ever seen,' he'd whispered, tapping her bottom.

The four of them lived in a town house at the end of a tree-lined street. It would have been far beyond their means if it hadn't been for the death of Denise's parents six years ago. They'd left the bulk of their estate to her and Daniel. Daniel loved The Rookery and didn't want to sell, whereas she was already married and living in London. She'd happily signed her half of the family home over to Daniel and with the proceeds, plus the equity they'd made on their previous property in a cheaper area of London, they'd bought their present house near Hampstead. Now her days were filled with housework, taxiing, childcare and coffee mornings with friends. Simon had been promoted to a senior level in the advertising company and enjoyed his work, so life was good. Nowadays she remembered her parents with a sad smile and fond memories, rather than tears.

'Look, they're leaving,' Peter shouted. He ran to a newly-vacated wooden bench on the brow of the hill. They all followed him and sat down facing the breathtaking panorama. The city's beauty silenced them all. Denise always read the view like a book, looking from left to right, taking in the familiar and much-loved sight before her. The rooftops of adjacent Highgate were bathed in the sunshine. Scanning right she saw St Paul's majestic dome, Docklands and the O2. Her gaze lingered on the London Eye that looked like a discarded bike wheel, turning lazily on its axis.

'I can see the BT Tower, see.' Peter pointed and they'd all looked past his finger towards the tower.

'I watched *ET*, didn't I, Mummy?' said Sam.

Peter guffawed, bending forwards and holding his stomach. 'You think it's the ET Tower, you baby!'

Sam had lowered his head and sulked. 'I'm not a baby. I'm four.'

'ET, phone home,' Peter squeaked, in his best alien voice.

Sam's lips twitched as he tried to suppress a giggle.

'Sam, do you know where ET comes from?' Peter asked, a mischievous glint in his eyes.

'No.'

'Uranus.'

'Where's your anus, Mummy?'

'Never mind.' She looked at her seven-year-old son. He'd reached the age when toilet humour beat any other joke.

'Behave, Peter. Let's just enjoy the peace for a few minutes and then we'll find the ice cream van.'

'But he's pointing at me and laughing,' whined Sam.

Denise looked at Peter with raised eyebrows.

'But, Mummy,' said Sam. 'Where's your—'

Peter hadn't been able to hold his sniggering any longer and exploded with laughter, rolling sideways onto the bench clutching his stomach.

'Okay, enough now. As ET said – be good,' Simon ordered, his mouth twitching to prevent a grin.

In the kitchen, Denise blinked out of her reverie. She realised she'd been smiling as she'd replayed the family's conversation in her mind. Her smile disappeared. The sun slipped behind a single white cloud, muting the colours of the bird that had transfixed her. With a sudden movement it flew onto the grass. She jumped, then staring at it as it ruffled its feathers, her thoughts returned to the harrowing events of the previous Sunday.

It had taken a shockingly short time since returning from their idyllic day out on Hampstead Heath, for Denise's happy, organised life, to turn upside down. After the boys had been bathed and their knees had been scrubbed clean of grass stains, she'd taken a long hot shower. She sang beneath the deluge of water as the rose-scented bubbles decorated her skin. Her mind had been full of their day out, her family, the bottle of wine she would shortly share with Simon and the bar of Galaxy chocolate secreted away from her sons.

What measure of time does it take to alter your life? It took one second to change Denise's. She'd felt it as she'd rinsed the bubbles from her breasts. A lump. It felt like a pea, fresh from the freezer. Hard and round. She remembered her heart crashing against her ribs while she rinsed her hair. She remembered trembling in the heat of the shower. After stepping out of the cubicle, she wrapped a large bath towel around her body and sat on the edge of the bath. She looked down at the patterns on the floor, watching water drip from her hair and splatter on the marble tiles. The tiles had patterns in them; swirls that contorted into hideous faces. She stood up. As if in a trance, she walked to the mirror. She wiped the condensation and let her towel fall. Denise looked at her body and felt her breast again. She closed her eyes as if to protect herself. The lump was still there. It hadn't been a mistake. She looked up at the reflection of her face. An older, paler version of herself looked back.

That evening passed in a blur of fake smiles and laughter for the boys. Of course she'd told Simon and he'd helped her get through the night with reassuring words and loving touches. The old adage was true, she thought, as she lay in bed that night. You never know what's around the corner.

Monday morning arrived after a sleepless night and Denise telephoned the surgery as soon as it had opened. Within an hour she'd been sitting in the waiting room, her stomach churning beneath her folded arms. After an agonisingly long ten minutes, she was buzzed through to see her doctor. Dr Gray sat at his desk reading, but turned to peer over his glasses when she closed the door behind her. Having explained her concern, Denise was asked to remove her blouse and bra behind a modesty curtain surrounding a narrow bed.

'I'm ready,' she mumbled.

Dr Gray, a tall, big-boned man, pulled aside the curtain and examined her. He stopped on the lump, pressing and manipulating it.

'Right oh! Get dressed, Mrs Harby and we'll have a word.'

Denise got dressed and Dr Gray indicated for her to sit down.

'You do have a small lump, but given your age, it's probably nothing to worry about. It's not unusual to feel lumps and bumps at different times of the month and they nearly always disappear. Hormones or lack of hormones have a lot to answer for. Now, if you still feel worried and it hasn't gone in a fortnight, make another appointment and I'll refer you to the Breast Clinic for a more detailed examination and scan. You have to remember, there are more sparrows in the sky than parrots.' He'd laughed and said goodbye.

'More sparrows in the sky than parrots,' she repeated to herself, five minutes later as she climbed back into her car. It was obviously meant to reassure her in a crass, arrogant kind of way. He was letting her know that she probably didn't have anything exotic or unusual, just a normal temporary lump caused by hormonal changes. But she hadn't found him funny or reassuring in any way.

Today, one week after visiting her doctor, Denise looked back at the bird that was sitting on her lawn.

It was a parrot.

Chapter Nine

Tess and Blake were sitting on the sofa watching the ten o'clock news. Tess was still reeling from having recently received the news from Blake that his test results had confirmed the doctor's initial thoughts. She'd felt incredibly guilty for having doubted him and now wanted to support him in any way she could, despite his protestations. The programme they were watching was reporting on NHS cuts, including care for cancer patients. The presenter looked straight in to the camera and Tess felt as if she were talking directly to her.

'Record numbers of patients are not getting vital cancer care on time because NHS England performance against waiting time targets has fallen to its lowest ever level, according to official figures. Hospitals are increasingly having to force patients to wait for care because they cannot keep up with the growing numbers being referred by GPs who fear they have the disease.'

'It's awful having to wait,' said Tess. 'How are you feeling?'

'Not too bad, just a bit tired.'

'I want to come with you for your next appointment.'

'There's no need.'

'I just want to let you know that I'm here for you. I want to give you more support. I don't want you to have to go through this alone.'

'I know you want to help, but I cope better when I'm on my own.'

'I wouldn't come in to the hospital consultations, if you didn't want me to. I'd just sit in the waiting room and be company on the journey to and from your appointments.'

'You're lovely and you're doing just the right thing for me already.'

'Like what? I don't even know much about what's going on, let alone doing anything to help.'

'You're kidding! You're doing so much. Just knowing you're here and you love me is all I need. So many girlfriends would have cut and run at the prospect of a sick partner, but you didn't. You're an amazing support.'

Tess hoped he didn't see her blush when he mentioned cutting and running. He had no idea how close she had come to doing just that. Granted, not because of his diagnosis, but she had been seconds away from turning her back on him forever.

'I understand that you might want to go to the hospital alone, but I need to know what's happening. Don't push me away.'

Blake sighed and impatiently ran his hands through his hair. 'What do you need to know?'

Tess laid a hand on his thigh. 'It's only because I care. Do you have any letters from your consultant that explains exactly where the cancer is? Can you show me your X-ray? Ask if you can take a photograph of it. It's your medical information and you're allowed access to it if you make arrangements.'

'How will *you* looking at some image help *me*?'

'You'll be sharing your problems and I'll understand more of what you're going through.'

Blake stood up. 'Okay, I'll see what I can do. Can we chat tomorrow? I'm going up now,' said Blake, yawning. 'Night.' He leaned forwards and gave her a perfunctory kiss on the cheek.

A few hours later, Blake checked the time on his Fitbit and tried to settle back to sleep. It was 01:53. It hadn't been an easy decision to lie to Tess. Before *that* meal, he'd even convinced himself that it wouldn't be necessary; a bit like his critical illness insurance. However, for the past few weeks following his lie, he'd slept badly and was anxious when staying over at Tess's. It wasn't that he didn't love her; it was just the endless questions. She was relentless. Somehow it seemed easier to live with his deceit when he didn't have to look her in the eye, and now gnawing guilt was ensuring that sleep remained elusive. Blake turned irritably onto his stomach and made a decision. He'd pretend to be cured quickly so that he could stop lying. Perhaps he could even say that the doctor had got it wrong. No. Tess would demand to know which doctor he'd seen and storm into the surgery.

He stayed motionless while Tess changed position, waiting until her breathing returned to the slow steady rhythm of sleep. He knew what he'd do. He'd play the brave boyfriend for a couple of months while staying positive and working hard. That'd show her that he was strong and dependable. Then when they were back on an even keel, he'd say the chemotherapy had worked and dramatically recover. The lie would be history. The important thing was that they were still a couple.

Blake sat up and thumped his pillow before turning sideways and curling into a foetal position. As he lay there, a thought occurred to him. A plan was taking form that would ease her suspicions. It could be the answer to all Tess's questions. He'd do it tomorrow.

The next morning Blake begrudgingly fed coins into the hospital car park's ticket machine, muttering about extortion. Having placed the ticket inside his car he strode towards the main entrance. Once inside, he studied a map of the hospital's layout showing directions to different departments, tracing the image of corridors and clinics with his forefinger. He didn't have far to go; just a five minute walk.

When Blake arrived at Oncology he lingered by the department's double doors, peering through the glass partition. It smelt of disinfectant and coffee. He felt anxious, his stomach churning at the thought of waiting with sick people who were sitting on the other side of the swing doors. He pushed one side open and stepped inside.

A few faces momentarily turned towards him before looking away again. Blake chose a seat in the corner of the waiting room with his back to the wall, where he could observe without interruption. The idea he was now putting into action had occurred to him the previous night and hopefully it would get Tess off his back for a while.

Over the next forty minutes, Blake observed the comings and goings of both staff and patients. No one seemed to notice him lurking at the back of the waiting area. Some patients were being pushed in wheelchairs, some must have been inpatients because they wore dressing gowns and slippers, and the majority appeared to be either bald or wearing a scarf. This observation set his mind racing once again.

There appeared to be a set routine to the clinic where every eight minutes or so, a nurse would pick up a set of medical notes from a pile on her desk and call a patient's name. She would then escort them through a side door and not return for a few minutes. Blake had also noticed people entering and leaving a small staffroom. Specifically, he noticed that a doctor had removed her stethoscope and left it hanging on a coat hook before leaving the department.

The nurse called out another patient's name and led the way through the set of double doors. Blake knew it was time to make his move. He stood up, stretched his aching legs and walked towards the staffroom. A quick glance at the two remaining patients assured him that they weren't looking at him, with one deeply engrossed in a magazine and the other texting on his mobile phone.

Within seconds Blake had removed the stethoscope, secreted it beneath his jacket and returned to his seat. He waited until the penultimate patient was called and led through to see the consultant. Retrieving the stethoscope from his jacket, he draped it around his neck, stood up and walked towards the front desk. He only had a minute at the most. He had to be quick.

With only one set of notes left for the morning session, Blake quickly scanned the pile of medical paperwork for that afternoon's appointments. Several X-rays were filed alongside the notes. The remaining patient coughed. Blake looked up. The man nodded and smiled before returning to his magazine. Feeling emboldened, Blake continued to shuffle through the notes. He glanced up at the door leading to the consulting rooms. They were still closed.

He lifted a black and white plastic film to the light. It wasn't clear what the image was of, so he took another. The second one clearly showed an X-ray of a skull. He looked once more at the door. He could only have seconds left. The third picture highlighted defined ribs with a small white smudge on one of the lungs. Perfect. He slid it back inside its brown envelope, hid it beneath his jacket, removed the stethoscope from his neck and walked out of the oncology department. All he had to do was to cut off the name of the patient at the top of the plastic film and Tess would get to see the image she'd been nagging him for.

Chapter Ten

Daniel picked up his jacket from the pew before shutting Goya and Gogh in the kitchen. December was months away, but he wanted to get everything in place so there'd be no panic close to Christmas. If he didn't find someone local to cater for his exhibition, he'd either have to provide all his guests with beans on toast or use a big impersonal company with set menus. He must come back from The Royal Oak with a name of a caterer.

Daniel closed the front door and checked that it was locked. He turned the handle a second time, then hesitated.

'You don't need to do this,' he said to himself.

He set off determinedly, yet after only a few steps he felt the familiar invisible elastic band tighten around his feet. Something was willing him to return to the door and check a third time. His strides became smaller. His inner voice goaded him.

So, you dare to leave the door checked only twice, do you? If something terrible happens to your loved ones now, you know it'll be your fault, don't you? Go back. If you check it one more time, one more protective third time, you can relax. Everyone will be safe.

Daniel swore. He marched back towards the front door. He hated this weakness in himself. Time and new friendships had tempered his anxieties and obsessions, but he still couldn't stop himself from performing some tasks three times.

Daniel grasped the handle and turned it. It was locked. His shoulders relaxed but his frown remained etched on his forehead. Rationale told him that what he was doing didn't make any sense, yet as he walked down his drive, he felt as if the protective shield had been raised once more around his family and friends.

The church bell tolled ten times as Daniel walked across Halston's cricket pitch in the evening gloom. The chimes drew his eyes to the distant spire of St Mary's Church, silhouetted against the sunset. Dark, wispy clouds obscured the apricot skies as if a vandal had smeared grey paint across a Turner sunset. Roosting birds chattered in the treetops that swayed and rustled in the cool breeze. Daniel relished the serenity of the evening and the fragrance of the blossoms and hawthorn hedges. Recently mown grass lay wilting and withering on the village green, sticking to the bottom of his shoes in damp clumps. A mournful bellow from a distant cow echoed across the empty expanse. His inner voice was now silent and forgotten – until the next time.

The lights of The Royal Oak grew brighter and laughter carried on the breeze each time the front door was opened. A smile played on Daniel's lips at the thought of the camaraderie and banter awaiting him. He stepped into the bar, leaving behind the peaceful village green. Artificial light, the musky smell of beer, the sound of Sky Sports on the television and cheery hellos, all greeted him as he entered the room. A group of men argued amicably in the corner, a barmaid flirted outrageously with two young builders who were still wearing their concrete-splattered overalls, and groups of women had their heads huddled together in conspiracy.

Daniel walked across the room and sat on a stool at the quieter end of the bar. Joe, the landlord, came smiling towards him.

'Good to see you, Daniel. How's life treating you?'

He held out his arm and the two men shook hands.

'Good thanks, Joe. Yourself?'

'I never complain when we're busy. What can I get you?'

'A glass of red, please.'

Joe slid a wine glass from the rack above his head and turned to fill it on the counter behind him. He looked over his shoulder as he uncorked the bottle. 'What are you up to these days? I haven't seen you for a few weeks.'

'Trying to keep out of trouble.' Daniel laughed and took a notebook and pencil out of his jacket pocket.

Joe turned and winked. 'Have you been in trouble with the ladies?' He placed the glass of wine on the counter. 'Is your book full of names and numbers?'

'Sadly not. I've almost forgotten what it's like to socialise. I've been busy with an art exhibition I'm presenting in December. It's a way off yet but time waits for no man, as they say. I've called in because I'm hoping to pick your brains about something.' He held the notebook up and gave it a shake.

'Be glad to help if I can. Wow, an art exhibition?' Joe whistled in awe. 'Are you holding it at The Rookery?'

'Yep, I'm using a few rooms around the back for a buffet and the main gallery. Then a marquee in the garden for dancing and a bar.'

'I think it's a great idea. Very *avant garde*.'

'More like *avant* got a clue, I'm afraid. That's why I need a little help.'

Joe laughed loudly. 'Be with you shortly, just give me a tick.'

Daniel began doodling spirals around the edge of his page while Joe turned to serve another customer. He picked at a bowl of mixed fruit and nuts on the bar, avoiding the shrivelled sultanas. He hated the grainy dehydrated fruit. They reminded him of Denise's teasing when they were young. He was five when he developed a liking for Garibaldi biscuits, so their mother would buy a couple of

58

packets at the weekly shop. Denise had hated the plain biscuits full of currants, so she'd hatched a plan to reinstate iced rings and pink wafers back into the pantry. While they'd been searching for caterpillars and ladybirds to keep as pets in jam jars in The Rookery's garden over a quarter of a century ago, his sister had pointed to a group of foraging ants. She told him that they were the black bits in Garibaldi biscuits. He'd been horrified and ran inside to ask his mother. Even when she'd assured him that Denise was only teasing, he'd never eaten dried fruit or Garibaldi biscuits again.

Daniel checked his notebook. He'd organised a marquee and a band, but needed to book a DJ and arrange a bar with seating. Denise had suggested flowers to decorate the tables for the diners and displays to be arranged around the areas of the house where the guests would be. She'd also urged him to make it festive, with a huge Christmas tree in the hall. If he could find a local caterer, it would be one more job to cross out in his notebook.

'Hello, handsome.'

Daniel had been deep in thought so when a voice spoke in his ear he looked up in surprise. The barmaid, who had been flirting with the builders earlier, was smiling at him.

'Sorry?' said Daniel.

'I'm Lizzy. Would you like my number for your little black book?'

Daniel laughed, politely. 'It's not that kind of book.'

She pouted. 'Shame. I was thinking... if you don't like sultanas you could try a date.'

He shook his head. 'You've lost me.'

'I was watching you pick out the nuts and leave the dried fruit. It was a play on the word, "date". Come on, a girl shouldn't have to explain.'

'Ah, very observant.'

'I finish at eleven.' She tilted her head in a coquettish manner.

'I'm actually working at the moment.' He shook his notebook again. 'Another time maybe.'

Daniel felt uncomfortable. He didn't want to be rude but nor did he want to flirt with someone so much younger than himself. Besides, he'd never liked the full on approach, even in his youth. He was old-fashioned when it came to getting to know someone; he liked it to be subtle and understated.

'Lizzy, another customer needs your attention,' said Joe.

She puckered her lips and frowned her disapproval at being interrupted. Straightening her skirt, she winked at Daniel and sashayed towards a middle-aged couple that were patiently waiting to be served.

'Sorry about that,' said Joe. 'She's only been here a fortnight and I actually think she's losing me business.'

Daniel grinned with relief. 'I was getting a bit hot under the collar, but for all the wrong reasons.' Daniel shook his head. 'I'm losing it, Joe. Even a young temptress leaves me feeling self-conscious and embarrassed.'

'I wouldn't compare Lizzy with other women. Most men would need their wits about them with madam on the prowl! She's still under review but I don't think I'll be keeping her on. She's scaring half my customers away.'

Bill, the local farmer, bustled his enormous belly through the pub door and was greeted by a chorus of welcoming cheers. He shook hands and exchanged a few words with several neighbours before joining Daniel at the bar.

'Evening. A pint, please, Joe.'

'Have you heard about Daniel's new venture?' said Joe, pulling down on the pump.

'No. What you up to, lad?'

'Trying to plan an art exhibition for December. I sell my artwork on the internet and occasionally to private collectors, but I was thinking that if the exhibition went well, I'd apply for planning permission to the local council and design a permanent gallery and maybe a small café.'

'Sounds great. We need a little enterprise here in Halston. Don't suppose you fancy opening up a village store as well, do you? Jackson's prices keep rising.'

'Sorry, Bill. I hate shopping at the best of times.'

'Pity. How's that sister of yours and her little 'uns?'

Daniel hesitated. He didn't want to divulge Denise's recent personal bad news. His sister had phoned him a few days earlier and told him that she had a hospital appointment to investigate a suspicious lump. She had been uppermost in his thoughts ever since.

'My nephews keep her busy. They're all fine, thanks.'

Daniel and Bill talked for half an hour, laughing into their drinks and occasionally greeting other regulars. The banter flowed as freely as the beer. Daniel relaxed with his friends and looked up, smiling. He caught the eye of the barmaid again, who waved back thinking that Daniel's smile was for her. With a jolt, he remembered that he'd come in for some information.

'I wonder if any of you guys can help me with something?'

'Of course. What's troubling you?'

'I want to put on a bit of food for my guests at the exhibition and I was wondering if anyone knew of someone local who can cook? I don't want to deal with a big impersonal company from the city.'

'My Mrs could knock you up a few steak and kidney pies,' said Bill.

Daniel was touched by the offer, but was thinking of a bit more refinement.

'That's a kind offer, Bill, thank you. But I'll be catering for a hundred or more people, so I think I'd better not ask your wife to bake fifty pies.'

Joe was frowning. 'Ooh, now what's her name? You know, that pretty dark-haired lass. She cooked some delicious food at a couple of charity events we've had here.' His face lit up when he remembered her name. 'Tess. Tess Fenton. I'm not sure where she lives in Halston and I don't have her number, but when she comes in next, I'll give you the nod.'

'That's great, thanks, Joe. I really appreciate it,' said Daniel. He made a note in his book.

Tess Fenton — FOOD.

Chapter Eleven

It was mid-August and the heat of the last six weeks had petered out. The long dry summer had left trees parched and wilting, and the grass on the village green was now beige and crisp.

It had been six weeks since Blake had revealed that he was sick, and Tess was exhausted from stocktaking at work and running around after Blake at home, although she had to admit she was impressed with his mental attitude and courage. He cooked her dinner occasionally and even bought her a bunch of chrysanthemums now and then.

Whatever medical treatment he was receiving, it appeared to be working wonderfully. When he'd shown her his X-ray last month, she'd been shocked. A shadow on his right lung was clearly visible without the need of an explanation from a doctor. Then, a week following that revelation, Blake had calmly walked through her front door with his fair hair cut so short that at first she thought that he was bald. He'd explained that as it was falling out anyway, he may as well cut it all off.

Tess was cautiously optimistic that his cough seemed to have almost disappeared and that he looked well. Yet again she'd offered to support Blake on his trips to hospital for treatment, but he'd told her it was a depressing place full of super bugs. They'd laughed at the thought that it'd sounded like huge insects were running round the hospital corridors, wearing pants over their tights and capes flowing behind them. She hadn't pestered him again. Some people preferred to be on their own to deal with things privately and that was okay.

Tess had arranged to meet Holly that evening at The Royal Oak. It had been a long time since their last girls' night out, and she was looking forward to relaxing and catching up on the latest gossip. Blake had sulked at first about her planned night out without him, and although Tess had almost given in when his cough had suddenly reappeared, she'd stood firm. Holly had been very supportive and understanding about their recent non-existent social life. So much so, that Tess had refused to stay at home and watch another repeat of *Star Trek*. Blake could stay in with Mr Spock, while she would boldly go where man had been many times before – the pub!

She heard Blake padding up the stairs.

'What're you doing?' he asked.

Tess was kneeling on the floor in her underwear with her bottom in the air, reaching under the bed. Clothes were strewn around the floor and she was mumbling inaudibly to herself.

'What?' she snapped.

'No need to bite my head off.'

She sat back on her heels. 'I'm sorry. I'm late and I haven't put a wash on for ages because I've washed your sheets and towels. I haven't got any clean jeans or T-shirts.'

'Why don't you stay in then?' His foot suggestively ran up and down her bare slender thigh.

Tess looked at his grey sock rubbing her leg. She noticed the worn heel and pink hint of big toe trying to escape an equally worn area at the front of his sock. She pushed his foot impatiently away and stood up.

'I haven't had a night out for ages.'

'Why do you want to dress up, though? You're only meeting Holly, aren't you?'

'Yes, but it's a girl thing. You wouldn't understand.'

'What about these?' He held up a yellow pair of cropped trousers. They'd looked great when she'd had a tan in the blistering heat wave of July, but Tess could hear the wind picking up outside. She looked at her watch.

'They'll have to do. I'm going to be late and no one will notice my legs under the table.'

She hopped around the bedroom floor, with one leg in her trousers and the other leg trying to find the second leg hole. Blake picked up a brown polo neck jumper and threw it to her.

'This'll keep you warm.'

Tess pulled it over her head, thankful that she didn't have to make a decision of what to wear on top. She turned to look in the dressing table mirror at her yellow and brown ensemble.

'I look like a geriatric Brownie!' she wailed.

'Just make sure you stay away from any Scouts with shiny toggles.'

Downstairs, rifling through the shoe cupboard, Tess wasn't having much more luck. Her first choice of footwear was outside the back door awaiting a good clean. Damn those cows! Her trainers would have been okay but they were at Holly's and she wasn't going to wear her work shoes. It would have to be her ankle boots. She looked down at the pale, bristly six-inch expanse of leg on show between her boots and cropped trousers. This really wasn't how she had hoped to be feeling just before going out with her best friend. As she only had five minutes before she should be there, it would have to do. At least Brown Owl would have been proud of her. She would have been presented with a *dressing as a vagrant for the sake of a neglected best friend* badge.

Inside The Royal Oak, Tess ordered herself a white wine and settled down at a quiet table in the corner of the pub in order to hide her legs. Ten minutes later, with her first glass empty and Holly still nowhere to be seen, Tess sent her a text.

Whr r u? I look desperate on my own. Pls hurry. X

Someone entered the pub, along with a chilly blast of wind that whipped around her bare calves. Trust her to be wearing cropped trousers when the next ice age was developing outside. She pressed *send* and read the word *delivered*, aware of noisy camaraderie and laughter at the bar.

Someone shouted, 'What are you drinking, Daniel?'

It couldn't be, could it? Could it be *the* Daniel who she owed two pounds to? The one who saw the messy contents of her handbag and the crusty fish scales on her cheeks? Could it be *the* Daniel who entered her thoughts as regularly as unwanted pop-ups on her computer?

Tess knew she looked dreadful. She could feel the heat of embarrassment prickle her face at the thought of seeing him again. She hadn't checked her make-up before she'd left home. Not since this morning in fact. *And* she was wearing these stupid cropped trousers with a healthy dollop of regrowth on her legs just for good measure. She lowered her head and prayed that she was far enough away from the bar not to be recognised. Please let their next meeting be after two hours showering, fake-tanning, plucking, filing, buffing, blow-drying, blending and shading.

She glanced up. It *was* him. Daniel was standing at the bar, tall, lean and magnetically good-looking. He was wearing loose jeans, an oatmeal T-shirt and a soft brown leather jacket – and God, he was looking back at her.

Tess looked down and pretended to text again. Her fingers were shaking as she silently repeated, please don't come over, please don't come over. Her heart was pounding.

'Shit! Shit!' she muttered at her mobile, still pretending to type a message.

'Are you okay?'

Tess looked up and was horrified to see Daniel standing

in front of her. She noticed that his eyes were the deepest moss green. The attraction was instant and undeniable. The bolt that ricocheted through her body was as real as the time she had touched Farmer Bill's electric fence as a dare. His dark hair was pushed behind his ears framing his handsome face and high cheekbones. She saw a smudge of a pale scar on his temple, highlighted against his tanned face. His lips were slightly parted with a hint of a smile on them. They were moving. Tess blinked. His lips were moving. He was talking to her.

'Wh— pardon?' It occurred to her that he'd only ever seen her red-faced and flustered.

'I said, it doesn't sound like you're very happy with someone.'

Tess remembered she'd been mumbling expletives in panic.

'Nothing that a pint can't put right,' she replied, trying to sound unfazed. 'I'm waiting for a girlfriend. She's late.'

Great! Now she sounded like a possessive alcoholic lesbian who suffered from a mild dose of Tourette's. This wasn't going well.

That same smile flickered across his lips.

Two dogs walked towards Daniel and started sniffing the air. Whatever scent they'd located, it was slowly drawing them towards Tess's ankle boots. She tucked her legs further under the table until she was leaning backwards.

'Meet Goya and Gogh.'

'You named them after artists,' said Tess, pretending to stroke their heads when she was really pushing them away from her bristly legs.

'Seemed appropriate at the time and now I can't imagine them being called anything else. They like you.'

'It might be my boots.'

'Your boots?'

God, now he was bending down looking under the table. Tess cringed.

Daniel stood up straight again. He was tall and Tess was refusing to stand up, so her neck ached from straining her head backwards to talk to him.

He frowned. 'Have we met?' He was tilting his head to one side as if he was studying some strange amorphous sculpture in a museum.

Tess cringed. 'I think I owe you some money.'

'You do?'

'At Jackson's. I didn't have any money for pasta.'

'Ah! That's it. Did the meal go well?'

'Yes, thanks,' she lied.

'The reason I've disturbed you is that I've heard you're a great cook. I've been asking around for someone local to cater for an event I'm holding in December. I'm hoping to exhibit some artwork. Joe told me that you've catered for some charity events here and that your food was delicious. He didn't have your number or address so he's just phoned me to let me know that you're here tonight. Can I give you my number? You can ring me at a better time so we could discuss it.'

Tess took the charcoal-grey business card from him. It was embossed in silver with the words, *Daniel Cavanagh. Artist. The Rookery. 0115 9407423.*

At least he knew she was good at something, she thought. Maybe not her dress sense, shaving or keeping a tidy bag, but he knew she could cook.

'Thank you. It sounds very interesting.'

'Do you have a dog too?' he asked.

'A dog?'

'You know, a small hairy animal with four legs.'

She smiled. 'Funny. I just couldn't understand why you asked.'

He leaned forwards and pulled several bits of hair and fluff from her jumper, showing them to her before dropping them on the floor.

She shivered at his touch and hoped he hadn't noticed.

'Dog hairs, I presume!' he said. 'I have double the problem with my two.'

'No, I couldn't find anything to wear and this had been living under my bed for a while.'

Daniel laughed, obviously mistaking her honesty for wit.

'I've got a goldfish called Bob, though,' said Tess.

'A goldfish?'

'You know, orange scales, a tail and with the added bonus that it doesn't need walking.'

Daniel guffawed, making Tess grin. She was surprised that conversation with him was actually becoming quite easy. He was warm and open and made her feel at ease.

Someone called Daniel's name from the bar, telling him that his drink was waiting.

'It was good to meet you. Don't forget to give me a call.' He smiled, turned and walked towards the bar before calling over his shoulder. 'Hope your girlfriend turns up.'

She watched him join a group of friends before sighing in to her glass.

Tess was still wound up when Holly arrived twenty-five minutes after their arranged time.

'Where've you been? You know I hate sitting in a pub by myself.'

Her best friend sat down opposite her, placing two glasses of wine on the table.

'Sorry, I couldn't start the car. What's the matter? You look a bit dazed.'

'I've been talking to Daniel.'

'What! *The* Daniel?'

Tess nodded, wide-eyed. 'I can't really remember what I said. Something about my goldfish.'

'Bob?'

'Yes. Mrs Campbell's budgie would have made more sense than me. He must think I need therapy.'

Holly looked around the pub's lounge. 'Where is he now? What did he want? What did he say?'

'He left after one drink, about five minutes ago.'

'Damn.'

'He wants me to cook for him.'

'No! As his personal chef?'

She showed Holly his business card. 'He wants me to cook at an exhibition he's holding at The Rookery. He must have rented a room there.'

'Can I be your sous chef?' She smelt his business card, checking to see if any cologne lingered on it.

'You've never helped me cook in your life.'

'I have. You were short of eggs once and asked me to pick some up on the way round to see you. Please, Tess. You could introduce me. It'll be my chance to meet him. We could be a foursome and go for a meal or dancing. It'll be great.'

Tess's smile uncurled. She had to stop fantasising about Daniel. She was with Blake. Sick Blake. She looked down at herself in her ridiculous clothes and then looked at her friend. Holly's blonde bob had been crimped, her eye shadow was perfectly blended, her lips shone with pink lip gloss and she was wearing a pretty pink T-shirt edged in imitation crystal beads. Tess felt plain and silly in comparison. Perhaps she shouldn't cook for him. The sight of him unsettled her and had awakened a passion in her that she thought had gone into hibernation years ago.

Holly suddenly appeared to notice Tess's outfit. 'What happened?' she asked, peering under the table.

'It was a mixture of cow pats, running out of washing tablets and Blake choosing this outfit for me.'

'How is the patient?'

'Amazingly resilient. Before he was diagnosed, I'd have to talk him out of dialling 999 if he had a blister. He's being incredibly brave. I still feel bad that I was horrid to him when he was suffering in silence.'

'Silence! He never stops moaning.'

'I mean, considering the enormity of his illness, he doesn't moan *that* much.'

'D'you think his treatment's working?'

'I think so but he doesn't like to talk about his hospital visits. I think it's his way of dealing with things. Anyway, I haven't come out tonight to talk about him. Let's order a bottle.'

Chapter Twelve

Although Tess was bored working at The Blue Olive delicatessen, she enjoyed working so close to Maddox Square. It was a busy fashionable part of town and had grown in popularity following a regeneration scheme. Over the past few years, boutiques and contemporary bars had moved into the area. The Square was a large stylish paved area, shared between several bars and restaurants. Four long cobbled streets all converged into the open space. Food and drinks were served on tables, each adorned with colourful umbrellas that protected diners from the temperamental elements. New apartments overlooked the bustling Square, swathed in huge advertising hoardings proclaiming, *stylish apartments offering a luxurious city chic lifestyle*. Several mature trees had escaped the demolition men and provided a natural canopy from the sun's intense rays. Their branches also made perfect supports for hanging fairy lights in the evenings. The atmosphere it created, along with a glass of wine, helped many a romance blossom as the lights twinkled above the diners, like a fibre optic galaxy.

The Blue Olive stood a short distance down one of the cobbled streets and had become popular and successful through being in the right place at the right time. It had been a rundown little newsagent's shop when Angelo Mancini had bought it and turned it into an Italian delicatessen.

Tess manoeuvred her grumbling Mini into a parking space a few roads away from work, locked her car and dropped her keys into her bag. Every morning as she walked from her car to the delicatessen, she'd stop and gaze into the window of her favourite teashop. One side was used as a dining area. The other side boasted bulging shelves that displayed the most amazing mouth-watering cakes. Tess imagined it was like looking into a bag of dolly mixtures. There were so many different colours, textures and shapes, no doubt all smelling so good that she didn't know which one to drool over first. There were decorated cup cakes sitting in silver cases, sponges filled with lemon cream, chocolate cakes decorated with marshmallows and fruit cakes bursting with nuts and cherries. Chewy-centred meringues exploded with whipped cream, a coffee cake decorated with walnuts and icing drizzled down the sides of an orange cake. In her dreams, she would own a teashop like this, but as usual, her dreaming could last only a few minutes before she had to hurry to work.

Tess pushed the deli door, but it was locked. She peered through the window, her cupped hand resting on her forehead in order to block her reflection. Spotting Margaret behind the till, she tapped on the window. Her colleague looked up and smiled when she saw that it was Tess, and scurried over to unlock the door.

Margaret was an attractive lady in her late fifties. She worked three days a week, mainly to cover Tess and Holly's days off. She was like Tess's surrogate mother here in Nottingham, while her own mother lived miles away in Cornwall.

'Morning, Tess. Sorry, I just locked the door while I was filling the till with change and notes. Holly's not here yet.'

'Guess what? They've got the lemon gateau in the teashop again.'

'Back by popular demand, no doubt. I'll treat us later.'

'I'll go and stick the kettle on. We've got ten minutes yet.'

'Lovely.'

Tess wandered into the staff room, took off her coat and threw her bag onto a settee. She filled the kettle and plugged it in. The settees were strewn with old magazines so she busied herself by tidying up for a few minutes as the kettle bubbled into life. A lazy bluebottle buzzed around the bin and she could hear voices in the shop. Assuming Holly had arrived, she reached for a third cup. The irritating fly buzzed around her head again and then landed on the rim of a cup she was about to use.

She looked for a weapon. Choosing the latest copy of *Heat* magazine, Tess spun round, her eyes darting round the room in search of the fly. It had settled on the settee. With one quick swat, the fly was squashed onto Katie Price's cleavage.

Tess heard a thud. She stopped and listened. Raised voices were coming from the shop. Were Margaret and Holly arguing? Tess hurried towards the staff room door, still clutching the magazine. She pushed it open and stopped in horror.

Two hooded men were leaning over the cash desk. One was threatening Margaret and the other was gripping the till and violently shaking it backwards and forwards, trying to dislodge it from its fixings. She noticed that the intruders were teenagers, long and lanky, wearing the latest high street fashion. The youths were shouting and Margaret was leaning against the wall with her hands covering her face.

Without thinking, Tess ran across the shop towards the men. All her pent-up frustrations of the past weeks were now focused on protecting Margaret and the shop's money. She batted the youths around the head, shouting and swearing with each blow from her magazine. The teenagers appeared not only shocked that someone else was in the shop but were confused by a screaming woman with a rolled up weapon. They cowered against the onslaught, arms raised and looking at each other for unforthcoming instructions. One of them pushed Tess out of the way, enabling them both to run out of the shop and disappear across Maddox Square.

Margaret was sobbing. 'I'm so stupid. I didn't lock the door again after I let you in. They must have seen the bags of money on the counter.'

'Don't you dare blame yourself,' said Tess. 'Leaving a door unlocked isn't a crime.'

Tess comforted Margaret with a hug. The door opened and they both jumped as Holly entered and saw their pale shocked faces.

'Did I miss something?'

Fifteen minutes later, two policemen were taking statements and advising against getting physically involved with criminals. Apparently there had been a spate of opportunist attacks in the area over the last few weeks, and leaflets were being printed to inform all local shop owners. Not a lot could be done immediately but the till couldn't be touched until someone had come and taken fingerprints. The police had some prints from a couple of other small shops that had been targeted and they wanted to see if they matched.

After the police had left, they were all feeling a little shaken and bewildered.

'We can't open the shop until the scene of crime chap has been,' said Tess. 'Why don't you finish making the tea and I'll go and buy us some of that lemon cake?'

This suggestion raised two smiles. Tess fetched her purse while Margaret sat down on the settee to recover. Holly made three strong teas and fetched her mobile phone.

A short time later Tess returned with a box containing three slices of lemon gateaux. She took three plates out of the cupboard and they all sat around the table, feeling a lot calmer.

'I've telephoned Angelo to tell him what's happened. His

cleaner said he's gone to visit family in Amalfi for a couple of weeks and that she'd call him,' said Holly.

'At least the little blighters didn't get any money,' said Margaret.

Tess was about to speak, when a loud knocking made them all look up.

'It'll be the fingerprint people. That was fast,' Holly said, getting to her feet.

'Don't open it unless they show you I.D.,' Margaret warned.

Holly smiled at her. 'We can't make everyone show us their I.D. Those youths won't come back now they know the police have been.'

Tess and Margaret finished their teas and were about to join Holly, when she came back in to the staff room.

'They're from the *Evening Gazette*.'

The woman was already removing the lens cap from her camera, while the man hovered by the door, pen poised for quotes.

'Hi, I'm Zoe and this is Jake. I've a mate who works in the local nick and he's just phoned me to say he'd got a story. Could we have a few words from you and take a couple of pictures? I hear one of you has been a bit of a hero.'

For the next five minutes Jake scribbled rapidly, his tongue protruding from one side of his mouth as he wrote down what had happened. Margaret was embellishing the story, telling of Tess's bravery and fight back against the hooded raiders with only a rolled up magazine as protection. Mortified, Tess was then asked to hold her *Heat* magazine in the air while grimacing for a photograph.

The next day, Tess popped out of the shop to buy the *Evening Gazette* from a nearby newsagent. The papers weren't available to buy until after twelve, so she and Holly had been clock watching all morning and looking forward to reading about her fifteen minutes of fame. Margaret wasn't at work that day so Holly urged her to hurry in case there was a rush of customers. Tess left her best friend jumping up and down and clapping her hands excitedly, like a wind-up toy.

The newsagent's shop was across Maddox Square and behind Caffè Nero. Tess hurried past the tables where al fresco diners were sitting. The restaurants were filling up with people meeting friends and entertaining clients for lunch. Wafts of garlic smelt wonderful as she passed a group of women who were tucking into their dishes of penne pasta. She crossed the road and walked past the bustling coffee shop.

Inside the newsagent's shop there was a long queue. She stood in line, becoming impatient as the minutes ticked by. She'd never been in the paper before, let alone for a heroic deed. Irritatingly, the queue had to wait while the cashier turned to shout through a hatch for some more change. Another customer was served and then it was Tess's turn. She bought three copies of the local paper.

Despite struggling with the papers that were slipping and unfolding, Tess managed to catch a glimpse of her photograph. She stopped, her jaw dropping in disappointment. Her mind was a fog of humiliation.

Tess reached The Blue Olive, turned and pushed the door open with her bottom.

'What's the matter?' Holly asked, noticing Tess's expression. 'Isn't it in?'

'Front page.' Tess dropped the papers next to the till.

'What's the problem, then? Let me see.'

The headline stood out in large bold letters. **DON'T MESS WITH TESS.**

Underneath the headline was the picture of Tess. She was wielding *Heat* magazine and grimacing with menace.

Tess groaned. 'I'll never be able to show my face in public again.'

Chapter Thirteen

As the week progressed, Tess's flush of embarrassment receded. New headlines had replaced hers and the photograph had now been relegated to recycling piles across the county. She was relieved that the paper hadn't been printed nationally and only to one small area of the country.

Evening light seeped through the window, dimming the colours in the lounge as Tess lay sprawled across her settee, relaxing in front of the television. A reporter on *East Midlands Today* was interviewing a local farmer about the difficulties of farming today. Tess was listening intently to the red-cheeked farmer while he explained how he'd set up his own fruit and vegetable shop on his premises.

Seeing boxes of fruit, Tess was reminded that she'd meant to pick blackberries from several huge bramble bushes growing alongside the village green. If she didn't do it this evening before the forecast of several days of rain, she'd be too late. Hauling herself up from the comfortable cushions, she slipped on her shoes and grabbed a Tupperware bowl.

The sun was slowly sinking, the green stretched before her and Halston looked bewitching. The village was bathed in an orange glow, as if viewing it through a Quality Street toffee penny wrapper.

Tess began picking blackberries. Every time she pricked her finger, she rewarded herself with a delicious sweet mouthful. She hadn't made Blake a pie or crumble for a couple of weeks now, so this would be perfect for Sunday lunch. He was visiting his mother this evening and then meeting a colleague in town for a drink. She wondered how his mother was coping with the knowledge that her son was ill. Her name was Joy, which seemed ironic. Tess had never met such a joyless woman. They weren't close, mainly due to Joy's jealousies and interference, but now wasn't the time to dwell on Blake's mother.

She continued to pick blackberries while humming contentedly, until footsteps made her jump and swing round suddenly.

'Is it safe to speak? You promise not to whack me with a magazine?'

That smile again. Daniel stood in front of her with his arms raised in mock surrender. Despite her hammering heart, Tess managed to speak calmly.

'Please, don't remind me. Why do you think I waited until it was dusk to come out?'

Daniel laughed. 'It wasn't so bad. I recognised you.'

'I'm not sure that's a compliment?'

Daniel smiled then suddenly looked more serious. 'Are you okay, though?'

'Yes, I'm fine thanks. Just a bit jumpy. When I heard your footsteps…'

'Sorry, I didn't think. Stupid of me. I should have whistled a tune as I got closer.'

'No, it's fine, really. I've never felt safer than I do since I've lived in Halston.'

'I think the last crime here was when somebody didn't finish their pint.' He winked at her. 'Were the culprits caught?'

'No, they wore hoods and apparently the CCTV cameras weren't working.'

'Typical. You were brave but you really shouldn't do it again. The next idiots might be carrying a knife.'

Tess felt light-headed at his concern.

Daniel turned and called his dogs. His two spaniels obediently came running to their master's side. Seeing Tess, they wagged their tails and went to investigate. Goya took a great interest in the bowl of fruit.

'They're lovely dogs,' she said, bending to stroke them.

'Yep. They're great company and they get me out the house.'

'I was going to phone you later this evening. I've jotted down some ideas for a finger buffet which I think would be easier if guests are wandering around looking at your art.'

'That's just what I had in mind. You're happy to come on board then?'

'I'd love to.'

'Great. That's a relief.' Daniel brushed a fly away from his face. 'So, why are you picking blackberries so late in the day?'

'Rain's forecast for a few days and I'm competing with the neighbours for collecting them. Unfortunately the best ones are too high for me to reach.'

He stepped closer. Tess's breath quickened. He reached past her shoulder towards the twisted and overgrown blackberry bush. He stood so close that she could smell a faint tang of soap on freshly washed skin. He stretched to the highest branches to pick a few berries from the top of the bush. She stepped to one side, watching his body bridge the distance between them, his T-shirt riding up above his waistband, revealing a taut stomach with a soft line of dark hair leading from his navel down an inch, until it disappeared beneath the waistband of his jeans. Tess reminded herself to breathe.

'Here you go.' Daniel dropped a palm full of berries into the bowl.

'Thank you. I was thinking of fetching a kitchen chair.'

'Now *that* I would have liked to have seen.'

The conversation stopped and their gaze lingered for a few seconds longer than was comfortable.

'I think I've got enough now.' She lifted up the bowl to show him.

'Are you making jam?'

'I'm going to make a crumble for my boyfriend.'

The words had tumbled out before Tess could stop them. She'd broken the spell and noticed Daniel's smile fade a little.

'Lucky chap. Well, you've got my number. Let me know your ideas.'

Her mind was whirring. Did he mean Blake was a lucky chap because she was making him a crumble, or because he was her boyfriend?

'I will.' Her mind went blank. She tried desperately to conjure up something interesting to say to him so that he'd stay and talk a little longer. Then, as if a switch had been turned, she unexpectedly became shy and self-conscious. No witty or interesting anecdote sprang to mind in order to keep him there.

Daniel said goodbye and turned away. She watched him walk across the village green towards the cricket pitch, his dogs bounding alongside. Was it her imagination, or had he looked disappointed when she'd mentioned Blake? She watched him until he was swallowed by the evening gloom.

Daniel trudged back across the grass feeling down. He didn't even know Tess. He'd only met her three times so why did the knowledge of a boyfriend disappoint him quite so much. She'd looked gorgeous tonight. No weird clothes, just jeans and a pale blue jumper. Her dark hair was spilling out of a ponytail and the escaping strands had framed her heart-shaped face. She had a little smudge of blackberry juice on her lips that he'd imagined kissing away. It had been a long time since he had been interested in a girl and it was just bloody typical that Tess was spoken for.

While he'd been travelling the world, he'd met many girls. Most had become friends, but a few became girlfriends and had developed into deeper relationships. He'd had a wonderful time getting to know them and enjoying exploring different countries with someone special. But his wanderlust had always grown stronger than each relationship, and Daniel had left several broken-hearted girls behind.

After his parents' death, Daniel had met Ellie. She was the daughter of one of his father's architect friends. Ellie had attended house parties his parents had hosted over the years and she'd also attended their funeral. She had rung Daniel a few times in the early weeks of his grieving. He'd kept her at a distance because he'd needed all his emotional strength just to get through each day. After a month, she'd called at The Rookery with a takeaway meal and they'd spent a pleasant evening together. She'd made him smile and had been a great support for him when he was feeling low. It was comforting to know that Ellie had been friends with his parents, and looking back, he believed that he'd been drawn to her through this connection. Their relationship had lasted more than two years. The end came shortly after she'd given him an ultimatum to take their relationship a step further. She'd wanted to move in with Daniel or become engaged. Instead of embracing a deeper closeness, Daniel had felt trapped. He thought he loved Ellie, but at the same time, he knew he didn't want to make things more permanent. That had been four years ago. He'd enjoyed several short-lived romances since then, but they'd mostly ended mutually and amicably.

Daniel opened his front door and ushered his dogs inside. He wondered if Tess was in her boyfriend's arms right now. He felt a pang of jealousy, then locked the door and checked it three times.

Chapter Fourteen

It was the eighteenth of August and Denise's appointment at The Breast Clinic had finally arrived. She was sitting in a waiting room elbow to elbow with several other women who were queuing to see a specialist. *This Morning* was on the television in the corner of the room and Philip Schofield was interviewing an actress who was promoting her latest book. The interview wasn't holding Denise's attention so she looked around the room.

It appeared that breast lumps weren't choosy. There were women of all shapes and sizes, races and ages: a large old lady sat knitting, knees apart and relaxing as if she were at home, a pale thin woman clinging to her husband's arm for support, a young Indian lady draped in a beautiful yellow sari.

Simon had tried desperately to change an important meeting in Dublin, but six other people had been involved and the timing had suited them all perfectly. She was alone, but she didn't mind. She felt calm. She was taking one day at a time. Why panic and jump to conclusions? She was young and healthy and had never smoked. Simon had made her laugh at the coincidence of seeing the parrot. He'd told her it was probably a parakeet that had escaped from its cage and that there were quite a few parrots living wild in London.

Denise found herself thinking of her mother. She missed her. If she were alive, would she be sitting with her now? Had she ever had a breast lump? A doctor had asked her this question but it wasn't something she'd ever discussed with her mother. They'd talked about family, memories, friends, shopping. The future.

'Mrs Harby,' called a nurse, reading the name from the set of notes she was holding. Denise felt the butterflies take flight in her stomach. She stood up and followed the nurse into an examination room.

'Take a seat, Mrs Harby. Mr Simmonds will see you soon.' The nurse indicated to a chair at the side of the table.

The room felt cool and clinical, making Denise shudder. There was a desk, three chairs, a stainless steel table with medical equipment on it and a narrow bed on wheels. There was a sharp knock on the door, followed immediately by a tall, well-built man wearing wire-rimmed glasses. A nurse stood to one side, attentive to any instruction he might give.

'Good morning,' he said.

'Hello.'

Mr Simmonds picked up her notes and rustled the pages until he found the referral letter from her own doctor. He read it, his head nodding slightly as he moved down the page, absorbing its contents.

'Right,' he said, looking up. 'If you don't mind sitting on the couch and removing the top half of your clothing, I'll examine you.'

Denise did as she was told. The doctor performed the same routine as her own doctor had done previously.

'Yes, I can feel a small lump,' he said. 'I just want to aspirate it.'

'What does that mean?'

'I need to draw out its contents with a syringe. If it is a common cyst, it will be gone as soon as I drain it. We'll need to scan the lump first.'

Within ten minutes, the radiologist was scanning her breast and the image was displayed in black and white on a screen beside her. She could see a small white lump on the screen. Mr Simmonds pulled on some tight latex gloves and inserted a needle into the lump. He pulled back on the syringe several times, but nothing drained. He laid down the syringe on the table.

'It doesn't seem to be a cyst, but that doesn't mean it's anything to worry about. It's not unusual for solid lumps to be absolutely harmless. I'll need to do another test to determine this. It's called a biopsy. I'm going to insert a larger needle that will remove a tiny piece of tissue from the lump. I'll give you a small local anaesthetic first to numb the area. Is that all right?'

Denise nodded, not trusting her voice.

The doctor injected her, making her wince. She felt a stinging sensation as the fluid was flushed through the syringe into her body. He turned and wrote in her notes while he waited a couple of minutes for the local anaesthetic to take effect. He then stood up and reached for a small instrument.

'When this takes a small piece of tissue, you will hear a sharp click. This is normal and it won't hurt.'

Denise nodded.

'Just relax, Mrs Harby. You're doing great.'

Mr Simmonds lined up the needle while looking at the image of the lump on the screen. She could see the needle on the display, slowly finding its way to the white highlighted area. A loud click made her jump even though she'd been warned. The needle was withdrawn and the nurse stemmed any drops of blood and put a plaster on the puncture wound. The doctor placed the specimen in a small jar and wrote on the label. He took off his gloves, walked to the sink in the corner of the room and washed his hands. As he lathered the liquid soap in his palms, he looked over his shoulder.

'It should take a week or so before the results are back. We'll be in touch with you as soon as they're through.'

He walked back to the table, drying his hands on two paper towels. 'Try not to worry unduly. You're very young for it to be anything nasty.'

Yeah, and there are more sparrows in the sky than parrots, thought Denise.

Chapter Fifteen

Tess sat wedged into the corner of her large settee, legs curled up into the deep feather-filled cushions, cradling a mug of coffee. She glanced up at the television every so often to watch a feature on *The One Show*. As the fire crackled in its grate, she nestled deeper into the cushions thinking that this free time was heavenly. She wiggled her toes while she sipped the hot liquid through its froth. No demands from Blake, a good supply of Jaffa cakes, and hours that stretched before her surrounded by cookery books. But best of all, she was reliving the conversation she'd had with Daniel earlier that evening.

She flicked through her books, jotting down a few notes from her favourite recipes and adding a few ideas of her own. Her pen hesitated above the paper. She remembered Daniel's T-shirt riding up his midriff. She shook her head to dispel the image.

'Finger food desserts,' she read, whilst stretching across the arm of the settee to reach another Jaffa cake. She nibbled around the chocolate perimeter, popped the circle into her mouth and sucked it until the sponge and chocolate melted away. This left the sweet tangy orange jelly disc to slowly dissolve on her tongue.

The shrill ringing of her mobile disturbed her peace as abruptly as a rugby tackle. She swallowed the lozenge of jelly, pressed the mute button on the television controls and stood up with a groan. Her legs were stiff from being curled up and sat on, so she limped to fetch her phone.

'Hello.'

'Is Blake there?'

It was Blake's mother, joyless Joy.

'No, he's out.'

'He's not answering his mobile.'

'He was meeting a colleague after work.'

'Poor boy. Working late while he's sick.'

'He's out socially, having a drink and relaxing. Is there a message I can pass on?'

'He looked so pale last week and the weight's dropping off him.'

Tess's mouth made an O shape as she gaped down the phone. The only weight that drops off him, she thought, was when he took his clothes off at night.

Joy continued. 'I really think you should be taking better care of him. It's not easy taking on all that new responsibility at work.'

Tess gritted her teeth and tried to remain polite. 'Blake gets a lot of support, so you don't need to concern yourself with that. Now was there a message I can give him?'

'Don't go getting hoity-toity with me, young lady. Lesley was always so polite to me.'

Not bloody Lesley again! Why did she constantly have to bring Blake's ex-girlfriend into the conversation? They had only dated for four months. Tess summoned a calm voice from the depths of her shrivelling reserve of diplomacy and patience.

'You can rest assured that Blake is eating well and getting plenty of support.'

'I need him to fix a missing tile on my roof and wondered if he can do it in the morning, before the rain sets in for a few days. I know how unwell and busy he is, but I'm sure he'd want me to ask him. My boy wouldn't want me hiring an odd-job man who would charge a fortune. What sort of a man does odd jobs instead of getting a proper job, anyway?'

Tess was in no mood to start defending odd-job men

or continue the conversation. 'If I don't see him tonight, I'll leave him a note. Sorry I have to dash, but I've got something bubbling on the hob. Bye.'

It was Tess's temper that was bubbling. 'Obnoxious woman.' She scooped up the Jaffa cakes' box and lukewarm mug of coffee. One minute she says that Blake needs to relax and then she demands he does a dangerous job for her.

Tess walked into the kitchen, dumping the box and mug angrily on the worktop. In her haste, her thumb became caught on the mug's handle, tipping the remnants of her drink over. It ran in rivulets along the worktop and dripped like a caramel-coloured waterfall onto the kitchen floor.

Five minutes. That's all it took to spoil an evening. Five minutes and Joy Snipes.

Blake showered having arranged to meet his colleague, Kent, at The Llama Lounge in town. He'd have a quick pint, maybe two, eat a curry and make his way to Halston to spend the night with Tess.

Blake was growing more comfortable with his lie. He was even convincing himself that he was justified in his deceit. After all, he thought as he rubbed his hair dry, it wasn't his fault that he'd been forced into such a difficult situation. Tess needed looking after and he was the one to do it. Wasn't he just protecting her from an unwise decision? He hadn't asked for all the extra pampering he was receiving from her. It wasn't his fault that she wanted to indulge him. Okay, he may have told a fib, but what was the harm in a little white lie if Tess still had him to protect her? In a month or two he'd tell her that he'd been cured and they could get on with a normal life.

Nottingham City Centre was busy for a Thursday evening. People bustled in all directions, some going home having worked late and others dressed up for an evening out. A group of short-skirted giggling girls hobbled by, their heels click-clacking on the pavement. Blake turned to admire their bare legs as they passed him. He made his way through the market area into Maddox Square. Wonderful smells of garlic and spices drifted along the cobbled streets and music blared out of doorways. He passed The Blue Olive and glanced over at the shop where Tess worked. Turning the corner, the square opened up before him. People were still sitting outside under the fairy lit trees even though autumn was fast approaching. He wound his way through tables and chairs and walked in through the swing doors of The Llama Lounge.

Leather settees and wooden tables dotted the lounge area. Black and white photographs of actors and singers decorated the walls, candles had been lit and George Ezra was singing through the sound system. Blake spotted Kent leaning on the bar, ordering a drink. He walked over and slapped him on the back.

'Alright, mate?'

'Blake, good timing. What can I get you?'

'A pint of bitter. I'll grab a seat.'

He wandered over to a battered but comfortable sofa near the window.

'Cheers,' said Blake, accepting the glass from his friend and taking several gulps.

'How's Tess?' asked Kent. 'I haven't seen her since the dinner party in June.'

'She's fine, thanks. Did you see her photograph in the paper?'

'Yeh. She's a pretty girl but the photo looked a bit weird.' Kent wiped creamy froth from his mouth.

'They told her to pose. She was a bit miffed about it. How's Randy?'

'You know she hates you calling her that! Miranda's fine, thanks. I've got a bit of a dilemma actually. Her sister's getting married on the third of November, on a Friday for God's sake. Who gets married on a Friday? That's the date we should be flying to Amsterdam for my stag break. Now Miranda's suggesting the stag party flies out on the Saturday instead, so I can go to the wedding. That'll mean no drinking at the wedding and a day less in Amsterdam. It's not as if Miranda's even close to her sister. She lives in Scotland and I've only met her twice.'

'Can't you move Amsterdam back a week or two?'

'No. The hotel's been booked so I'll lose the deposit.'

Blake thought it would have suited him to put back the stag weekend. If it were moved into December he would have had another payday.

'D'you think you're going to make it to Amsterdam?' asked Kent.

'If Halcott Manor sells. To be honest, I might be struggling if it doesn't. I could really do with the commission.'

'I shouldn't think it'd take long to sell.'

Blake drained his pint and got up to get the next round in. 'Same again?'

Kent pointed to his half full glass and shook his head.

Blake turned towards the bar then looked back over his shoulder at his friend. 'You could always dump Randy!' He winked. 'Then you could go to Amsterdam when you want.'

Leaning against the bar waiting to be served, Blake noticed a barmaid with red hair and a shapely figure. The giddy buzz of alcohol made Blake stare unselfconsciously. He'd drunk a large glass of wine before leaving home and had downed his first pint quickly on an empty stomach. Blake raised a ten-pound note and smiled when the girl came to serve him. He noticed a sign behind her that read,

Delicious New Pear Cocktail – Ask for Details. Great, he had a conversation starter.

'What can I get you?'

'Tell me about your lovely pear.' Blake raised an eyebrow at his innuendo.

'What?'

Blake pointed to the sign.

'Oh. It's made from Poire Williams liqueur, Grand Marnier with mandarin and pear juice. It's quite sweet and usually the ladies drink it, so if you prefer a more bitter drink you should go for a gin based drink, like Bitter Bomb or Fallen Angel.'

He smirked while lounging across the bar. 'A Fallen Angel sounds intriguing.'

The girl turned her back on him and began making the cocktail, leaving Blake wondering why his charm didn't seem to be working with her. It worked on many women whose houses he valued.

Ninety minutes later, Blake had drunk four pints of beer, one cocktail and two Jack Daniel's. He felt his eyes roll out of focus whenever he looked at his colleague.

'Not driving to Tess's place tonight, then?' asked Kent.

Blake slurred his speech. 'I'll shee how I feel later. A naan bread and rice will mop up most of the alcohol.' Blake hiccupped loudly, forcibly jolting him back into his seat.

'I think you'd better get a taxi. A sponge the size of a bucket wouldn't soak up what you've put away in the last couple of hours.'

Blake was feeling relaxed and happy although his eyes weren't focusing too well. They returned to discussing their first topic of the evening, but hadn't reached any conclusions to the dilemma of Kent's stag do.

'Ah, dilemmash.' Blake leant back in his chair, raising his arms and clasping his hands together behind his head.

'Do you ever find yourself cornered?' asked Kent.

'I have my momentsh.' Blake leaned forwards and tapped the side of his nose, knowingly.

'Go on then. Spill the beans.'

'No, mate. It's a secret.'

'I might be able to help.'

Blake blinked slowly, feeling very tired and a little emotional. Kent was a good bloke and had been a friend for many years at the agency. Perhaps he should share his secret and get a little support and understanding for his tricky predicament.

'Okay, but promise you won't tell a shoul.'

His colleague nodded and leaned forwards.

Blake swayed slightly. 'I've told Tess a lie.' He put his forefinger to his lips and exaggerated a shushing sound.

'What about?'

'She was going to dump me. Me!' He pointed to his chest and looked incredulous at the thought. 'What could I do?'

'So what did you say?'

'I told her I was sick.' Blake nodded, smugly. 'Mate, I've got to tell you, it sheems to be working like a dream. I know, I know,' he said, holding his hands aloft in mock surrender. 'You don't need to tell me. It was a bit shneaky, but she needs me.' He wagged his finger at Kent.

'Let me get this right,' said Kent. 'You're telling me that you're letting Tess believe that you're ill, when you're not?'

Blake stifled a burp that jerked him backwards again. He finished his Jack Daniel's with a single gulp. 'Well, putting it like that, it shounds bad. But I'm thinking of her. Buying a bit of time.'

Kent shook his head slowly. 'What did you say you were suffering from?'

'Cansher.'

'What!'

'Shhh!'

'I can't get my head around this.'

'It'sh not a big deal. In a few months I'll tell that her I'm okay. I only did it because... I love her. I want to look after her. Protect her. How can I do that if she dumpsh me?' Blake raised his shoulders and extended up-turned palms in question.

Kent raised his voice. 'But you're lying to her.'

'Only temporly... tempily... only for a bit.'

'That's okay, then,' said Kent, sarcastically. 'Hey, Tess, I'm lying to you and worrying you sick, but it's only temporary.'

'You know what I mean, mate. Come on! You musht have lied to Randy now and again.'

'A couple of times—'

'There you go then.' Blake leaned back and rested one ankle on his bent knee.

'If you'd let me finish, I was going to say when I'd booked a secret weekend away and I didn't want her to find out where we were going. And then when I needed her to book a day off, so I could propose in a hot air balloon.' Kent shook his head. 'I need some fresh air. I'm feeling claustrophobic in here.'

'Let'sh go for a curry then.'

'You know what? Suddenly I don't feel very hungry. I'm calling it a day.'

'But you asked me to explain. You shaid you could help with my problem.'

'That's not a problem. That's you being a complete and utter manipulating bastard.' Kent scraped his chair back and stood up. 'She's too good for you.'

Blake looked up at him and tried to focus. 'Have another drink before we go to Ghandishh.'

'How about you just fuck off, Blake!' Kent threw a twenty-pound note on the table, punched the door open and left.

Blake turned a little unsteadily and shouted after him, 'Don't tell anyone. I said it was a shecret.'

He ordered another whiskey and started to feel sorry for himself. He shouldn't have told Kent. He wouldn't understand. Now he had a headache and could do with one of Tess's magical massages. He'd pay up after this drink and make his way over to Rose Cottage.

Blake stumbled through Maddox Square. He found his car after a few wrong turns and then hunted for his keys. They weren't in his trouser pockets. Damn. Had he left them in the bar? He jumped up and down in the gutter. This made him feel sick and attracted giggles from three girls who were walking past with linked arms. His drunken gymnastics worked. His keys jingled inside his jacket pocket. He opened the door and slumped into the driver's seat. Blake shook his head, feeling very tired and a little nauseous. Maybe he was a little over the legal limit for driving, but the roads were quiet heading towards Halston. If he took it slowly, he'd get to Tess's safely.

He started his car and gingerly emerged from his parking space. Turning left, he headed for the roundabout that would take him in the direction of Halston. The lights seemed to confuse him as he struggled to stay in his lane. The bright yellow streetlights and red brake lights made him squint. He slowed down when he saw an amber light and stopped when it turned to red. Blake decided to close his eyes for ten seconds. He was so tired.

A sharp knocking on the window woke him with a start. He opened his eyes and saw flashing blue lights. Now what part of the traffic light sequence were they?

The following morning Tess woke up at seven fifteen when her alarm clock beeped. She pressed the snooze button that gave her another five minutes. Slowly remembering Joy's unpleasant phone call, and Blake's night out, she rolled over to see if he'd slipped into bed beside her while she'd been asleep. The other half of the bed was still tidy and cold, the pillow still plump. She reached over to her bedside table and picked up her mobile. No missed calls or messages. He must have drunk too much and sensibly stayed at his own place in town.

She heaved herself into a sitting position with her legs dangling out of bed and rubbed her eyes. Stifling a yawn, she slid her feet into her slippers and walked to the bathroom. A shower always revived her and within twenty minutes she was humming a tune while rubbing cream blusher onto her cheeks. Tess dried her hair, got dressed and ran downstairs to make some breakfast. She was just pouring milk onto her cornflakes, when her mobile rang at five past eight. She really should have left five minutes ago and it could well be Joy again. Then again, it could be important.

'Hello.'

'Tess, it's me.'

'Blake? Why didn't you call me? Have you got a sore throat, you sound awful?'

'Can you come and pick me up?'

'I'm late for work. Where are you?'

'At the central police station.'

Chapter Sixteen

September arrived, bringing with it grumbling mauve clouds that bruised the sky. A watery sunshine pushed its way through fast-moving clouds and shone upon Halston. During the night, a violent storm had swept through the village, loosening roof tiles and knocking over fence panels. This morning the gales had subsided, but the aftermath had woken the villagers early. Swathed in coats and scarves, neighbours righted upturned wheelie bins, collected snapped branches and rescued laundry that had been left on the washing line and was now decorating trees.

It had been a couple of weeks since Daniel had spoken to Tess. He hadn't seen her in the village since he'd helped her to pick blackberries and some days he even lingered self-consciously by the same bramble bush, while walking his dogs. Plans for his art exhibition were progressing well, but now he had to contact Tess somehow. He kicked himself for not getting her number because all he knew was that she lived close to the blackberry bush.

Daniel had slept through the alarm he'd set himself that morning. He'd painted until the early hours the previous evening, while listening to the buffeting of the tall trees in the garden. The rain had lashed against the windows and the thunder had rocked the room when the storm had passed overhead. The intensity of nature had inspired him to paint, smear, rub, daub and splatter. This morning he'd slept until nine thirty, waking in a panic and rushing downstairs to find the dogs sulking and desperate to be let out into the garden. It was now nearly eleven and he was fastening their harnesses.

'Come on, girls, let's go.'

Having left The Rookery, Daniel turned to lock the front door with difficulty, as one arm was outstretched behind him restraining his two excited spaniels. They were pulling towards the enormous metal gates and the village green beyond. Daniel pulled them back the obligatory three times while checking that the front door was definitely locked.

'Whoa!' he shouted as the dogs strained on their leads. 'Who's taking who for a walk here?'

Daniel pulled open one of the front gates that creaked on its hinges. He was disappointed to see that the electric fence and Farmer Bill's cows had been moved to the front of The Royal Oak. The groundsman was working on the cricket pitch and several families were flying kites, kicking footballs or walking dogs. He decided to walk through the village to a smaller field that still had plenty of room for the dogs to have a good run.

The clouds were school-jumper grey and yellow leaves fluttered to the floor with each gust of wind. Daniel stopped to read a planning application notice, holding it down with a finger as a corner of the paper flapped. He kicked a fallen apple and waved to a neighbour. Cows bellowed and rooks flew overhead, cawing their displeasure at the blustery weather.

He spotted Mabel, taking in some washing. Mabel was a widow, a silver-haired old lady who reminded Daniel of his late grandmother. As a small boy he would always receive a lavender-scented hug and silver foil-wrapped chocolate coins whenever he visited his mother's mother.

'Morning, Mabel. You're taking your washing in. Do you know something about the weather that I don't?'

'How nice to see you.' She tottered towards him, tipping several pegs into a basket. 'I've been listening to the local radio station and they say that another downpour is on its way. We do need some rain though, don't we? We've had a long hot summer.'

'Yes, we've been spoilt this summer. I suppose it couldn't last forever.'

'Sadly not. I saw the poster for your art exhibition in Jackson's window. You'll be leaving us for London before long.'

'Not me. Too many memories here in Halston to ever leave, besides, I love it at The Rookery.'

'Yes, I suppose that's true.' Mabel daydreamed over Daniel's shoulders.

'Penny for them?'

'Oh, I was just thinking of my husband, George. When loved ones pass on, you feel closer to them if you don't move away.' She turned and pointed to a neat little border edging the lawn. 'George spent hours planting and weeding. If I close my eyes I can see him there on his kneeling cushion with his spade, winking at me before asking for a cuppa. He built that barbecue over there and the bookshelves in the dining room. It's comforting, you know?'

'I do, Mabel,' he said, touching her age-spotted hand.

Daniel was jolted sideways. Goya and Gogh were growing impatient and pulling.

'I think they're trying to tell you something.' Mabel chuckled.

'I pretend I'm in charge, but we all know different.'

They laughed and said goodbye.

The cricket pitch and village green were behind him now. He continued along the narrow main road that was flanked on either side with cottages. A short way ahead, Daniel recognised the small hunched figure of Mrs Campbell chatting on a neighbour's doorstep. He couldn't see whom she was talking to because the figure was hidden from view by a rose bush. As he reached the gate where Mrs Campbell was in conversation, a gust of wind took his breath away and blew his jacket wide open like leather wings. He looked up and felt an unexpected rush of excitement. Tess was standing in the doorway. Cursing to himself for blushing like a teenager, he raised an arm and smiled. He saw her return his wave. He'd have loved to stop and talk, but Mrs Campbell was mid-flow, so he continued on with the dogs. His pace picked up with a smile on his face. At least he knew where she lived now.

Tess had been preparing a home-made pizza for lunch. Blake was calling in before going to his mother's later in the afternoon to finally replace her roof tile. Tess had been happily kneading and punching the dough when a knock at the front door had disturbed her.

'You're early,' she shouted, wondering why Blake hadn't let himself in.

She shook the loose flour from her hands into the sink and hurried towards the front door. Gingerly she opened it with doughy fingers. Tess smiled weakly when she saw Mrs Campbell at the door, knowing that the old lady didn't do two-minute chats.

'Hello, Tess. I see you're baking again,' said Mrs Campbell, pointing to Tess's hands covered in sticky mixture. Despite acknowledging that Tess was busy, it didn't stop the old lady from launching into a tirade of gossip about several neighbours, Chippy's latest escapades, her rheumatism and the change in the weather. After ten minutes, Tess felt dough drying and tightening on her fingers. She was about to make her excuses to escape, when something moving in her peripheral vision distracted her from the conversation. She turned to look and caught her breath. Daniel was walking his dogs past her house. Had he come to visit? He waved. Tess now had no idea what Mrs Campbell was saying. She waved back to encourage him to interrupt her

101

neighbour, but disappointingly he continued walking until he disappeared along the lane.

'Damn!' Tess sighed.

'Pardon, my dear?'

'Erm… pan. I've left a pan on the hob. I'll have to dash, I'm afraid.'

'I do go on a bit, don't I? I'll leave you in peace.'

'I'll pop over in the week to catch up.'

'Lovely. See you soon.'

Daniel and the dogs turned left at a huge oak tree and walked on to the village's smaller grassy area. He let the dogs off their leads and watched them bolt across the expanse of grass. The wind had grown stronger and colder and he wrapped his jacket tighter around his body. The trees' branches whipped and fought as they swayed violently and the sky grew darker. Mabel had been right about an imminent downpour.

He was halfway across the field of grass when he felt the first splat of a raindrop. Seconds later, the heavens opened. His jeans stuck to his legs and his T-shirt welded itself to his body. The sky flashed, followed by a hollow rumble. Goya and Gogh came running towards him. They all ran to a large tree in the middle of the field but it didn't offer much shelter because half its leaves had already fallen. The thought crossed his mind that he shouldn't be standing under a tree in a thunderstorm, but it was their only source of shelter, however minimal.

The deluge continued and the dogs huddled close to Daniel's feet. He couldn't see clearly because the rain streamed through his hair and down his face. The sky flashed and the thunder roared once again. The dogs looked forlorn, their ears wet and hanging like damp socks on a washing line. They shivered and pressed closer against Daniel's legs.

Tess had walked back into the kitchen and washed the sticky mess off her hands before starting to knead the dough again. Thoughts of Daniel in his leather jacket filled her mind. She pressed the mixture into a circle and smeared tomato paste over it. If she was quick, she could run upstairs and wait by the bedroom curtains until he walked back. She tutted at the idea; she wasn't a silly schoolgirl, nor was she a stalker.

When the mushrooms, pepperoni and mozzarella had been arranged on the dough base, she sprinkled some grated cheese on top. She gave the pepper grinder a few twists and placed the pizza on the top shelf of the oven.

Tess rinsed her hands again, glancing up when she heard tapping on the window. Silver raindrops were decorating the glass. After drying her hands, she started stacking the dishwasher just as the tapping turned to a loud hammering. The rain beat down on the windows with ferocious strength. Tess was thinking that a second deluge of water in twenty-four hours would be good for her sun-baked lawn, when she remembered Daniel. He'd passed by with the dogs and the only place for dogs to run in that direction would be the little green, which had no shelter.

Without hesitating, she grabbed her car keys and an umbrella from under the stairs and ran down the garden path. She jumped in her car and accelerated along the road with her wipers waving frantically in front of her. The rain pounded against the roof of her little car, deafening the music from the radio. She turned the corner and saw the expanse of grass and wild flowers being battered by the downpour. Standing in the middle of the green was Daniel and his dogs. They were hunched together under a tree. She beeped her horn and saw him turn to look towards her car.

Realisation dawned. She'd driven to Daniel's rescue without giving it a second thought. Any moment now he would be sitting in her car. They would be enclosed in this tiny metal box, inches away from each other. Daniel was running towards her car. She began to hyperventilate. It was thrilling and terrifying. He was a few feet away now. She rolled down her window, feigning nonchalance.

'Climb in. You look like you're drowning. It's a tiny ark, but you're all welcome aboard.'

Daniel opened the door, pulled the passenger seat forwards and let Goya and Gogh leap in. He climbed in the front and shut the door, his broad shoulders already brushing up against her slender ones. The dogs shook themselves on the back seat, showering them both and making them both laugh, breaking the ice.

He turned to face her. 'It's the best ark I've ever seen. Thanks.'

Tess looked at his wet, handsome face. She felt awkward and shy now that he was sitting so close in such a cramped space. She hoped he couldn't tell her heart was hammering inside her chest, so she made up an excuse for passing by.

'I was on my way to Jackson's Store for mushrooms.'

'Sorry to hold you up, but thanks for stopping. I was beginning to think I'd need a snorkel.'

He was tantalisingly close. She could feel his breath on her skin when he spoke and could smell a faint citrusy fragrance as she manoeuvred the car into reverse.

'What about your mushrooms?' asked Daniel.

'Oh, they're not important. I've left something in the oven. Would you mind if I call in home before I drop you off? If you have time I could put the kettle on.'

'That would be great.'

They pulled up outside Rose Cottage and made a dash to the front door. Tess unlocked it and a delicious smell of dough and cheese welcomed them. Hurrying into the kitchen, she bent double and peered into the oven. The pizza needed another five minutes for the cheese to turn golden.

She stood up and faced Daniel. Seeing him clearly for the first time in the last hectic five minutes, Tess was taken aback. He was peeling his leather jacket from his shoulders. His wet jeans clung to his thighs and his black T-shirt was stuck to the contours of his muscled stomach. His hair hung in dripping tendrils, raindrops decorating his face like tribal markings. Tess felt light-headed and incredibly confused.

'I'll fetch a towel.' She ran upstairs. 'Please let there be clean towels in the airing cupboard. Please don't let Blake have used the last one,' she muttered, under her breath.

'I love your house,' Daniel shouted up to her.

'Thank you. Feel free to put the kettle on.'

'Can I let the dogs out the back? The rain seems to have slowed.'

Tess yelled back through the spindles. 'Of course.'

She opened the airing cupboard. One white bath towel sat neatly folded on the shelf. It smelt of jasmine and fresh air. She hugged it and whispered, 'Thank you, thank you.' Back downstairs she saw Daniel was shivering as he filled the kettle. Tess passed him the warm towel. Should she suggest that he remove his wet clothes? God no, what was she thinking?

'Thanks.' He wrapped the towel around his shoulders and used one corner of it to rub his dripping hair.

Tess busied herself getting two cups out of the cupboard and spooned ground coffee into her coffee pot. What had possessed her to invite him in? She knew the answer; she felt good whenever she thought about him, let alone being in his company. She filled the coffee pot with boiling water and immediately the kitchen was filled with the intoxicating aroma of fresh coffee. Tess gripped the tray to pick it up and carry it to the table, when Daniel appeared at her side.

'Let me,' he said.

'Thank you.' She wasn't used to such chivalry. Tess felt his fingers brush against hers as he took the tray from her. A million watts of electricity passed from his skin to hers.

'My pleasure. I really am grateful that you rescued us from the flood. Can I call you Noah?'

'You're welcome, but as I said, I was on my way out anyway.'

'Ah yes. Mushrooms.'

Tess cringed. She could see him looking at an unused number of mushrooms on the worktop.

'Do you cook for a living?' he asked.

'Sadly not. Perhaps one day.' Tess pushed down the filter with the palm of her hand. 'I work in a boring deli in town. It's not very interesting, but I work with nice people and it pays the bills.'

'You're doing well. You have a lovely house.'

'Thank you. I rent it. Houses rarely come up for sale in Halston. Once here, no one wants to leave. But I can understand that, it's a beautiful village.' She lifted the coffee pot. 'How do you take it?'

'Black, no sugar. Thanks.'

Tess pulled out a chair and sat down at the table next to him.

'I really like the initial ideas you gave me for the buffet,' said Daniel. 'How's the final menu coming along?'

She poured milk into her coffee. 'I was going to phone you this weekend about it. I've made a list I'd like to show you.'

'That's great. I can't believe it's only a couple of months away.'

Tess looked at him cradling his coffee cup, peering over the rim and meeting her gaze. With immense effort, she pulled herself away from the table and crossed the kitchen. Opening a drawer, she brought out a list of recipes that she'd scribbled onto a pad. She laid it on the table in front of him. As he studied the recipes, she looked at his dark hair pushed behind his ears and noticed the scar on his temple. She wondered what the story was behind it, but thought better of asking. Instead, she studied the tiny fair hairs on the skin of his neck. When he bent forwards to read her list, his hair fell forwards revealing a small freckle just above the neckline of his T-shirt. Tess quickly looked away when he leaned backwards.

'This sounds fantastic. What's a filo cigar?'

'Oh, it's just a posh name for rolled up paper thin pastry that can be stuffed with a sweet or savoury filling.'

'Why don't you cater for a living, if that's what you really want to do? I'm sure you'd have no trouble cooking privately for dinner parties or even opening a little shop. Joe said your food was delicious. Life's short. It has a way of coming up behind you when you're not looking and pulling the rug out from under your feet.'

Tess saw his expression change for a split second. She wondered if he'd had a bad experience, maybe with an old girlfriend. She decided that she'd try to find out a little more about this man who'd walked into her life and occupied a large percentage of her daydreams.

'Do you live locally?' she asked, trying to appear casual while sipping her coffee.

'Yes, you could say that.'

'Just you?'

'Just me and my two girls.'

Tess fought to keep her smile in place, imagining a wife and daughter.

'Talking of which, they're ominously quiet. What're they up to?' He stood up and peered out of the kitchen window.

Tess held in a sigh of relief. 'Do your family live nearby?'

'My parents died some years ago now, in a car accident.'

She gasped. 'That's dreadful. I'm so sorry for prying.'

'It's okay. You weren't prying, just asking a perfectly normal question in conversation. Do you live alone or does your boyfriend live here too?'

'Just me and Bob the goldfish.'

'Ah! The elusive Bob. Where is he?'

'He lives in the bathroom, with a rubber duck and plastic dolphin.'

'A chap can never have too many friends.'

'Do you have a girlfriend?' Tess could have kicked herself for being so blunt.

'No, I'm far too busy at the moment with my art. I'm a bit of a hermit, to be honest. If it wasn't for the girls taking me on a walk twice a day, I'd probably grow a long beard and become a recluse.'

They laughed.

'I suppose you could try internet dating.' Tess couldn't believe how her mouth was taking control of this conversation instead of her brain. What was she doing trying to enrol him at a dating agency?

'Too scary. I've had friends who have dabbled in it. Apparently the odds are good, but the goods are odd!'

Tess swallowed her mouthful of coffee with some difficulty, trying not to giggle. She swallowed loudly, waving a hand in front of her face as if fanning herself. 'Don't make me laugh.'

Daniel rubbed her back as she gave a few tickly coughs. His touch was thrilling but she hid any reaction.

'What about *your* family?' Daniel asked.

'Mum and Dad live in Cornwall. I'm their only child.

Apparently I arrived in my own good time after seven years of them trying. How about you?'

'I have a twin, but Den lives in London.'

'A twin? How wonderful. Are you identical?'

He laughed. 'No, but we both have Mum's nose and eyes and Dad's colouring, so there's no mistaking that we're related.'

Tess thought that his parents hadn't used much imagination calling their twins, Dan and Den. It must have been very confusing having two boys with such similar names.

'Will Den be coming to the exhibition?'

'I hope so, but the family's been going through a rough patch recently.'

'I'm sorry.'

'Den's not well at the moment and is waiting for test results.'

Tess nodded, knowingly. 'That's awful. My boyfriend has cancer, but he's making good progress.'

'I'm sorry, I didn't know. That's rough.'

'He's coping physically, but mentally he's not so good. Short-tempered, impaired judgment, tired. He spent the night in a cell a few weeks ago for drunk driving. He's never done that before. He must be stressed. Now he's waiting for a date for a court appearance to find out what his punishment will be.'

'Poor bloke. Sounds like he's got a lot on his plate. But he's got you.'

Tess smiled weakly but didn't reply. They held each other's gaze for a few seconds. The intimate moment was interrupted when the front door slammed. Tess jumped. Footsteps marched down the hall.

'Bloody weather! Wipers aren't working properly, so I'll—'

The kitchen door swung open and Blake stopped mid-sentence. His last harsh haircut had left one millimetre of fair hair on his scalp. 'What's this?'

Daniel stood up and held out his hand. 'Hi, I'm Daniel. Tess kindly rescued me from the storm.'

'Did she?'

Since being with Daniel, Tess had totally forgotten that Blake was coming for lunch. She saw that he'd noticed the dining chairs she and Daniel were sitting on were at an angle, facing each other.

'I'm Blake. Tess's boyfriend.'

'Pleased to meet you, Blake.'

'This is the Daniel who's asked me to cook for his exhibition. He's an artist.'

'So I hear.' Blake sounded uninterested.

'Do you want a coffee?' Tess asked.

'No, thanks. What's that smell?'

'Oh no!' Tess hurried across the kitchen. She opened the oven and was greeted by a plume of smoke. The pizza looked like a huge dirty bronze penny.

'Sorry, it was my fault,' said Daniel. 'I asked Tess about some recipes and distracted her. I'll be off and get out of your way.'

Tess saw Blake open the fridge, looking for an alternative lunch. She looked at Daniel and pulled a face, hoping it would convey an apology.

Goya and Gogh were called from the back garden and hurled themselves excitedly across the kitchen floor into the hall. Blake looked up in disbelief, mumbling something about fleas and allergies.

At the front door, Daniel unwound the towel from his neck and handed it to Tess.

'Thank you. I meant what I said about life being too short not to change what isn't right.'

Tess wondered if he was talking about her career or if intuition had told him that she and Blake were having problems. 'I know. My best friend has said the same thing.'

'I love your food ideas. Give me a call and we'll arrange a time to meet up at The Rookery.'

'I will.'

Tess hesitated. She didn't know whether they knew each other well enough for a friendly hug or a kiss on the cheek? She felt awkward and clumsy. To cover her embarrassment, she opened the front door and watched Daniel walk down the path with his two bounding spaniels by his side again. That's where she wanted to be.

He closed the gate and looked over his shoulder towards her, lifting an arm to wave.

Tess closed the door and hugged the damp towel. It was still warm from his skin. She pressed her nose into the softness, closed her eyes and inhaled.

Chapter Seventeen

A letter dropped onto Blake's veneered flooring. Before picking it up, he pushed the last piece of toast into his mouth, swapping his half-smoked cigarette into his other hand. With his cheeks bulging, he carried the envelope towards the kitchen sink where the light was brighter on this grey morning. He turned it over to look for a clue to the identity of the sender. He stopped chewing. The address of the Magistrates' Court was printed on the back.

'Shit!'

As he hadn't heard from them for a couple of weeks, he'd begun to believe that it had all gone away. Scanning the black type, too afraid to read it in detail, he picked out a few phrases.

In charge of vehicle with excess alcohol... mitigation... endorsement code DR40... fine... ban... imprisonment.

Visibly shaking, he searched for Tess's number on his mobile.

Tess was singing along to the radio. She stopped only to gently slice the top off her boiled egg. A thick slice of toast popped out of the toaster and she smeared a generous amount of butter onto its golden surface. She wiggled her bottom to the music while cutting the slice into six fingers, before dipping a hot oozing soldier into her egg. This caused a volcano of yolk to slither down the shell. She chewed the delicious mouthful while carrying her plate and mug of tea to the table, enjoying the banter from the team on the radio. To add to her good mood, she had phoned Daniel last evening and they had arranged to get together tomorrow morning to discuss the list of party food.

Her mobile vibrated against her mug.

'Hello.'

'Tezza! I've had a letter that says I could be disqualified. How can I do my job without a car? How can I pay the mortgage without a job? What shall I do?'

'Who's the letter from?'

'The Magistrates' Court.'

'Oh.'

'What do you mean, "oh"?'

'Nothing. I suppose a letter was inevitable.'

'Shit, Tezza, it looks so formal.'

'Bring the letter over tonight after work and I'll read it.'

'It says I could go to jail.'

'Blake, that won't happen. It's your first offence and you didn't hurt anyone. I'm pretty certain you'll get points on your licence and a fine.'

'You think? Bloody hell, I'm actually shaking.'

'Calm down. Breathe deeply and slowly. It's the jargon they use. It can be quite intimidating if you don't understand it. I remember when Margaret at work was threatened with a CCJ. The letter she read out to us sounded as if she was about to be transported to Alcatraz.'

Tess heard Blake take a few deep breaths. 'Better?'

'Yeh. Thanks, Tezza. I do love you, you know? I'm sorry about all the stress I'm causing at the moment.'

'Don't be silly. I think you're being incredibly brave and positive under the circumstances. I'm very proud of the way you're coping.'

'Shall I pick up a takeaway?'

'No, save your money. I've got some salmon in the fridge.'

'See you later then.'

'Bye.'

So much for a new month. It felt as if the first line of the new exercise book had been blotted, never mind the first page. She had tried to sound positive on the phone to Blake, but she'd never received a letter from a court so she wasn't really sure of her ground. Tess reminded herself that Blake must feel vulnerable. The shock of the letter couldn't be good for his recovery. Not for one moment did she condone what he'd done, she'd been stunned by his stupidity and had told him so when she'd collected him from the police station. He could have hurt or even killed an innocent person. She knew drink drivers should be punished, but also believed that Blake hadn't been himself at the time. It must be so stressful, struggling to recover from a serious illness while working full-time.

At seven that evening, Blake sat on the arm of a chair in Rose Cottage, picking at a cuticle until it bled. Tess sat reading and absorbing the letter's contents. A fire blazed and crackled in the hearth, but she didn't feel comforted by its warmth. Outside, the purple haze of dusk descended, subduing the village with fading colours. Gusts of wind spat leaves and rain against the windowpane as Tess finished reading the letter. Despite her limited knowledge on court summons, she smiled reassuringly.

'There's still hope you won't get a ban. For drink driving offences, the court must take into consideration any mitigating circumstances at the time of the offence. It'll also help your case that you haven't been in trouble with the police before and that you're stressed due to your illness.'

Blake sighed and slumped into the chair, throwing a palm full of peanut M&M's into his mouth.

'I'm not saying that you won't be punished in some way.'

'I know. I'll pay up and take the points.'

'I'll write a letter to the magistrates for you explaining your circumstances at the time of arrest. I'll write it as if it was from you, but you'll have to sign it. I don't think the judge would be too impressed with a letter from your girlfriend. Hopefully it'll help if they know a little more background.'

Blake lifted his face to the ceiling, closed his eyes and took a deep breath. He'd take all the help he could get. If Tess wrote a letter explaining that he'd forgotten to eat before having a few drinks, that he knew he should have pulled over if he was tired, and that he was a good guy with an unblemished criminal record, he may even receive a smaller fine. What would he do without her? It didn't bear thinking about. After his hearing he would make it a double celebration. He'd tell Tess that not only had he been given the all-clear by the magistrates, but the doctors too. Things were going to be different. He would never take her for granted again. He'd get his finances and fitness in order, and who knows, he might even propose on New Year's Eve.

Tess sat at the kitchen table typing the letter on her laptop. She tried to concentrate over the noise of the canned laughter while Blake watched *You've Been Framed*. You had to give him credit, she thought. He was incredibly brave to be so positive for the majority of the time.

She spent twenty minutes typing, explaining to the magistrates that Blake had recently been diagnosed with cancer and had been working full-time while receiving intensive treatment. She'd told them that the stress of his job and coping with the illness had made him act out of character and that drink on top of medication could have contributed to his breathalyser reading. When she'd finished the letter, she printed it and carried it through to Blake. He was lying on the settee, chewing chocolate and sniggering at the silly antics on the home-recorded videos.

'I've finished the letter. I just need your signature.'

He signed his name at the bottom, leaning sideways to see the television behind Tess. Back in the kitchen, Tess clicked the kettle on and unplugged her laptop. She sat at the table waiting for the kettle to boil when a sudden sadness descended like an autumn leaf. What would she be doing now if Blake had never become sick and she'd ended things months ago? Would Daniel be lying on her settee now? What was he doing this very minute? Tears welled, making her throat feel as if she'd swallowed a pinecone. She wiped her eyes. This wasn't the time to get maudlin. It wasn't her that was sick. Blake needed her support. She slipped the letter into an envelope and addressed it to the Magistrates' Court.

Tess placed two mugs on the coffee table and put another log on the dying fire, before slumping into an armchair. She needed chocolate. Leaning over the arm of the chair, she reached for the bowl of M&M's on the coffee table. It was empty.

After a few minutes her mood calmed. It was like a pendulum these days. One minute confused and indecisive, the next, optimistic and cheerful. Some days she wished Blake would take his problems and leave, and on others she'd think how stoical and resilient he was being. Would *she* have the strength to laugh at the television if she knew she'd been diagnosed with a serious illness? He wasn't feeling sorry for himself, or asking, 'Why me?' Okay, so she had a crush on someone else. But it was a secret and she wouldn't act on it, so it was harmless, wasn't it? It was human to find someone attractive. You can't control your feelings, but you can control what you do with them. Tess decided that she should try harder to show Blake more affection.

'Move over, make room for a little one.'

He shuffled backwards and Tess squeezed onto the edge of the settee with her back to him. Blake nestled his chin into her neck so he could continue to watch the television. His breath smelt of stale tobacco and sickly chocolate and he continued to laugh at the ridiculous antics on the screen. The best thing she could do was to fall asleep. She closed her eyes. A few minutes later, she heard the theme tune drift from the television as the credits rolled.

Tess was in that indistinct moment between dreaming and wakefulness. Her back was being rubbed by a gentle touch. A hand was massaging her skin beneath her jumper. In her sleepy consciousness, she felt her stresses being stroked away. Was it Daniel touching her? In her mind, he was gently slipping his fingers beneath her bra and caressing her breasts. She conjured up memories of Daniel's mouth as she felt her jeans being undone. With one leg out of her jeans she pulled his body towards her, urging him on. He was now on top of her, moving rhythmically. Tess pictured Daniel's smile. She imagined she could smell the lemon soap on his skin. Tess could feel delicious waves of pleasure slowly building up inside her body…

Blake groaned, loudly. He sighed, suddenly feeling very heavy on top of her. Tess opened her eyes, reality hitting home like a slap. He rolled sideways and stood up, removed a condom and fastened his trousers.

'I'll get rid of this. Don't want a screaming kid just yet, do we?'

Tess blinked at the bright light of the lamp. Thank God one of them was thinking clearly.

'No.' Tess sounded calm but her thoughts were chaotic. Had she seriously just had sex with Blake without checking beforehand that he'd taken precautions? She had to get over this silly crush on Daniel. It was dangerous.

Tess pulled her jeans on and lay back down on the settee. She felt frustrated and disappointed while staring at the ceiling in disbelief.

The next thing she knew was when Blake woke her up again.

'I've got a valuation first thing in the morning my end of town. I've got to make tracks.'

'What time is it?' She groaned and stretched.

'Ten thirty, the news has just finished.'

'What! That means I've slept for two hours.'

'Yep. Although, if I'm honest, I slept for an hour too.'

Tess sat up and Blake pulled her to her feet. They walked unsteadily to the hall, arms around each other's waist for support. Spotting the letter, he snatched it up.

'I'll drop it in the post box on my way.'

'Don't forget it. It's important.'

'I won't.' He gave her a quick kiss. 'Bye, sexy.'

Tess stood waving goodbye until the red lights of his car disappeared down the road. Her emotions felt very different from when she'd stood waving goodbye to Daniel, having been left holding his towel. Was it too late to phone him now? She needed to know what time they were meeting tomorrow. She snuggled into a pile of cushions in her armchair as bubbles of anticipation made her smile to herself. Holding Daniel's grey business card up to the light, she tapped out his number even though she'd added him to her contacts. Daniel answered on the third ring.

'Hello.'

'Hi, it's Tess.'

'Hi. I'm glad you called.'

'You are?' Tess hugged a cushion.

'Yes, I'm going to London for a couple of days so I'll have to cancel our meeting tomorrow.'

Tess released the cushion and the smile fell from her lips. She tried to sound upbeat. 'Oh, okay. We can rearrange.'

'Yes, how about next week?'

'I'm not sure what day I'll have off, but it should be fine.'

'Great. I'll check my schedule. I passed your door earlier while walking the girls, but I didn't knock because I recognised Blake's car. I didn't want to disturb you both.'

'You could have done. We were only watching television.'

She blushed. What if Daniel had knocked on the door while she and Blake were...

'I must go and pack a few bits because I'm leaving early,' said Daniel. 'Have a good weekend.'

'And you have a good trip. I'll be in touch next week.'

'Bye.'

Tess finished the call and sat in silence for a few minutes, going over their short conversation. He had cancelled their meeting. He'd have to check his schedule. He didn't want to disturb her and Blake. It had been like a business conference call. Quite obviously she was living out a fantasy when she imagined the two of them having a special connection. The warmth of their last conversation was missing, instead it had sounded like a customer and contractor exchange.

Chapter Eighteen

Daniel turned into Denise and Simon's driveway and parked beneath the dappled shade of a large fig tree. Dark fruit hung from its branches, like sleeping bats amongst autumn's yellowing leaves. He looked up at the double fronted house with its hanging baskets and wooden window surrounds, each one painted the colour of vanilla ice cream. It had been several months since he'd visited his sister and her family in Hampstead and this time it wouldn't be solely a happy, sociable occasion. He'd come to offer his sister support and love. She had called him the previous day and it was obvious from listening to her, that she was struggling with the apprehension of receiving her results.

Daniel climbed out of his Land Rover, pushed the door to and clicked the lock. His emotions were fraught and anxiety gnawed at his thoughts, causing him to click the lock twice more. Lucky number three. Everything would okay.

He walked towards the front door along a paved sandstone path bordered with pruned lavender bushes, knocked and waited. Frantic pounding on the bay window caused Daniel to take one step back, where he saw Sam grinning and waving. His nephew disappeared from view but could be heard calling his mother from inside the house.

'Mum! Uncle Daniel's here. Muuum!'

The front door opened. Denise pulled it wide, allowing Sam to run outside and wrap his arms around Daniel's waist.

Daniel leant forwards and hugged him, while looking up towards his sister. He winked.

'He's been driving me mad all morning asking when you were going to get here.'

Daniel stood up and walked inside holding Sam's hand. 'No nursery today?'

'No. I was sick in Mummy's slippers last night.'

Daniel pulled a face. 'Poor Mummy.'

Denise continued on into the kitchen. 'Yes, especially as poor Mummy was wearing them at the time.' She turned to her brother. 'He's been fine today, but I thought I'd keep him at home just in case.'

'When's Peter back from school?' asked Daniel.

'I'll meet him from the school bus at four. Simon should be back around half six.'

She turned to her son. 'Sam, darling. Why don't you finish your Lego house so you can show Uncle Daniel?'

Sam ran through to the lounge leaving brother and sister standing beside each other. Daniel moved first, opening his arms wide and immediately Denise fell into them. He held her securely, rubbing her back.

'How are you?'

'Terrified.'

He hugged her more tightly. 'How can I help?'

'This is helping.'

They stood together for another minute until the kettle clicked off. She pulled away giving Daniel a tight-lipped smile. 'I'm coping. As long as the boys are unaware that anything's worrying me, I'll be fine. Actually, sod the coffee. It's after twelve. Wine?'

'I'll keep it a secret if you do.'

They moved to two armchairs close to a log burner and both sunk into the cushions. Daniel played with the stem of his glass while speaking. 'I'm so sorry this is happening to you, Den.' He looked up at her. 'If I could take the worry instead of you, I would.'

She smiled, sadly. 'I know.'

'Have they told you what's next?'

'I'm just waiting for the biopsy results. A pathology report will be sent to my consultant.'

'How long will they take?'

'They're going to phone me. They said up to two weeks.'

Daniel nodded, unable to trust himself to speak.

Denise continued. 'I keep telling myself it'll be fine. I'm too young. I don't smoke. Hopefully I'll get a call to say it's nothing to worry about and the boys will never know anything was wrong. It's just when I think of them...' Denise's voice broke.

Daniel was beside her in seconds, kneeling on the carpet as he hugged his sister. 'I'm here.' He gently rocked her in his arms. 'You did everything right. You didn't wait. You went straight to your GP. I'll stay with you until the results come through. My neighbour, Mabel, has got the dogs overnight, but I know she'd willingly have them longer.'

Denise took a deep breath and sat up straight. She wiped her eyes. 'You'll do no such thing.' She smiled, retrieved a tissue from up her sleeve and blew her nose. 'I'm fine. It's just when I think of the boys and protecting them. You have an exhibition to get ready.'

'The exhibition can be delayed.'

'No, it can't. Besides, it's something to look forward to when all this is behind me. I've no doubt it'll be great and it's very important for your future career that it goes well. I'm fine, honestly. Sit down and get comfy.'

Daniel sat back down as Sam came running in carrying a multi-coloured box made from Lego bricks, its sides dotted with small plastic windows.

'Wow, that's fantastic,' said Daniel.

Sam handed it to his uncle. 'I made it all by myself.'

Daniel studied his nephew's construction. 'It's sturdy with a strong roof. Four windows, oh, where's the door?'

'There isn't one. That way the big bad wolf can't get in.'

'Ingenious,' said Daniel, rubbing Sam's hair. 'If only it worked in the real world.' He looked at his sister. 'No doors to let any bad news in.'

'I'll have a word with Simon and see if he'll block them all up,' said Denise.

Sam laughed. 'Silly Mummy.' He turned to Daniel. 'Uncle Daniel, one of Peter's teeth fell out yesterday. It was wiggly for ages. He can stick his tongue through the hole, like this.' Sam stuck his tongue out a short way through his pursed lips.

'Very impressive. Did the tooth fairy come?'

'Yes, but Peter said it was Mummy really, but it wasn't, was it?'

'Certainly not. I hope Santa's elves didn't hear him say that.'

'I don't know. Daddy says they're watching us to see if we're being good or not.'

'If you're good for your mummy and tidy up your toys and do as you're told, I'm sure you'll go to the top of the good list.'

'And get a scooter?'

Daniel glanced and Denise. She nodded. 'Yes, I'm sure Santa will bring a scooter if you're very good.'

A few days later, Tess, Blake and Holly had arranged to share a takeaway. It had been a sunny but cold day, with the smell of autumn bonfires suffusing the air. The skies had remained cloudless as evening fell, making the temperature plummet. The bells of St Mary's Church tolled seven when Tess heard a knock on the front door. It was Holly.

'Brrrrr! I think we can safely say that summer's gone. My bloody heater isn't working in the car. I'll have to dig my old coat from my winter clothes suitcase. I'm freezing in my denim jacket.'

'Come in. There's a roaring fire for your toes and G and T for your stress.'

'I feel better already,' said Holly, hanging her jacket on the banister post and hugging Tess.

'My turn.' Blake came out of the lounge and hugged Holly.

'Hi, Blake.'

'Can you get Holly a drink while I fetch the takeaway menus from the bedroom?' Tess ran upstairs to hunt for the leaflets. It was an odd place to keep paperwork, but her underwear drawer made perfect sense to her. Every week she'd scoop up her letters and bills from the kitchen, take them upstairs, and shove them in with her knickers and bras. Safe, out of the way and private.

She found the menus and was about to leave her room when she heard voices on the pavement below. She caught her breath and dived behind a curtain when she saw Daniel talking to another dog walker beneath the streetlight. So, he was back from London. He was wrapped in a thick coat with the collar turned up against the cold. His head was covered with a woollen hat that had been pulled down over his ears. His hands were thrust deep inside his coat pockets and the golden glow from the street lamp highlighted his face with an apricot hue. Tess's breath steamed up the window, obscuring her view. Would he catch her watching if she wiped it? She gingerly rubbed the glass. It squeaked beneath her finger and Blake shouted upstairs making her jump.

'Have you found them yet? I'm starving.'

She hurried away from the window and called from the landing. 'Won't be a second.' She heard him walk into the kitchen and open the fridge door. The chink of the tonic bottle suggested that he was pouring another gin. Tess waited until she heard him close the lounge door again and tiptoed back to the window.

The pavement was empty and the glow from the lamp

shone desolately onto the ground. Daniel had gone. Had he looked at the house before he'd left? Had he wondered what she was doing? Tess picked up the menus and went downstairs, pushing such thoughts to the back of her mind. She threw a selection of different coloured pamphlets onto the coffee table.

'Top up, Holly?'

'I'd better not. I don't want to get tipsy. It's my Saturday at work tomorrow and I've got to drive home—' Holly blushed and looked at Blake. 'Sorry, I wasn't having a dig.'

'S'okay. Tess has written me a letter. Hopefully I'll just get a slap on the wrist.'

'Don't think it's all going to be plain sailing,' said Tess. 'Not everything has a fairy tale ending. We don't all get what we want. You need to be prepared to face some consequences.'

'I have faith in you.'

Tess felt irritable. 'Don't be flippant. You can't heap pressure on me to save your skin.'

'I'm paying you a compliment. I'm saying I have faith in you and trust you. I just can't win with you, can I?'

'I'm just trying to explain that it's not up to me. Okay, I've written a letter, but it could be totally inconsequential. It's not a *get out of jail free* card.'

Blake sat forwards. 'You said I wouldn't go to jail.'

'It's just an expression.' Tess sighed. 'But you'll get some punishment.'

'I expect to. I know I'll get three points.'

'I can't believe we're going over this yet again. Can we drop it and enjoy the evening?'

Holly jumped up. 'I'm getting a Diet Coke. Does anyone want anything from the kitchen?'

'I'll have the same, please,' said Tess.

Blake mumbled from behind a large menu. 'Sorry. I know

I must be a pain to live with. It's just work's so busy, the court case is hanging over me and I'm overdrawn at the bank... and you know.'

'Look, we're stressed and hungry. We all say things we don't mean when we're anxious. Let's order some food and try to relax and have a nice evening.'

Blake stood up, walked to the settee and kissed her on the mouth. 'All I meant was that I'm grateful you wrote the letter. I won't mention it again.'

Tess snatched at his hand as he started to walk back to his chair. 'Sorry I was snappy.' She shook his hand playfully. 'You choose what takeaway we'll have.'

Holly walked back into the living room, placing Tess's drink on the coffee table in front of her. Tess caught Holly's eye as her friend mouthed, 'Are you okay?'

Tess shrugged and pulled a face, before nodding.

'I think we'll have pizza tonight,' said Blake.

'You know what, Tess?' said Holly. 'You should practice your recipes for the exhibition and have a little party.'

'You've actually read my mind. I've been having restless nights thinking about the timings and storage. I can't stop planning and cooking in my mind. If you'll be willing participants, I wouldn't mind a practice run on a few dishes.'

'It's my birthday on Saturday,' said Blake. 'Let's do it then. It'll save some money if we're not going out for a meal to celebrate.'

Tess knew it wouldn't save money because she had expensive ingredients to buy, but she would feel better having practiced the recipes.

'That's a date then, you're both invited to Halston's Gallery Preview Buffet next Satur— I can't next Saturday! Mum rang and asked if I was free to travel down there.'

'What for?' asked Blake.

'No idea. She said she wanted to show me something.'

'Cornwall isn't just around the corner, and besides, I'm going to the match on Saturday afternoon. We'd have to go on the Sunday and we can't go to Cornwall and back in a day.'

Tess grimaced, guiltily. 'I'm going on my own. I'm leaving Friday afternoon and coming back Monday afternoon. I sorted the rota with Margaret this morning. I was going to tell you, but you only arrived a couple of minutes before Holly.'

'It'll be lovely for you to see your mum and dad again,' said Holly. 'Wasn't it your birthday in June when you last saw them?'

Tess was grateful that Holly was trying to diplomatically calm the situation. 'Yes, and I do miss them. And Padders. And the sea.'

Padders was her parents' scruffy little mongrel dog. He was named Padstow, but his name had been shortened to Padders over the years.

'We'll do the buffet one evening the week after next and we'll celebrate your birthday when I'm back, I promise. Now, what pizza do you want?'

Chapter Nineteen

The windscreen wipers squeaked backwards and forwards, slicing through the drizzle. Tess had left Nottingham behind and the motorway was clear. Despite looking forward to seeing her parents and Padders again, she couldn't help feeling disappointed that Daniel hadn't been in touch since returning from London. True, she hadn't phoned him either, but that was because when she'd called him a week ago, he'd sounded distant and business-like. If only her feelings for him would fade and disappear painlessly, like a grazed knee.

However, Tess was relieved to be spending a few days away from Blake. Recently he'd been pestering her to move in with him, but she'd no intention of leaving Halston. She couldn't imagine sharing a house with his numerous diecast models and action figures of Captain Kirk and an army of Klingons. Models of the Starship Enterprise decorated any flat surface and it didn't help that a poster of Mr Spock looked down on her whenever she sat on Blake's toilet.

Tess sighed at the complexity of her situation. Determined not to feel down, she switched on the radio to stop her mind from wandering. Paolo Nutini blasted from the speakers and she sang loudly, wishing away the miles and impatient to get there. It had been nearly four months since she'd seen them and she longed to feel the salty spray of the sea, the cry of the gulls and the smell of the lobster pots. She looked forward to falling asleep to the sound of the waves crashing onto the shore while snuggled under her duvet.

Five hours, a service station break and a bag of fruit pastels later, Tess negotiated the winding hedge lined roads of Cornwall. Stone houses edged the narrow lanes and the traffic became lighter as she got closer to St Merryn. Dusk was falling and Halston seemed a long way away. She followed the signs to Padstow, looking out for all the well-loved landmarks she knew so well. Within half an hour, the night was as black as tar. Tess followed a narrow lane with only her headlights to pierce the darkness. It was all so familiar and wonderful. She turned right into a private road that was lined on either side with half a dozen houses, all spaced generously apart. Continuing to the end of the cul-de-sac, Tess stopped outside her childhood home. A warm yellow glimmer seeped through the gaps in the drawn curtains, making her feel safe and welcome.

She turned off the engine and climbed out of her car, standing and listening for a moment. The sky was inky black, punctured by millions of stars. She could smell the sea and hear the hush of the waves in the distance. Closing the driver's door, she retrieved her bag from the boot and locked the car.

Her parents, Celia and Graham, opened the front door and Padders ran outside. He barked with excitement and jumped up at Tess, almost knocking her off balance.

'I've missed you too.' She dropped her bag and made a fuss of him while trying to dodge his wet tongue. Still grinning, Tess hurried into her parents' arms and hugged them tightly.

'Hello, darling.'

'Hello. It's so good to be here.'

'Did you have a good journey? How was the traffic?'

Tess laughed. Dads were always interested in the journey. 'It was fine, Dad. No hold ups or diversions.'

Roast pork was cooking in the oven, sending mouth-watering aromas wafting around the house. Tess dumped her bags on her bed and kicked off her boots. Before long they were all sitting in the lounge in front of an open fire, relaxing on soft deep-cushioned sofas and catching up on news. Padders had wrapped himself around Tess's feet and was snoring gently.

'How's your job, darling?' her mother asked.

'It's okay, I suppose. A bit boring. I feel like I'm ready for a change.'

Tess noticed her parents exchange glances.

'And Blake, how's he doing? Is he on the mend?'

'I think so. To be honest he doesn't like talking about his illness. He's coughing less and I like to think he's doing well.'

'That's good to hear.'

'How have you two been?' asked Tess. 'Did you book the cruise for next Easter?'

'Yes. We're so excited, aren't we, Graham? We've booked a three-week cruise and have a berth with a balcony.'

'How are you after the drama at work?' her father asked.

Celia leaned forwards. 'It's such a worry knowing you're in the city with all that violence and robbery. You should live somewhere safe and quiet. Somewhere away from the rough elements in society.'

Tess saw her parents exchange another furtive glance. 'Am I missing something here?'

Her mother's face broke into a huge smile and she clapped her hands together.

'You'll never guess what's come on the market in Padstow. I was walking along the far side of the harbour, you know, the road that leads up the hill. I'd just passed Crimpton's Tea Room when I noticed a 'For Sale' sign that had been hammered onto the fence. I went inside and asked a few questions. I mean, if they were closing down because business was bad, it wouldn't be any good, would it? But Jimmy Crimpton says they are retiring to Barnstaple to live closer to their daughter. They've found a lovely bungalow where Jimmy says he wants to start growing his own vegetables and buy a dog now he'll have time to train it. The teashop does very well in the summer and business keeps steady enough in winter to pay the bills. Well, it would, wouldn't it? Padstow is so popular with tourists. There's a two bedroom flat above the shop and a small yard out the back. The views are amazing and—'

'Steady now, Celia. The poor girl can only take in so much.'

Tess sat open-mouthed listening to her mother's news. She had mentioned to her mother in a recent telephone conversation that she was thinking of a change from her humdrum job and her dream would be to own a teashop, but she hadn't imagined it would become a reality for many years.

'Gosh, Mum. I don't know what to say.'

'I'll take you tomorrow. You can see it for yourself. I just know you'll love it.'

Tess's thoughts fell over themselves in the jumbled rush to the surface. What would this mean for her and Blake? She'd moved to Nottingham with Holly, so would Holly come back home to Cornwall too? She'd be hundreds of miles away from Halston. And Daniel. She looked up at her mother's expectant face. 'It won't hurt to look, I suppose.'

The following morning, Tess woke to the sound of gulls crying outside her bedroom window. She stretched and wiggled her toes, smiling at the aroma of coffee and bacon drifting upstairs. It felt good to be home. The stresses of work, Blake's illness and the court date were all a long way behind her.

Shafts of autumn sunlight shone through the V-shaped gap at the top of the curtains, hinting at a beautiful day. She slipped out of bed, grabbed her dressing gown and stood in front of the curtains. She knew what view would greet her when she pulled them open. The image was as clear in her mind as a photograph. She pictured every tree, every rock pool and every undulation of the cliff top in her mind's eye. With a flourish, she swept aside the curtains. At first the sunshine and blue skies blinded her and she shielded her eyes, but as her eyes adjusted to the light, she drank in the beauty of the scene she knew so well.

Her bedroom overlooked a long lawn, enclosed with a white picket fence. Ten steps led from a gate at the far end of the garden, down onto the soft yellow sand beyond. The damp stretch of sand sparkled as the sun reflected in the rock pools left behind by the receding waves. The sea shushed up the shore and a few surfers were braving the chill of the early morning. Sharp vertical cliffs framed her view of the beach. She could see a few people walking along the cliff top path, heads bowed like Lowry figures against the wind that whipped up the cliff's steep sides.

It was wonderful. It was home. She wished she could share the view with someone. Blake had seen this vista several times, but had never understood her passion for it. What would Daniel think of the view? No. She mustn't think about him. It would only make her sad and wistful and she didn't want to feel down while she was back at home. She pushed the image of his dark hair and green eyes from her mind. She wasn't going to spoil this wonderful weekend by giving way to indulgent crushes.

Sliding her feet into her slippers, she skipped downstairs to the kitchen where her father turned towards her with a beaming smile.

'Good morning, love. You're up early. Did you sleep well?'

'Like a log. It's so good to be back.'

'Bit chilly though. I popped out half an hour ago for a paper. Would you like some bacon?'

Tess was looking out of the kitchen window towards the sea. 'No thanks, Dad. I think I'll have a walk along the beach first and beat the weekenders before breakfast.'

'Good idea, it soon gets busy on a Saturday. You could take Padders and I'll put some bacon on a low heat. It'll keep warm until you're back.'

'Perfect, thanks.'

Tess planted a kiss on his cheek and ran back upstairs to get dressed. Within minutes, she was running back downstairs and whistling for Padders. 'Come on, boy. Let's go.' She buttoned up her coat and yelled goodbye to her father.

The chill wind bit her hands and cheeks, making her shiver and push her hands deep into her pockets. She walked around the side of the house and down the length of the garden. Padders waited for her at the gate, panting with impatience. Once the gate was opened, he bolted down the steps, across the sand and towards the sea. Tess followed him, stepping over the rocks that threaded their way through the sand like an ancient bony arch of dinosaur vertebrae.

At the water's edge, waves flowed over her boots and washed the damp sand from them. She watched bubbles of water playing around her feet and felt the wet sand sucking her boots deeper. She waded backwards a few steps, struggling to keep her balance. While walking along the shoreline, Tess threw driftwood for Padders and teased him with straggly pieces of seaweed. She climbed some rocks, searched for crabs in the hidden pools and collected pink shells that would look nice on her bathroom shelf back at Rose Cottage. After half an hour and with her coat pockets bulging, she turned back home for hot tea and bacon.

The smell of fish and chips wafted around Padstow's harbour. Brightly-coloured boats bobbed up and down on the water and as usual, the seagulls were out in force pestering the weekend visitors.

The sun shone weakly through a thin veil of clouds as Tess and her parents stopped outside the teashop and looked up at the whitewashed building. It was a small two-storey café directly facing the beautiful harbour. There was no doubt that its position was perfect. It had black paintwork and a sign hanging over the door that read, Crimpton's Tea Room. Below the name was a painting of a teapot with a cup and saucer.

Celia linked arms with Tess. 'Isn't it perfect, darling?'

'It's very pretty, Mum.'

'A manageable size. Not too big to start off with.'

'Let's take a look inside.'

They followed each other up two steps and pushed open a glazed door. The room buzzed with conversation and smelt of marzipan and coffee. They wound their way past several tables and stood in the queue. Tess looked into the cabinet that displayed insipid and unappetising cakes. A colourless coffee cake looked dry, the shortbread was broken and the blueberry muffins looked stodgy. She could definitely improve on that meagre display. Eventually they got to the front of the queue.

'Hello, what can I get you?' asked the assistant.

'We've come to view the property. We have an appointment at eleven.'

'Just a second.' The girl yelled through a door behind her. 'Jimmy! Someone to view the property.'

The room quietened and Tess cringed. 'Now the world knows why we're here,' she whispered.

Tess and her parents stood to one side while the next customer was served. The door behind the counter opened and a large man with a ruddy face walked into the room. Balanced precariously on the end of his nose was a pair of half-moon glasses. He boomed a hearty greeting, shook hands with each of them and invited them through the internal door.

'Not one for tact, that one,' Jimmy wheezed as he climbed the stairs. He beckoned them to follow him. 'Face of an angel, voice of a fog horn.'

Having viewed two bedrooms and the bathroom, the final room to see upstairs was at the front of the building, directly above the teashop. Tess was taken aback when the door was opened. Sunshine streamed into the room through a large bay window, highlighting a cream cornice edging the high ceiling. All the furniture in Rose Cottage would fit in this one room. Tess and her parents were drawn to the large bay window overlooking the harbour. It was a scene that could grace any postcard. In the distance she could see the ferry that travelled backwards and forwards across the estuary to Rock. She watched the hustle and bustle of the holidaymakers going in and out of the gift shops. The reds, blues and yellows of the painted hulls reflected in the water and bunting flickered in the breeze. Tess's mind buzzed at the opportunity this could give her, in a place she loved.

'Just the kitchen to show you now,' said Jimmy, leaving the room.

Back downstairs the kitchen was quite roomy, but disappointingly old-fashioned. The odour of onions accompanied the burnt liver-coloured walls. Cupboards were lopsided and the upright oven looked sad and unused. The Crimptons obviously bought their cakes in from elsewhere. Tess's imagination was in overdrive again. She imagined revamping the kitchen and bringing it alive with the smells of lemon, vanilla, cinnamon and chocolate.

'Well, that's your lot.' Mr Crimpton scratched his head. 'If you're still interested you can come back and have another look when we're closed one evening. The agents have all the accounts for serious buyers to look at.'

Tess shook his hand. 'Thank you. I'll give it some serious thought.'

That evening, having collected paperwork from the estate agents, Tess and her parents were mulling over the tearoom's figures.

Celia pointed to the expenditure on cakes and pastries. 'You'll save money here by making your own.'

'That's true,' said Graham, 'but before Tess starts planning a menu, she'll need to make a checklist because every step will be crucial to its success.'

'Dad, I'm not thinking of planning a menu. I'm not sure I want to move back to Cornwall. I've had a look today and I can see how it would be a great business for someone, I'm just not sure it's me.'

'Why ever not?' asked Celia.

'I'm not experienced enough. I haven't baked commercially or run my own business.'

'But you've made beautiful food for your local pub and now you're cooking for an exhibition, and besides, once upon a time Richard Branson hadn't run a business. Everyone has to start somewhere.'

'Your mum's right, and one huge benefit is the café's location. Padstow's full of visitors throughout the year and the building's already fit for purpose. All the plumbing and electrics are in place, the fridges, display cabinets and seating are included in the price and the permits and licenses won't be a problem.'

Tess felt excitement and fear plaiting together to form a tight knot in her stomach. In her fantasies, she imagined handing over a delicious piece of homemade chocolate gateau and a floral china cup of tea to a customer, before accepting a five-pound note in grateful exchange. Her dreams didn't include licenses, a supply chain, hiring staff, security systems, marketing and promotions.

She let out a long breath. 'I promise I'll think about it over the next week or two.'

Chapter Twenty

Distracted by his mobile phone ringing, Daniel stopped stuffing paint-splattered clothes into the washing machine.

'Hello?'

'Hi, Daniel, it's Denise.'

'I don't believe it. I was just thinking about calling you.'

'Anyone would think we were twins with a psychic connection.'

'How are you?'

'I've had a phone call and have an appointment to get my results on the third, that's Tuesday. I'm feeling more positive because although it might be my imagination, I'm sure the lump's got smaller. Simon's been great. I don't know how I'd have got through the last few weeks without him.'

'I'm thinking of you and hoping it'll be good news. All the same, get lots of rest and look after yourself.'

'I will. You okay?'

'Yes. Good thanks. Things are running smoothly for the exhibition. I've emptied the room next to the main dining room and had it repainted ready to hang my canvasses.'

'Wow, that's a huge room. Do you really have enough artwork to fill it?'

'You're joking. I could do with two rooms but I've decided to keep the guests to one area of the house.'

'Good idea. How's the catering coming along?'

'I took your advice and asked Joe at The Royal Oak. He put me in touch with someone local who's shown me a few ideas over a cup of coffee. I think she fits the bill perfectly.'

'Fits the bill for what? A girlfriend or a caterer?'

Daniel laughed. 'Don't start.'

'Is she pretty?'

'She is actually.'

'Hmm!'

'She also has a boyfriend.'

'That's a shame. Girlfriends won't come knocking on the door looking for you, you know? You have to get out there and meet people. You're no spring chicken at thirty-two. If you don't socialise you'll turn into a grey-haired recluse with long fingernails.'

Daniel distractedly looked down at his nails and nibbled off a smudge of paint. He heard a beep on his mobile that meant someone else was phoning him. He ignored it. They'd leave a message.

He pacified his sister. 'Let me just get this year and the exhibition out of the way and we'll see what happens.'

Denise's husband, Simon, shouted down the phone, 'About time we had a pint.'

'Tell him to get his lazy butt down here if he wants a pint.'

Denise passed on her brother's reply. 'Simon's giving you the thumbs up, but I hardly see him myself during the week so I'll be hanging on to him at weekends, if that's okay?'

Daniel was delighted that Denise was sounding much brighter than when he saw her last week. Hopefully the results would be clear, the exhibition would go well and then they'd all have a great Christmas in London. He loved spending Christmas with his sister. He could play with all his nephews' new toys and he got on well with Simon.

'I'll let you get on then. Let us know if we can help with anything for your big night.'

'It's all in hand, thanks. I'm looking forward to you all coming to stay for a few days.'

'We are too. Perhaps I can have a word with your attractive caterer when I'm down there, and tell her she's crazy for liking anyone else but my gorgeous brother. What's her name?'

'Tess.'

'You're usually hopeless at remembering names. You've got a soft spot for her, haven't you?'

Daniel squirmed. Denise had an uncanny knack of appearing to see into his innermost thoughts.

'Like I said, she's seeing someone else and besides, I'm far too busy to get involved with someone right now.'

'You don't fool me, but I'll stop teasing. Sorry must dash, Peter's stuck on maths homework and Simon's useless at anything that isn't creative.'

'Den,' said Daniel, more seriously. 'I'll be thinking of you. Will you let me know straight away?'

'Of course I will. Love you. Bye.'

Daniel ended the call and looked pensively at his mobile. He couldn't bear it if he lost his sister too. He shivered, suddenly feeling cold. He threw the last few socks into the washing machine. Goya and Gogh were asleep, curled nose to tail in front of the Aga, making little twitching movements as they slept. His phone beeped, reminding him that he'd a missed call. Whoever it had been, they'd left a voice message.

'Hi. We're having a tasting on Tuesday evening, as a practice run of the food for your painting night. You're invited. It's just a casual thing, any time after sex... six. See you there. Rose Cottage. Hopefully you're free. I mean, you know, no plans kinda free. Bye.'

He frowned. It didn't sound like Tess, but who else could be inviting him around to Rose Cottage to taste food for his painting night. He imagined his invitations reading, *An Invitation to Daniel Cavanagh's Painting Night*. It sounded like an open evening for a nursery school.

Chapter Twenty-One

'Answer your damn phone!'

Blake threw his mobile on to the passenger seat while pressing his foot on the accelerator. That was the fourth time he'd tried calling Tess. He was approaching traffic lights that had turned to amber but he couldn't afford the time to stop, so pressed his foot harder on the accelerator. With one hand on the wheel, he bit the cuticle around his thumb until it bled. It had become a regular habit, leaving him with red and sore fingertips. Why couldn't Tess stop bloody interfering?

He turned a corner and stamped on the brake as a man stepped on to a zebra crossing ahead. Impatiently, Blake moved back up the gears and knew he was travelling too fast for a residential area, but what choice did he have? He had been sitting at his desk at the office when he received a text from Tess.

Calling in at the library to borrow some cook books for tomorrow's tasting. It's near your GP so will call in and see if a prescription is waiting for you. It's the least I can do to help. X

She could be so irritating. What if she asked the receptionist questions? What if she demanded to speak to a doctor? Why couldn't she leave him to get on with things and recover from this supposed illness by himself? He wished he'd never lied. Living with the stress and anxiety of his deceit was spoiling everything and affecting his concentration at work. Look at him now. Stressfully negotiating traffic to get to his GP surgery before she'd finished in the library. He wasn't supposed to have left the office.

He stopped in the surgery's car park sending a flurry of

gravel spraying along the ground. 'Shit.' He could see Tess leaving the building and she looked angry. He climbed out and went to see how he could salvage the situation.

'What are you doing here?' asked Tess.

'I was valuing an apartment nearby when I got your text. I thought I'd say hello.'

'I'm livid.'

Blake felt sick – really sick. 'Why?'

'I don't believe what I've just been told.'

'Tess…'

'I asked a woman in the pharmacy section whether you had a good supply of tablets. I was checking to see if a prescription was waiting for you. I didn't know if you were running low so I told them that as I was in the area, could I check on your medication. I said you were ill and it would save you a journey. Do you know what she told me? I'm bloody fuming.'

Christ, thought Blake, feeling a rush of heat to his head in panic. Tess rarely lost her temper. He could see that she was shaking with anger. Did she know something? Did she know everything? He had to smooth it over right now. 'Tess, I'm so sorry—'

'She said I should ask *you* what medication you're on and bring in the correct tear-off counterfoil from your last prescription.'

'Is that all?'

'No, it gets worse.'

'Christ. Tess, I can explain—'

'She said that she couldn't let me know because of patient confidentiality. She didn't even look on the computer. She made me feel like a stalker instead of your girlfriend who's trying to help. She had such a superior attitude. It's wrong that some stranger should know more about your medication and illness than your girlfriend.'

Thank God for patient confidentiality, thought Blake, forcing himself not to sigh with relief. He put an arm around her shoulder.

'Thank you for trying to help, but I can manage.'

Tess sighed loudly. 'I'm sorry for ranting. I just feel so helpless because I can't even collect your prescription.' She paused. 'What did you mean when you said you could explain?'

Blake surprised himself with the speed of his reply. 'I knew you wouldn't be allowed to discuss my personal details so I was hoping to save you the journey.' He pulled her to face him and kissed her gently on the lips. 'There, that'll keep me going all day now,' he said.

She smiled at him. 'Softy.'

Chapter Twenty-Two

October had arrived and on Tuesday afternoon, Denise and Simon climbed into the car and fastened their belts in silence. The boys were at school and were going to be collected by a good friend who also had children there. Thankfully, Peter and Sam were oblivious to the maelstrom of emotions their parents had been feeling recently. Before Simon turned the ignition, he reached over and laid his hand on top of his wife's clenched fingers.

'You can do this, love. I'll be with you every step of the way.'

'I know.'

He squeezed her hand then started the engine. Within an hour they'd know the results of her biopsy. Denise felt lightheaded. She had the same churning feeling in the pit of her stomach that reminded her of the anxious minutes before an exam or an interview. Looking out of the window, she couldn't focus on anything in particular. Her mind was elsewhere. Would she see her boys grow into young men? Would she see them choose a wife and be a proud mother at their weddings? She took a deep breath to ward off tears that were threatening. No, it would be fine. She must remain positive. Chances were that they'd be driving back in an hour's time with relieved smiles on their faces.

Simon parked the car in the multi-storey car park that was connected to the hospital. They walked purposefully towards the lift, focusing on each footstep. The doors squeaked open and they stepped inside the small dimly lit lift. It smelt of pine disinfectant. The lift reached the ground floor with a jolt and the doors once again squeaked open.

They held hands and walked in silence towards the main reception area.

It was bustling with people. Patients were strolling in dressing gowns, porters scurried on errands, people were asking for directions, visitors were buying flowers from a little kiosk and nurses weaved their way through the melee. Denise remembered the way and turned towards the long corridor that led towards the Breast Clinic. As she walked towards the reception desk, she noticed that the waiting room was much quieter today. The receptionist looked up from behind the desk and smiled.

'Good afternoon. Do you have an appointment?'

'Yes. At two thirty with the consultant, Mr Simmonds.'

The receptionist ticked off her name from the list and pointed to a door. 'If you go through there and take a seat, someone will call you shortly.'

They took a seat and looked at each other, resting their foreheads together for a few comforting seconds. Denise breathed deeply trying to keep her nerves in check. She shivered involuntarily and looked around the room. They should replace the carpet in their hall with this lovely warm oak flooring, she thought. So much easier to clean when the boys come running in from the garden.

Her thoughts were interrupted when a nurse walked through the swing doors from the main reception room. She smiled at them and knocked gently on Mr Simmonds's door, then leant inside. Denise heard a mumbling and the nurse turned to them.

'You can come through now.'

Taking a few steps towards the consultant's door, Denise stopped. Her eyes were drawn to a colourful poster at the far end of the room. She felt a surge of adrenalin rush through her veins, making her heart pound. Goosebumps prickled her skin as she absorbed what she was looking at.

She turned to look at Simon. He had seen it too. The poster was full of exotic brightly-coloured birds under the heading, *Parrots of the World*.

Denise somehow managed to make her legs move again and walked into the consultant's room. The nurse continued to smile and hold open the door. Mr Simmonds was sitting behind a highly-polished desk in a high-backed leather chair. Two further leather chairs had been placed in front of the desk and Mr Simmonds indicated for them to sit down. He reached over the desk and shook their hands.

'Hello, please take a seat.'

Denise and Simon sat down.

'It's nice to see you again. How have you been?' he asked.

'Okay. Worried, but okay, thank you.'

'That's only natural. I'm sure it's been difficult.'

'Yes, it has.'

'Well, Denise. May I call you Denise? What do you prefer?'

'I don't mind. Friends call me Den or Dee Dee.'

'And are you Denise's husband?' he said, looking at Simon.

'Yes. Simon.'

'Pleased to meet you, Simon. I'm glad you could come.'

He turned back to Denise and paused. 'We've received the results of your biopsy and I'm sorry to tell you that it's not the news we were all hoping for. Unfortunately the pathology lab did find cancerous cells in the breast tissue.'

Unfortunately… unfortunately. The word repeated in her head. Her skin felt hot. She heard the words but couldn't help but fixate on Mr Simmonds's tie. Here was an eminent consultant sitting in a grand office, telling her that she had cancer, and he was wearing a Mickey Mouse tie. Lots of tiny Mickey Mouse characters were printed upside down, on their sides and standing up, all over his tie. What was he thinking this morning when he got dressed? *'Today I'm going to tell someone that they have cancer and might die young. I think I'll wear my Mickey Mouse tie to cheer them up.'*

'Darling, are you listening?' Simon touched her hand and brought her out of her reverie.

'I'm sorry to be giving you this news, but the outcome should be very positive. You were very wise to have the lump checked in its early stages. The lump is small and there's an excellent chance it hasn't spread. We can arrange for an operation next week to remove it. We'll take a little extra tissue from all around the lump, which will then be examined. If there are some cancerous cells in this tissue, we'll have to remove a little more until the microscope sees only healthy cells. Because you detected the lump so quickly, I'm optimistic that it won't be necessary for further surgery. I know there's a lot to take in, but do you have any questions I can help with?'

Denise sat numbly, still trying to take in the fact that she had cancer at thirty-two.

Simon gently squeezed her hand. 'Honey, do you have any questions?'

She blinked. 'How long will I be in hospital for? I have two little boys.'

'It should only be an overnight stay.'

'What are the chances it might have spread?'

'We won't know until we test the area around the lump. However, as I said, you caught it early and it's a small lump.'

'Who will do the operation?'

'I will, with my team.'

Denise looked down at her hands and fiddled with her wedding ring. 'How long will I have to wait to find out if it's spread?'

'It's usually quite quick. I'm afraid I can't give an exact time because it depends on how busy the pathology lab is.'

Simon shifted in his seat and asked, 'If the surrounding tissue is clear, is Denise cured?'

'There are no definite answers with cancer – for any of us. As an added precaution, even when the surrounding tissues are clear of cancerous cells, Denise would receive six to eight sessions of chemotherapy and a course of radiotherapy.'

'Will I lose my hair?'

'It's likely you will. You'll also feel very tired and you'll need a lot of family support.'

She didn't care about losing her hair. Not much anyway. All that was important was that she recovered for her boys. She thought of her mother, wishing she were here with her.

'What do I do now?'

'Go home and try hard to relax and take in what's happened. Sometimes it takes a while to sink in. The nurse will give you some printed information about what to bring in with you, and about not eating after six o'clock the night before your operation. She will also give you a leaflet about the actual surgery and recovery time. You'll need to have a blood test first which I'll book in for early next week. Is there anything else I can help you with?'

Denise shook her head.

Chapter Twenty-Three

Tess was in the kitchen adding the final touches to her finger buffet. She had worked on this trial run all day and was just thinking that she must have a quick shower and change out of her food splattered clothes, when there was a knock on the front door.

'Come in, it's open,' she called.

After a few seconds, Holly poked her head around the kitchen door. 'It's only me.'

'Hello.' Tess turned to greet Holly and gasped, 'You look amazing.'

Holly was dressed in a black sequined vest top and a pair of skin-tight dark jeans that looked like they'd been spray-painted onto her slim legs. She'd had her hair cut into an even shorter bob, which she'd then painstakingly straightened. Her make-up was more glamorous than usual and she wore some strappy stilettos on her painted toes. It also looked suspiciously like she'd had a spray tan.

'You look like you're expecting Prince Charming to appear.' Tess laughed. 'You can't have gone to that much trouble for me and Blake.'

Holly shifted guiltily. 'I hope you don't mind, but I *have* invited someone to join us. I didn't want to play gooseberry to you two, as usual.'

'Of course I don't mind. We could do with another dozen people to eat all this food,' she said, sweeping her arm sideways to reveal worktops laden with platefuls of food. 'Who've you invited?'

'It's a surprise. Someone I've had my eye on.'

'Ooh! How exciting. Is it Doug the delivery bloke you keep going on about?'

'Doug? No. I think he's dating. He says "we" a lot when we talk about what we've done during the week. But if my date turns up, he'll more than make up for Doug.'

'I'm intrigued.' Tess looked down at her messy jeans. 'I must run upstairs for a quick shower and change. Blake shouldn't be long. He's just popped out to Jackson's to buy some more tonic water. I shan't be more than ten minutes.' Tess ran upstairs, before stopping halfway to shout, 'Sorry, I forgot to say help yourself to a drink.'

Tess continued up the stairs and ran into the bathroom. What she would give for a long soak in Radox bubbles. Instead she turned the shower on and jumped backwards before the jets of water sprayed her hair. She peeled off her clothes and threw them all into the wicker linen bin. After the quickest shower she'd ever had, she was rubbing in her Sanctuary Body Souffle when she heard Blake let himself in.

'Tezza, I'm back. Where are you? I've... bloody hell, Holly! You look fantastic. Come here for a hug.'

Holly squealed. 'Not so tight.'

'But I've never seen such tight jeans before. How did you get them on, and how will you get them off? You can give me a demonstration if you like. Just wait while I get a gin and tonic.'

Tess smiled and crossed the landing to her bedroom. He was incorrigible, but she was pleased her best friend and boyfriend got on well. She hadn't got time to wash her hair so she pulled off her shower cap and brushed her hair into a ponytail. She wrapped it into a bun and pulled some strands of hair out of the elastic in different directions. She left her eye make-up on because the steam of the shower had smudged it slightly, making her eyes appear sexily smoky. Having smeared some pink gloss across her lips, she pulled on some clean jeans and a pale pink angora mix jumper. Next she sprayed Jo Malone's Pomegranate Noir into the air and stood under the falling mist. She'd read in a magazine once that it was a good way to smell lovely without suffocating your guests.

Tess was walking along the landing listening to Blake and Holly singing along to Madonna, when she heard a knock at the door. She was hoping to nip into the bathroom before going downstairs, but they obviously couldn't hear the knock with all the noise they were making. Still, it was a good opportunity to get a look at Holly's new man before she whisked him into a corner to chat. Tess ran downstairs and jumped the last two steps before opening the door with a welcoming smile.

It was Daniel.

He was holding a bottle of wine and a small bunch of flowers. He wore loose jeans and a black jumper. His hair, which was still slightly damp, had been pushed back away from his face and curled onto his collar. His eyes twinkled cheekily as he held out the flowers and wine.

'Hello, Noah. I come bearing gifts... although I think I'm mixing up my Bible stories.'

'Hi. How...?'

'Oh.' He looked disappointed and dropped his gifts back down to his sides. 'It wasn't you who left the message on my voicemail, was it?'

'No, but I have a sneaky feeling I know who did.'

'This is awkward, sorry.'

'No, don't be silly. It's great you've come. The food's a trial run for your exhibition, after all. I should have invited you.' Tess stood back. 'Come in out of the cold.'

Daniel and Tess stood facing each other in the hall. He smelt delicious and looked amazing. There was another uncomfortable pause, each standing wordlessly without moving. Daniel offered her the bottle and the flowers again.

'Thank you. You shouldn't have,' said Tess. 'Come through and I'll introduce you to the mystery voice.'

'Should I be afraid?'

'I'll let you be the judge of that.'

Tess could have happily spent all evening with him standing by the hall radiator, but she turned and opened the lounge door.

The first thing Daniel saw was the back of a bald, overweight man, dancing with a skinny girl. He recognised Blake but not his dance partner. Tess's boyfriend had one arm on the girl's hip and the other holding a drink that was splashing everywhere. The girl was wearing a lot of make-up and was dressed in painfully tight clothes. They were dancing suggestively to Madonna's 'Erotica'.

After a few seconds, they noticed him and stopped dancing. The girl turned to him with a wide grin, her eyes sparkling with excitement. Blake's smile seemed to have disappeared. He turned the music off and an atmosphere descended like a winter fog.

'Hello again.' Daniel offered his hand to shake.

Blake shook it limply. 'Didn't know Tess had invited you.'

'I didn't,' said Tess. 'But I should have. These recipes are all for Daniel's exhibition so it makes perfect sense that someone invited him.' Tess looked directly at her best friend.

Holly hunched her shoulders, looking embarrassed and flustered.

'Thanks for the invite,' said Daniel.

Holly blinked her eyelids rapidly. 'Sorry, I hate leaving voice messages. I'm not good at it.' She grinned, coquettishly.

'Well, this is nice,' said Tess, trying to act as if this was all very normal and pretending she hadn't noticed her boyfriend's rudeness or her best friend making a very obvious play for Daniel. It made her stomach churn with jealousy.

'Any more drinks?'

'Could you top up my glass with tonic please, it's a bit strong,' asked Holly, passing her glass to Tess.

Tess took the glass and smiled at Daniel. 'What would you like?'

'If you've got a bottle of red open, that'll be great thanks.'

Tess sensed Daniel following her into the kitchen. She put the flowers and bottle of wine on the table and turned towards him.

'I'm sorry he was rude. Remember I told you about the court case? He's been given a date now, so he's a bit jumpy.'

'It's okay,' said Daniel. 'Stop frowning.' He raised his hand and stroked her forehead with his thumb. 'It'll give you wrinkles.'

Tess caught her breath at his touch. 'I just want you to feel welcome here.'

'Tess, you worry too much.'

She loved hearing him say her name. It felt intimate. They were standing facing each other, close enough for her to reach out and touch him. She clenched her fists by her side to stop herself from doing just that. She picked up the flowers and began to unwrap them in order to keep her hands busy.

'Look at all this! It's amazing,' said Daniel, turning towards the food on the counter. 'It's just what I'd hoped for. What are these called?'

'They're blinis with smoked salmon and crème fraiche. This is halloumi with chilli. Try some.'

Daniel chose the smoked salmon appetiser. Tess watched his mouth open and close as he took a bite, noticing how his lips shone with crème fraiche as he chewed. She imagined the smooth soft sensation of kissing them. With a quick movement he licked his top lip, the sight of his glistening pink tongue quickening her pulse.

'That's delicious,' he groaned. 'My guests won't leave the food table. They'll have no interest in my paintings.'

Tess glowed with pleasure and pointed to a few more dishes. 'These are chicken tikka, mango and coriander on sticks and those over there are crispy vegetable spring rolls with pickled lemon salsa. Remember you asked me about filo cigars when you came for coffee? These are they! I've filled them with feta and cranberries.'

'May I?'

'Of course.'

He picked one up and closed his eyes momentarily as he swallowed. 'And what are those little beauties called?' Daniel pointed to a tray.

'They're called, one-bite Bloody Mary cherry tomatoes.'

'Tess, you're amazing. Would you like to move in and become my resident chef?'

'Sorry, am I interrupting something?' Blake was leaning against the doorway.

Tess blushed. 'I'm showing Daniel the food.'

'Really? I thought he'd brought you flowers and was asking you to move in with him.'

Daniel held up his hands as if he'd had a gun pointed at him. 'Hey, I was just complimenting Tess on this amazing food.'

Blake said nothing.

'Daniel was joking. And it's just a polite tradition to take flowers for the hostess.'

Blake stood up straight. 'Holly is wondering where the tonic water is.'

'Daniel, do you mind?' asked Tess, handing him Holly's glass and a bottle of tonic water.

'Of course not.' He took them from her and left the kitchen.

'How dare you?' she hissed. 'How do you think that

made Daniel feel? That was *so* embarrassing.' Tess sunk her face into her hands and groaned.

Blake stepped closer to her. 'I don't like him and I don't trust him. I can see what he's doing. I'm not blind – just sick.'

Tess was silenced by Blake's metaphorical slap. Hadn't she been enjoying every second of Daniel's conversation? Hadn't she almost physically swooned at Daniel's touch? She reached out and rubbed Blake's arm.

'It's not what you think. He was just pleased with the food and relieved that I've actually got round to sorting it out. He's waited a long time for me to finally put this menu together.'

'But why did he have to come over?'

'Holly invited him.'

'But you invited him in for coffee a few weeks ago.'

'Blake, he's asked me to do a job for him and you know I need the extra cash. He'll write me a good reference that will come in handy one day when I've saved enough to open my own little teashop. It's called networking. I know you wouldn't have this problem if a woman had asked me to cook for them.'

'Of course that would be different.'

Holly popped her head into the kitchen. 'What's going on?'

Tess smiled. 'Nothing. Just chatting.'

'We can't work the CD player and the music's stopped.'

'Blake will have a look. I'll just get a glass for Daniel.'

Blake opened his mouth as if to say something further, but stopped. He followed Holly into the lounge, leaving Tess alone in the kitchen. She looked at the ceiling, closed her eyes and exhaled deeply. Why was everything so stressful? Couldn't she just enjoy a new friendship? After all, she'd decided to stay with Blake instead of relishing freedom, hadn't she?

Alicia Keys's voice drifted into the kitchen, giving her the impetus to reach for the bottle of red wine. She took a glass out of the cupboard, pushed escaping tendrils of hair behind her ears and went into the lounge. Jealousy zipped through her body like an electric current when she saw Daniel and Holly deep in conversation. Holly was sitting on the floor leaning against Daniel's knee. She was gazing up into his face.

'I think you're right,' whispered Blake. 'He may have only come for the food, but I bet you a fiver Holly goes home with him tonight.'

Tess gave a stiff smile and placed the glass on the coffee table before pouring the wine. She crossed the room and handed it to Daniel, making him sit forwards and forcing Holly to sit up without the support of his leg. Daniel took the glass.

'Thank you. I hope you don't mind, I put another log on the fire before it went out.'

'Of course not. I'm always forgetting.' Tess made a show of warming her hands against the fire while she listened to their conversation.

'So who trained you?' Holly asked Daniel.

'Trained me?'

'You bring flowers, you make a good waiter and you stoke the fire.'

Tess couldn't bear it. She turned her back on them, missing his response to Holly's flirting. She couldn't help but feel resentful that her best friend was holding Daniel's attention and being brazen enough to lean against him. Tess knew that her secret infatuation was just that – a secret. Maybe if Holly knew how she felt about Daniel, she wouldn't be making such a play for his attentions. It was a strange emotion. Not only feeling jealous, but feeling jealous of her closest friend. Tess looked over at the sound of their laughter. Another tight knot of jealousy wound around her stomach. Could she bear it if he dated Holly?

Tess knew without a shadow of doubt that her and Blake's relationship was floundering. She still loved him, but it was more the love of a concerned sister. Her passion for him had died and this was underlined whenever she looked at Daniel. She had never experienced such a powerful emotion before and it made her feel considerably out of control. However, she couldn't face the guilt of leaving Blake in a heap when he needed her so badly. How would she feel if he became sicker because she'd left him just when he needed some emotional support? Didn't they say that a positive frame of mind helps you to recover? She had no real option. She had to stay with him until he was better. She surely owed him that much after two years. If Daniel were still single in six months, a year – however long it took for Blake to recover – she'd let him know how she felt.

Considering the way the evening had started, the next hour passed amicably. Daniel spoke about his travels and Blake regaled the room with some stories about characters at his office. The food had been brought through and lay depleted on several plates. A steady flow of alcohol had mellowed the atmosphere and soothed Blake's mood considerably. Just before nine o'clock, Daniel's mobile buzzed. He excused himself and walked into the kitchen to take the call.

'Probably his secret wife,' said Blake.

The girls ignored him. A few minutes later, Daniel came back into the lounge looking pale and shaken. 'Thank you for a lovely evening but I've had some bad news and have to go.'

Tess noticed his eyes sparkling with tears. She longed to comfort him.

He cleared his throat. 'Sorry to dash. The food is perfect for the exhibition, Tess. Thanks.'

Tess walked with him into the hall. She gently touched his arm. 'I hope everything will be all right.'

'Thank you. Me too. Bye'

Later that evening, Tess had cleared away the food and was busy tidying the kitchen. Holly had left in a whirlwind of happiness and declarations of love for Daniel. Blake was mooching about, by now a little drunk after copious amounts of gin and tonics and several Jack Daniel's. He grabbed Tess around her waist from behind as she bent to put some glasses in the dishwasher.

'Come here, gorgeous.'

'Blake, I'm clearing up.'

'Leave it. I'll do it later.'

Tess was in no mood for sex with her intoxicated boyfriend. She was worried about Daniel's phone call, on edge due to Holly's flirting and Blake smelt like an ashtray. He was being insensitive to her quiet mood, but she supposed that alcohol blurred sensitivity. His hands grasped her breasts. Irritated by his touch, she escaped his arms with a swift turn and opened a cupboard to look for a dishwasher tablet. She placed the tablet in its container on the dishwasher's door and felt Blake grasp her hips and press himself against her. Tess swung round and faced him angrily.

'Stop it. You're drunk and I'm not in the mood.'

'I'm not drunk! I've only had three gins.'

'And about six Jack Daniel's.'

'Daniel. Daniel. We can't escape from fucking Daniel, can we?'

'Now you're being pathetic.'

'I bet you wouldn't say no to Danny Boy, would you?'

'I'm not playing this silly game.'

'Oh Danny, kiss me, Danny.' Blake puckered his lips.

'I'm serious. Stop it before you go too far.'

'Look at my cakes, Danny.'

Tess's patience snapped. 'Blake, I want you to leave. I can't talk to you when you've had too much to drink.'

'Tough. I can't leave because apparently I'm drunk. And we all know what happens when you drink and drive.'

'I'll phone a taxi for you.'

Tess dialled the number of her local taxi firm.

'Well, thank you very much. Kick a sick man out. Thanks a million.'

Tess was livid. His emotional blackmail didn't dissuade her from continuing the phone call. She wanted him to go home and leave her to think by herself and try to piece together her fragmenting life.

'Hello. I'd like a taxi from Rose Cottage in Halston. Yes. Into town, please. Yes, as soon as possible. Thank you. Bye.'

Blake swayed in the doorway. 'You've changed.'

'I'll speak to you tomorrow when you have a clear head.'

'If I'm alive.'

'That's below the belt. I'm trying so hard here,' shouted Tess. 'You won't let me in regarding your illness. You won't talk to me about your treatment or your medication. You won't let me come with you to the hospital. I'm fighting a battle with my hands tied behind my back. I do what I can for you. I look after you as best I can. I'm here for you, but you're pushing me away.'

'I've just tried to get close to you and you pushed me away.'

'I'm not talking about sex. I'm talking about sharing and talking. We don't communicate any more. We just seem to work, eat, clear away, sleep and then go to work again.' Tess raked her hand up through her hair. 'I'm tired of it.'

Blake's bottom lip quivered. 'I love you, Tezza. I don't know what I'd do without you.'

Tess sighed deeply. 'Please don't call me Tezza.'

'Don't leave me.'

'I'm here, aren't I?'

'I feel like I'm losing you. You seem so far away these days.'

Tess held out her arms. Blake fell against her. She held him numbly, feeling no emotion. Minutes passed and neither of them moved. Blake occasionally sniffed and the kitchen clock ticked. Tess's mind reeled with images: her parents opening their front door, the whites of Blake's eyes glaring at her earlier and Daniel standing at the door holding wine and flowers. She felt as if she was going mad. It really was time to sort her life out.

The sound of a car horn pulled them apart. The taxi had arrived. Blake kissed Tess on her cheek, walked reluctantly towards the front door and left. She walked back into the silent kitchen, the dam of anxiety and uncertainty burst. Sobbing into her arms, Tess leaned against the kitchen worktop. Her body shuddered with anguish. She cried for wasted years, for unrequited love, for the evil touch of illness and for her helplessness in all these things.

As the minutes ticked by, her body shook less and her gasps became quieter. Her breathing became easier and she became aware that she was leaning on something uncomfortable. She stood up and looked to see what was pressing into her forearm. It was a mobile phone. It wasn't hers or Blake's. Holly had lost hers last week and couldn't afford to buy another until payday. In an instant she realised that it was Daniel's. He must have put it down after the phone call telling him the bad news. Tess picked it up and held it in her upturned palms. Lifting it to her face, she pressed it gently against her cheek and closed her swollen eyes.

Chapter Twenty-Four

Tess slept deeply that night and was surprised to wake up at half past eight to the sound of a cyclist ringing their bell. The breeze from a small open window occasionally made her curtains billow like an intake of breath. She'd gone to bed imagining a night of torment and tears, but had fallen into a deep dreamless sleep within minutes.

This morning she felt calmer and more determined to get her life in order. It looked like Holly and Daniel might become an item and she wasn't sure how much longer she could stay with Blake. She could still support him through his illness as a friend, couldn't she? Tess made a mental note to telephone her parents later to arrange another visit to Crimpton's Tea Room. She groaned loudly and stretched like a starfish beneath her duvet. Thank goodness she'd booked two days annual leave this week.

What could Daniel's bad news have been? How was Blake this morning? What should she do about Daniel's mobile? She'd slept with it beside her on her bedside table, sitting alongside her own phone. She reached to pick it up. It felt smooth and cool as she gently ran her fingers over the buttons. How could a collection of metal and plastic seem like a priceless object to her? She pressed the screen to her lips, letting it rest there.

Brrrrrr! Tess was startled when it vibrated. Involuntarily, she threw it across the bed. With her hand shaking she picked it up again and took a second to steady herself.

'Hello.'

'Hi, Tess. You found my phone, then? I'm calling from my landline.'

'Yes. It was on the kitchen table. Are you okay?'

She heard him sigh.

'Could be better, to be honest. Is it alright to call by and pick it up at lunchtime?'

'I've got to go to the supermarket in an hour. I could drop it round to you.' Tess was impressed that she'd instantly conjured up a plan to see where he lived.

'That'd be great. I've got a busy morning framing some artwork.'

'Where shall I drop the phone off?'

'I'll be at The Rookery most of the day.'

Damn. He was working at The Rookery, so she still wouldn't find out where he lived. She tried not to sound disappointed.

'Okay, see you about ten.'

'Great. Bye.'

Placing the phones side by side on the bedside table, Tess swung her legs out of bed and sat dangling them over the edge. She sat there feeling slightly overwhelmed. How was she going to find the energy to begin to sort out her complicated life?

By ten o'clock, Tess had washed her hair and had taken the time to blow-dry it, instead of her usual quick and easy ponytail. She pulled on some clean jeans and tucked them into some black boots. She slipped on a charcoal-grey blouse and an olive cardigan. A quick spray of perfume and she was ready.

The sun-tinged edges of the clouds looked like they'd been dipped in honey. A cool breeze ruffled her hair, causing flyaway strands to stick to her lip-gloss. As Tess walked alongside the cricket pitch, butterflies took flight in the pit of her stomach. Would Daniel or the owner answer the door?

She pushed open huge iron gates that squeaked on their hinges. Dew-laced cobwebs quivered in corners of the ornate ironwork and crows cawed their annoyance at her presence. She noticed Daniel's black Land Rover Defender parked by the side of The Rookery, making her squeeze his phone between her fingers in nervous anticipation.

Tess passed huge mature trees and high rhododendron bushes. Then The Rookery came into view. Her eyes opened wide in wonder. A huge turret that had been hidden from the road by abundant foliage, rose up three storeys high like Rapunzel's tower. A gleaming glass orangery clung to the side of the building, revealing itself as she walked the curve of the gravel drive. The leaded windows glinted in the autumn sun and seemed to watch her approach. Finally the hidden treasure of architecture was now in full view. Tess thought it was wondrous.

The sand stone facing was veined like marble, and layers of bricks added texture and pattern. Stone mullions framed the pointed arch windows, which diminished in size with each floor. Ornate chimneystacks stretched into the sky, with rows of terracotta chimneys perched on top. A twisted and gnarled wisteria wound and grasped at the stonework growing over the top of the enormous arched oak front door. The front door itself was studded with black bolts and the growling face of a brass lion doorknocker looked back at her with sightless eyes.

Tess lifted it and let it drop heavily. The noise disturbed the crows, drawing her eyes skywards. She turned back quickly at the sound of the door opening. She was about to explain her presence to an imagined old wizened owner, but Daniel stood holding the door open. He was wearing faded canvas trousers and a T-shirt with a tear on the front, both splattered with paint. She also noticed that he looked tired and pale.

'Hi. Sorry for disturbing your day off. Come in,' said Daniel.

'Don't be silly. You didn't. Wow, this place is amazing.'

She'd stepped into a huge double height hall that was overlooked by a glistening planet of a chandelier. The lower half of the hall's walls were covered with warm oak panelling. Above the panelling the paintwork was warm claret red. Paintings and ornate gilt mirrors hung at intervals and at the far end of the hall an impressive staircase divided into two, curving left and right before disappearing from view. Behind the staircase was a huge window that spilled citrus sunshine onto the stairs and hall.

'Is the owner out for the day? What a wonderful place to hold your exhibition.'

Before Daniel could answer, eight paws pitter-pattered across the stone flagged flooring. Goya and Gogh wagged their tails in delight at seeing Tess. She bent to stroke them.

'So, you lucky girls are allowed to come for the day too.' Tess looked up at Daniel from her crouched position. 'It's a devil wondering what to do with a dog when you need to go away for more than a few hours. When I lived at home, if Padders couldn't come with us overnight somewhere, we wouldn't go.'

'Come through and I'll put the kettle on. Who's Padders? I thought you only had Bob the fish.'

'He's my dog, but he stayed with Mum and Dad when I left Cornwall.'

'When did you leave?' Daniel walked through the hall followed by Tess and the dogs.

'I suppose you could say I followed Holly, eight years ago. She wanted to move to a busy city with plenty of nightlife and invited me for the summer. We had a wonderful time. We were only eighteen and squashed into her tiny flat, but it was great to go out five nights a week without our parents worrying and pointing at the clock. It was the first time we'd really let our hair down. The Blue Olive was new and hiring staff, we both got a job and rented a couple of rooms above it. We've both moved twice since then.'

Daniel filled the kettle. 'Do you miss Cornwall?'

'I miss all of it. Mum, Dad, Padders, the beaches, the raw elements and the peace. That's why I moved out to the countryside here in Nottingham and commute into the city. I'm a simple country girl at heart. In fact, I took your advice. Remember the day I rescued you in my ark?' Tess smiled. 'You said I should follow my dream because life is too short. Well, I've seen a little teashop for sale in a lovely small harbour town, close to Mum and Dad. There's an opportunity to buy it, with their help, of course.'

'What about Blake?'

Tess bit her lip. 'I don't want to sound disloyal behind his back, but things haven't been good between us since last Christmas. I feel like we've both changed; both moved in different directions. Now he's ill and in trouble with the police, so, he needs me at the moment.'

'He seemed pretty robust yesterday evening. How is he this morning?'

'I'm really sorry about last night. We had an argument and I asked him to leave. I hate it when he's drunk. He changes character. Yeah, I think he's improving. He keeps me at arms' distance when it comes to his health.'

Daniel frowned. 'Maybe he thinks he's protecting you.'

'But don't you think you need a huge amount of support when you have cancer? It must be a very scary and lonely experience.'

'It must be.'

Tess noticed Daniel's eyes glistening. She watched him turn and sniff as he rinsed the coffee pot. He spooned fresh coffee into the pot and then poured in boiling water. Tess felt uneasy and didn't know what to say next. She wandered around the room, grimacing to herself for talking too much.

It was nervous excitement at being with him. She ran her fingers along the gigantic smooth fridge and along the front rail of the Aga, before noticing a watercolour. It was a framed picture depicting a jug full of pink tinged daisies. It was simple but painted beautifully.

'What a beautiful painting. I love daisies. Do you think the owner would sell it?'

'Never. It's very precious to him.'

'Do you know him well, then?'

Daniel placed the coffee pot, cups and a plate of chocolate biscuits on the table. 'Sit down, Tess. I have some explaining to do.'

Tess sat down with a frown of worry. He sounded serious and looked subdued in a pensive Byronic way, as if remembering a painful memory. He poured out two coffees.

'This is *my* house. I'm exhibiting in my own house. Remember on the day of the flood?' He smiled softly. 'I told you my parents had died in an accident? This is the house I grew up in. It was left to Den and me, but Den was living in London, married with a young child and they didn't want to move back to Nottingham. Den got the equivalent monies transferred from our parents' estate and bought a bigger house in the capital.'

Tess sat in stunned silence trying to comprehend what she'd just heard. 'I don't know what to say. I feel silly. It never occurred to me.'

'In fairness, why should it? I'm just surprised that some gossiping neighbour hadn't mentioned it.'

Tess remembered how close she'd come to hearing where he lived from Mrs Campbell. He stood up and walked to the painting that she'd just been admiring.

'My mother painted this. I remember the very day, like it was yesterday.'

Tess was mortified. 'Daniel, I'm so sorry. I can't believe

how rude I was asking if it was for sale. I'm so embarrassed.' She stood up and walked the few steps towards him. She laid her hand on his arm and said again quietly, 'I'm so sorry.'

'Don't be.' He smiled and patted her hand. 'You don't know how pleased I am that you love it. It means a lot. You have great taste.'

She looked into his eyes and watched his smile fade.

'There's something else,' he said.

'What is it? Is it the phone call last night?'

He nodded. 'Den has cancer too.' A tear fell on to his cheek and without thinking Tess lifted her hand and wiped it away. She stepped forwards and wrapped her arms around Daniel's shoulders, hugging him tightly. At that moment, her thoughts were only to offer comfort to a new friend who had received terrible news.

'I'm sorry,' she whispered. She felt his arms fold around her waist and hold her tightly in an embrace. She could feel herself falling in love with this man. A man who could cry with love and concern for his family, without feeling embarrassed.

Inevitably, they pulled apart.

'We'll support each other through this. After all, that's what friends are for,' said Tess.

'That would be good.' He squeezed her hand then let it go. 'Coffee?'

'Please.'

After coffee and biscuits, Daniel offered to show Tess around his home. They walked towards the back of the hall and under the sweeping staircase, heading for several large oak doors. Daniel opened one and led them down a long dining room that smelt of beeswax. Tess had never seen such a long dining table. It stretched nearly the length of the entire room and seemed to have twenty or more seats arranged around it. Four candelabras stood proudly on the table, spaced several feet apart. More oil paintings and watercolours decorated the walls, along with family photographs. She'd have liked to stop and look at his parents and Den, but she followed him through another door at the far end of the dining room. It led to yet another spacious room, smelling of fresh paint. An enormous white marble fireplace stood in the centre of the far wall and a delicate cornice of gilt oak leaves edged the top of the walls.

Daniel's voice echoed around the empty room. 'I've cleared this room of furniture and painted all the walls with a fresh coat. This is where I'm going to hang my work.' He swept his arms expansively in a curve.

'It's huge. Are your paintings big?'

'Some are. Some are quite small. I'll show you later. Come and look at the garden.'

Tess walked to the bay window and stood looking out of the French doors. She imagined the bay to be the size of her whole kitchen. The garden looked like a corner of Kew Gardens and petered out into the distance. A large paved area led to an immaculate velvet lawn that extended as far as she could see. To the left was a circular lily pond, backed by banks of shrubs. Mature trees dotted the lawn and boxed hedging punctuated the lawn in different areas.

'I'm going to have a marquee out the back for music and dancing.'

'You're going to make it a party?'

'It was Den's idea because it's our birthday on the exhibition day. What does everyone do when they've looked at the artwork and had a bite to eat? If I'm not careful, everyone will have left after an hour. Den came up with the bright idea of extending the night with dancing and I thought, why not? That way everyone can walk in and out, looking at the paintings and prints more than once.'

'Very clever. They won't want to leave.'

He laughed. 'That's the idea.'

Tess was relieved to see him laughing and the colour return to his cheeks. Thank goodness he had this project to keep him busy.

'What an amazing house and garden to grow up in. No wonder you didn't want to move.'

'I'll never sell The Rookery. I'm here for the rest of my life. There's nowhere else I want to be. I've seen a lot of the world and still want to see a lot more, but I'll always come back here. All the memories I have of my parents are here, living in every room. That lawn,' he said pointing out of the window, 'played a big part of my childhood. It was my ocean, my sky and my racetrack. I learnt to ride a bike on it. The bushes were my caves and dungeons and the trees were my flying machines, or dinosaurs I rode on the backs of.'

'I wish I'd known you then. It would have been fun playing kings and princesses.'

'Ha! There were no princesses in my games. My games were macho and all about saving the universe.'

They grew relaxed and comfortable in each other's company.

'Come and see my work. It's in my studio.'

Tess followed him back through the dining room and up the staircase. Her eyes couldn't take everything in at once. At the top of the stairs, a large landing had six doors leading off it. The staircase continued to curve up to a second floor, but Daniel opened the first door and held it open for her. They exchanged smiles as she passed him.

The room was high and light, despite the walls being painted a rich dark plum above waist height. The lower half was covered in stylish Art Nouveau pressed paper, with Tudor roses on long stems, the colour of whipped cream. A bitter chocolate leather settee edged one wall and an easel and desk stood by the window. Canvasses leant against the far wall and the room smelt of oil paint.

'This used to be my father's study. He was an architect. I feel close to him when I'm working in the same room.'

'It must be very comforting.' Tess wandered over to the canvasses propped up against each other. 'Are all your paintings in oil?'

'No, not all of them. I do some work on my Mac and then print it. I do a little watercolour, but I'll never be as good as Mum was. Why don't you have a look at some of those while I see if I've got any emails.'

Tess knelt down on the floor. She reached for the first painting. She wasn't sure what she'd been expecting to see, but her smile was soon replaced by open-mouthed awe. She'd presumed they might have been modern stylish pieces with streaks and dashes of vibrant colour, but she couldn't have been more wrong.

A river scene depicting a woman waist deep in water caught her attention. She could feel the heat of the summer sun on the woman's warm damp skin. The luminosity of her skin must have been captured with a glaze of some sort. Tess could almost smell the river and hear the hushing of the water over the shallow gravel on the riverbank. She tried not to think who the woman could be. This wasn't the time for jealousies to interrupt her private viewing.

The next painting was of a cityscape, silhouetted against a night sky full of stars. Another was an oil painting of elegant Cypress trees, clinging to a steep hillside that sloped towards the sea. A portrait of an old lady took Tess's breath away. It depicted poverty, tears, dirt and tragedy. The background resembled a post-apocalyptic landscape, barren and infertile. Daniel had captured her raw emotion as if it were a photograph.

Canvas after canvas revealed snow capped mountains,

verdant forests, lush vineyards, children playing, people suffering. Each painting told a story with atmospheric intensity, their hues, tones and textures drawing the eye to particular areas of the picture. Dimly lit backgrounds showed figures in the foreground, bathed in sunlight. Mountains which were shadowed in the deepest greys and mauves on one side, exploded with whites and lemons on the sunlit side of the rock face. Bands of paint in a juxtaposition of vibrant colours, all painted in perfect perspective, made Tess shake her head in admiration. She pored over many more prints, paintings and sketches, amazed at Daniel's imagination and talent.

Daniel interrupted her silence as he was unscrewing the lens cap from his camera. 'What do you think?'

'I think you're incredibly talented. They make me smile, they make me think and they make me want to empty my piggy bank and buy them all.'

'Right answer.'

Tess spotted a cabinet stuffed full of comics. There were so many that the doors wouldn't close properly. 'I'm curious about this huge pile of comics over here.'

Click! Daniel took her photograph.

'Hey, I didn't say cheese,' protested Tess.

'Photographs are so much better if they're not posed.'

'Anyway, stop changing the subject and explain these comics.'

'It's a bit embarrassing really. You've found my Achilles heel. I collected *The Dandy* for more years than I care to remember.'

'You're an anorak! A bona fide collector.'

'Hey, don't knock my namesake.'

'Who's that?'

'You don't know that Desperate Dan lives inside *The Dandy*?'

Tess giggled. 'Was he the one who had big muscles and ate lots of cabbage?'

'Now you're really showing yourself up. That was Popeye and he ate spinach. But Desperate Dan had muscles all right. He could lift a cow with one hand and his beard was so tough he had to shave with a blowtorch. He didn't eat vegetables. He ate cow pie with horns sticking out of them. Desperate Dan was a real man.'

'Thank you for enlightening me. Tell me, how is Desperate Dan these days?'

'Like most things, the political correctness police have got hold of him. He's been told to calm down and turn vegetarian.'

'No! Seriously?'

'He's not allowed to eat cow pie any more. I'm guessing it's because of the new trend for healthy eating and cutting obesity and all the medical problems that goes with it. I bet mad cow disease had a lot to do with cutting it out of his diet and the comic as well.'

'They'll have him training to be a social worker next.'

Daniel laughed and turned off his computer. 'Are you hungry?'

Tess realised she was feeling a little hungry and looked at her watch. 'It's nearly twelve. I can't believe I've been here nearly two hours.'

'You know what they say. Time flies when you're having fun.'

Tess *was* having fun. She felt happy and relaxed sharing Daniel's private world.

'How about scrambled eggs on a toasted English muffin?' he asked.

'Do you have any cow pie?'

Chapter Twenty-Five

Tess's day at The Rookery continued to pass in a happy blur. She and Daniel had eaten lunch together and shared memories about their lives and travels. For the past twenty minutes they'd been walking with the dogs in the house's beautiful back garden and enjoying the unseasonably mild day. They walked in an easy silence, winding their way towards the far end of the garden.

A light aircraft droned overhead and sheep bleated in a distant field. Birds sang high in the trees and a white butterfly, enjoying the last heat of the day, danced in front of them. The area of the garden where they were now walking had been left to grow semi wild. Looking over a fence at the end of Daniel's land, they stood and watched caramel-coloured cows chewing grass and wafting flies away with their tails. In the distance, behind the cows and high in the sky, a white hot air balloon drifted silently in the air streams, resembling an impatient moon.

'It's lovely it's so mild today after the recent chilly weather,' she said with a sigh, leaning on the mossy fence. 'It can't stay like this for long now it's October. It always used to rain when I dressed up on Halloween evenings to go trick or treating.'

'What did you dress up as? It's something I never did.'

'You're joking! You don't know what you missed. One year I was a witch with a green face but I was frightened of my own reflection. So the year after that I was an orange pumpkin. Stop it. I looked great.' Tess playfully thumped his arm as he bent double holding his sides laughing. Goya and Gogh ran excitedly in circles around them.

'You wouldn't laugh if you'd seen the treasure I collected. If you'd seen the mountain of Haribos, sherbet fountains, fizzy snakes and flying saucers I took home, you'd soon be pulling your orange tights on.'

'I'm sure I would.' He wiped his eyes. 'You must dig out some photographs for me.'

Tess couldn't quite believe that she was spending the whole day getting to know Daniel. She hadn't felt this relaxed and happy for a long time. Secretly she was studying every laughter line around his eyes, the tan flecks in his irises, the sexy prominent bone on his wrist and his long slim artistic fingers. She'd felt the occasional pang of guilt because she'd purposefully left her phone back at Rose Cottage, just in case Blake had decided to ring and apologise for his behaviour last night. How was she to have known that she'd be spending the whole day with Daniel?

'Let's go back this way,' said Daniel, pointing to a copse of trees. 'This is the orchard. The trees are breaking under the weight of apples but I've only picked a few dozen. They're past their best now. I usually take several boxes across to the pub, but I've been too busy this year with the exhibition.'

'Is that why a ladder's propped against that tree?'

'No, I just like climbing trees.'

Tess looked at Daniel who winked back. 'It really wouldn't have surprised me,' she said with a giggle.

'Are you saying I'm childish?'

'Stop!' Tess yelled. 'Don't walk under it. Seven years bad luck, or is that breaking a mirror?'

'I'm not superstitious, are you?'

'No. Touch wood!'

'Do you think some people believe that touching wood really stops bad things from happening?'

'Some people do. Why?'

Daniel breathed in and opened his mouth to speak but exhaled noisily instead.

'What?' asked Tess.

Daniel shook his head. 'It's crazy. I don't want you to think I'm crazy.'

'I won't, honestly.'

'It's nothing. Really.'

Tess looked at him and raised her eyebrows questioningly. She smiled gently to encourage him to continue.

'Promise not to think I'm a mad man and run away?'

'Promise.'

'I... no, this is ridiculous. I can't. Let's change the subject.'

'What can be so bad that you can't speak about it?'

Daniel's expression changed, but Tess couldn't read its meaning. 'Let's sit over there and I'll try to explain.'

Tess followed him to a wooden bench beneath a pear tree. They sat down a few inches apart. Daniel was hunched forwards on the edge of the seat with his hand squeezed together between his knees. He turned to face her.

'It's not a superstition as such.'

'What isn't?'

'What I did. What I do.'

'I don't understand.'

He rubbed his palms together, making a shushing sound. 'Shit,' he said, ruefully.

Tess remained quiet and let him take his time.

'I count things.'

'Count?'

'Yes. I count things. Three times. I can't stop myself. I'm not crazy. You think I'm crazy, don't you?'

'No.'

'Really, you're not just humouring me?'

'Daniel! I'm not humouring you?'

'I'm not as bad as I used to be. I just need to do some things three times.'

'Like what? Give me an example.'

'I pick up the third newspaper in a pile. I check I've locked the door three times. Lather my hands with soap three times, choose the third carton of milk at the shops, check the lights three times... I could go on. I've managed to stop doing several repetitions over the years, but some things I *need* to continue doing. You probably hadn't even noticed. It's not something that looks out of the ordinary. I suppose you'd call it a private addiction.'

'Have you done it since you were a child?'

'No.'

'Can you remember when it started?'

'Shortly after my parents died. It made me feel safer; more in control of mine and Den's destiny.' He shrugged. 'So much for that hypothesis. Look at Den now, diagnosed with cancer. I've been thinking since yesterday, that maybe I brought it on because I stopped counting to three on some occasions. As I'm saying the words to you, I can hear that they sound ridiculous, but maybe that's what caused the cancer.'

'Have you spoken to someone professional about it?'

'Christ, you *do* think I'm mad.'

Tess placed her hand on his. 'I *know* you're not mad. It sounds like an obsessive compulsion. I've seen a documentary about it on the television. Some people can't touch anything without scrubbing their hands and some people have to check that the gas is off hundreds of times a day. It can ruin lives if it gets out of hand without professional help.'

'I suppose I'm lucky, then. I could be obsessed with the number thirty-three. What sort of help do you mean? A psychiatric hospital?'

'No. Nothing that drastic. You ought to see your doctor and he'll arrange an appointment to see someone. Sometimes it just helps to talk. Have you told anyone else?'

'I told Den shortly after it started but I've never mentioned it since.'

'Do you have any idea why you count to three over any other number?'

'I don't want a third accident to happen.'

'A third one?'

Daniel held his head in his hands and gripped clumps of hair in his fists. 'Sean.'

'A friend?'

'An ex-friend.'

Tess spoke softly. 'What happened to him?'

'It was my fault.'

Tess didn't answer. She waited for him to continue in his own time.

'Sean Connors was my best friend since the age of five,' said Daniel. 'He'd been paired with me at school, you know, to show him the ropes. I'd been there a term and new kids were coupled with older kids. We became inseparable.'

Daniel appeared to drift off into a painful distant memory, his eyes staring sightlessly into the distance. Tess waited patiently. He cleared his throat and shook his head as if trying to dislodge the heavy burden of guilt that was weighing him down. He subconsciously rubbed his scarred temple and continued.

'Sean was a fantastic artist. It was because the two of us stuck together like glue, that I went with him to galleries and evening art classes and discovered that I'd inherited my mother's talent for painting.' Daniel wafted his hand in the air as if dismissing an irrelevant idea. 'My stuff was child's play compared to Mum and Sean's work. Sixteen years ago, on bonfire night, I wanted to skip an evening class and go to a firework party. He wanted to go to the class and finish a painting.' Daniel took a deep juddering breath.

Tess almost believed that he'd forgotten she was sitting

there. His thoughts and visions were in another time, another place.

'I suggested we tossed a coin. I won. We caught the bus to the bonfire.' Ten long seconds of silence passed. 'A firework shot sideways into the crowd. It hit Sean's face.'

Goosebumps spread down Tess's arms and neck like a rash. She slowly lifted her hand to cover her mouth. Tears pricked her eyes as she tried to comprehend the immense misplaced culpability that Daniel must be feeling.

'He lost an eye. I did that to him. He might only have been blinded in one eye, but I killed his future as an artist. All I got was this burn which healed.' Daniel rubbed his scar.

Tess knew that his physical injury had healed, but his psychological wound was still sore and open. 'Where is he now? Do you keep in touch?'

Daniel looked up at her. He was pale and drawn. 'I visited the hospital every day for the first few weeks he was there. When Sean left hospital his family sold up and moved to America. They had family there so moved to be with them. We were inseparable for eleven years and then he was gone.'

Tess turned towards him and held both of his hands in hers. 'Listen to me. Look at me. Terrible things happen to wonderful people every day. It was an accident. It wasn't your fault. The coin could have come down on the other side and an accident could have happened in the art class. Would you have let Sean blame himself? And listen, Daniel.' She gently shook his hands to make sure he was listening. 'From my point of view, you'd already had three tragedies, not two. Your mother. Your father. And Sean.'

He looked deep into her eyes. 'I hadn't thought of it that way.'

'So Den's illness is a fourth negative thing to happen, not

third. None of this is your fault. It's just life. It can be cruel sometimes.'

Tess could see his mind whirring with this fresh look from a new perspective. She continued, eager to un-crease a few more frown lines from his brow. 'Blake is suffering with cancer just like Den, so you must stop thinking that something you have, or haven't done, has caused Den's illness. Every day people wake up without a care in the world, and by the time the sun sets on the day, they or a loved one have discovered that they're sick. It's out of our hands, Daniel. The luck of the draw. No matter what number you count to, it won't alter people's destinies.'

'It sounds so logical when you explain it. And I hadn't looked at it from the point of view that three tragedies have already happened.'

'Will you give your doctor a call?'

'I'll think about it. I can't believe that I didn't realise that three people had already had accidents. It sort of makes my counting – irrelevant.'

'Phobias and obsessions don't always make sense, but there's always a reason for it.'

Daniel lifted his hand and gently moved a stray wisp of hair away from Tess's face. He then stroked her cheek with the back of his fingers. 'You're incredible,' he whispered.

Tess's fingers tingled and her heart raced. She could see his eyelashes blinking over his pained moss-green eyes. He was looking directly at her. They were still holding hands, a current of electricity passing between them. Could he see her body shaking from his touch? His lips opened slightly and he leaned slowly towards her. Her body moved towards his, their faces inches apart. Tess could feel his warm breath on her face. She knew without any shadow of doubt, that if she let him, he would kiss her in the next second. She wanted him to, but like a drowning man letting go of his only life support, she moved backwards and raised their hands to come between their chests as a barrier.

Daniel continued to look at Tess, but a deep sadness fell over his eyes and his shoulders fell. 'I'm sorry. I shouldn't have tried… I know you're with Blake. Forgive me?'

'Don't be sorry. There's nothing to forgive. I wish things were different, but Blake needs me at the moment. I was going to end things between us a few months ago. But he got sick.'

'I understand, but like you told me, nothing you do now will change his destiny.'

'It's just that he has no one else. He hasn't many friends and his mother isn't much help.'

'Like I said, you're incredible.'

By mentioning Blake's name, the spell had been broken. Reality hit home like a thump in the stomach. This was just a magical day that she would relive for months to come, perhaps years. She couldn't live with herself if she left Blake in order to follow her own selfish longings. She couldn't be that cruel and not suffer the consequences. It seemed that she and Daniel shared something in common. Guilt.

Tess spoke quietly as she looked at her watch and then at Daniel. 'I ought to be making a move now, it'll soon be half three.'

He didn't answer but stood up pulling her to her feet. He stuck out his elbow for her to link arms, which she did. They strolled in silence back towards The Rookery. After a few minutes Daniel spoke.

'Thank you for listening and understanding. You've really helped.'

Tess squeezed his arm in reply. They walked back through the patio doors retracing their steps. At the front door they stopped and faced each other once more.

'Please don't think I'm crazy.'

Tess smiled and held up a forefinger. 'Stop it.'

'Okay, okay, enough of the crazy talk.'

'I've an idea that might help.'

'What idea?'

'I'll phone you. Thank you for lunch and a wonderful day.'

'I've really enjoyed it.' Daniel opened the front door.

'I'll phone.' She smiled and waved, before turning and heading back down the gravel drive. As she walked, she wondered if Daniel was checking the door three times.

Chapter Twenty-Six

One. Two. Three. Four. Five. Denise silently counted the lights on the ceiling as the trolley she was lying on was pushed down a hospital corridor. She shivered in her lightweight gown under a thin sheet. It wasn't the cold that was making her shiver. It was anxiety. The hospital was warm with a pungent smell of antiseptic and cooked dinners lurking in the corridors. It wasn't a good mixture when you were feeling sick and anxious. Simon was holding her hand as she was bumped down the corridor.

'Hang on tight. I don't want to lose you,' the hospital porter joked. He slammed the trolley through a double set of plastic doors.

Denise screwed her eyes tightly and braced herself. The doors opened easily and the trolley passed through smoothly. They turned a corner and waited at a large lift. A sign above it read *Operating Theatres Only*. She looked up at Simon who smiled back at her and squeezed her hand tighter. She noticed his hair. It was sticking up where he had obviously raked his hands through it.

'It's taking its time today, must be on a go slow like the French.' The porter laughed.

Denise heard Simon grunt in response.

'Weather's turned, hasn't it?' continued the man. 'Soon be Christmas, you'll see. No sooner is October here than Christmas is round the corner. Have you got kids?'

'Two boys.'

The lift stopped at their floor. After a few seconds the doors opened and Denise was rattled inside. The doors closed and all that she could see were the chrome walls and handrail. Soon she was pulled out backwards and wheeled down another white featureless corridor. The porter stopped at a thick red line that had been painted on the floor. She read another sign. *Patients Only Beyond This Point.*

'I can't go any further, darling,' Simon whispered. 'I'll be by your side when you wake up. Everything will be all right. I love you.'

'I love you too.' A tear rolled down her cheek and Simon kissed it away.

From the other side of the painted line, two nurses came out of a plastic double door.

'Mrs Harby?'

'Yes.'

'Lovely. Can I just check a few details?'

The nurse asked her full name and date of birth and then checked her hospital wristband.

'Are you hubby?' asked one of the nurses, looking at Simon.

'Yes.'

'We'll take good care of her. You go and have a cuppa and we'll buzz the ward when your wife is back out of theatre.'

Inside the anaesthetic room, Denise was slightly raised into a half sitting position. It was a small room full of shelves and boxes. A man walked through a set of swing doors in front of her towards her trolley. Before the door swung closed behind him, she could see the operating lights and table in the room beyond.

'Hello, my name's Rupert Goldsmith. I'm your anaesthetist today. Have you had a general anaesthetic before?'

'No, just two epidurals.'

'I see. An epidural blocks the pain sensors, but as I'm sure you're aware, you stay alert and awake. Today, we're going to make you fall into a peaceful sleep and you'll wake up and wonder if we've even started.' He smiled reassuringly. 'A strange question, but do you have any false teeth, crowns or veneers?'

'No.'

'Good. In a minute I'm going to inject some fluid in here,' he explained, pointing to a taped needle protruding from the back of her hand. 'You'll be asleep in no time. Just relax.'

Denise took a deep breath. The anaesthetist flushed something cold into her arm. She could feel it sting as it was forced into her vein. The anaesthetist turned and picked up another syringe.

'Okay, Denise, this is the one that will send you off to sleep. Count to ten and I bet you don't get past lucky number seven.'

Please let me wake up, she thought. One. Two. Three. I feel like I've drunk a few glasses of champagne. Four. Five. This is really quite pleasant. Six.

Chapter Twenty-Seven

It had been a few days since Tess had spent the day at The Rookery with Daniel. During this time she had searched the internet looking for as much information as she could about Obsessive Compulsive Disorder. She'd made copious lists with snippets of information that might be useful, but all the time a nagging thought chipped away at her. She had willingly invested many hours researching ways to help Daniel, but before Blake had been diagnosed, she'd never once googled his symptoms. She was sitting at her kitchen table and foremost in her mind was the thought that if she'd cared more, maybe she might have detected Blake's illness sooner.

Tess was relieved to read that Daniel's compulsion was mild, which meant that it didn't stop him from leading a normal life. It didn't keep him housebound or afraid to go out at night, like some unfortunate sufferers she'd read about. Tess had discovered two main therapies that could help him overcome his compulsion. The first was behavioural therapy, where sufferers are gradually and repeatedly confronted with the situation that they fear the most. In Daniel's case, this was fireworks and *not* repeating some action three times. The second therapy was cognitive therapy. Tess read that this was talking through and analysing why the sufferer feels such a compulsion to repeat things. She supposed that their conversation in the orchard had been a good start. Daniel knew that he counted to three on occasions because he felt it kept him and his loved ones safe. So he must be making headway already.

Tess had also searched for Daniel's friend, Sean Connors, on her computer. It had only taken twenty minutes of research to find something very interesting. Something that might just help Daniel that little bit more. She printed the article and then sent off an email.

The following day, Daniel decided he would finally make an appointment with his doctor. Although his obsession with the number three was considerably better than it used to be several years earlier, he trusted Tess and wanted to show her that he was taking her advice seriously. He wanted to get better, not only for himself, but for her.

He knew he was falling for Tess. Who wouldn't, he thought, looking at his reflection in bathroom mirror? Beautiful, funny, thoughtful. He knew his feelings for her were growing each time they met and that he would probably end up getting hurt. But he felt relaxed and even a little mischievous when they were together. He was enjoying their friendship, even if it must remain platonic. He did regret one thing though. He spoke to himself in the mirror. 'Idiot.' He cringed at his insensitivity in trying to kiss Tess. He shut his eyes in embarrassment, unable to look at himself. He groaned aloud with humiliation when he remembered her lifting their hands as a barrier to his advance. Shaking his head, he turned his back on the mirror and went downstairs to find his jacket.

Daniel found it on the kitchen pew just as he heard a knock on the front door. 'Be good and no chewing the table legs,' he said. Slipping his arms into his jacket sleeves, he crossed the hallway and unlocked the heavy oak front door.

'Morning.'

'Hello,' said Tess. 'Lovely day for a trip to the supermarket.'

'I can think of a few places I'd rather we were going.'

'C'mon.' Tess turned and walked towards the Land Rover.

Daniel looked over his shoulder in the hope that Tess wouldn't see him checking the door. She had her back to him so he quickly ensured that the door was locked three times, before following her.

It was Tess's second day of annual leave and she'd come up with the idea of driving to a supermarket in order to put some therapy into practice. They pulled out of the drive and Tess tried to concentrate on the matter in hand. However, the excitement she felt by sitting next to him in his Land Rover, made her feel more like she was off on a wonderful holiday. She tried to keep her eyes on the passing country scenery, but occasionally they strayed to Daniel's hands gripping the steering wheel or shamefully, his thighs.

Daniel parked his Defender in the supermarket's car park and climbed down. She heard him click the central locking three times before watching him squirm with embarrassment.

'I feel such an idiot. Can we just buy some sticky pastries and head back home?' he called over the bonnet.

'Of course we can, but you have to give it a go first.'

'Spoilsport.'

They walked towards the main entrance. Tess asked, 'What do you usually do now?'

'What would I do now? Stand on my head and yodel. Seriously though, you're making me sound like a total freak.'

Tess linked arms with him and laughed. 'We've been over this already. I don't think you're weird, crazy or mad. Now be good, or there'll be no pastry for you. What would you usually do first?'

Daniel squeezed her arm with his. 'I like it when you're strict.'

'Are you taking this seriously, Daniel Cavanagh?'

Daniel cleared his throat. 'I'd pick this trolley because it's from the third stacked line.'

'Okay, you've got to choose another one today.'

Daniel looked along the six lines of stacked trolleys and slowly let out a deep breath. He pushed a pound coin into the fourth line and a trolley clicked free. They walked through the main entrance in silence and through the automatic barriers into the fruit and vegetable area.

'It doesn't feel right,' said Daniel, shaking his head.

'What doesn't?'

'The trolley. I can't explain it. It just feels wrong.'

'We'll be quick.'

'It's like having your shoes on the wrong feet. You have to stop and change them because it's all you can think about.'

'But what's the worst that can happen? Continuing with your shoe analogy, it feels wrong but you can still walk. Put a few things in the trolley. We don't have to be more than five minutes.'

'Five minutes. I'm timing it.' Daniel looked at his watch, breathed in and braced himself. 'Danish pastries, this way.' He rushed through the store as if he'd won a trolley dash and had a few minutes in which to collect what he wanted. He clipped a couple of other trolleys in his haste, but soon arrived at the cake section. Tess caught up.

'What pastry do you want?' he asked.

Tess surveyed the display. 'Apple and raisin, I think,' she said, picking up the pastry with a pair of tongs and placing it into a bag. 'How about you?'

'A cinnamon whirl.'

Daniel inhaled deeply and let out a long breath, as if he were blowing out a candle. 'Let's go now.'

'Are you okay?'

'If I'm honest, I'm feeling a bit anxious.'

'What about?' asked Tess.

'This bloody trolley.' He tried to laugh but it sounded more like a groan. 'I can't explain except to say that it feels wrong.'

'I know it feels like this isn't working, but you've successfully chosen some food in a trolley that wasn't the third in line. How long is it since you've done that?'

'Years.'

'Do you think we could pick up a bottle of wine before we go to the checkout?'

He set off once again at speed.

They continued to meet each other throughout October. They used the excuse that their get-togethers were a sort of therapy. Tess had said it would be a good idea to try some cognitive therapy, in other words, to have a chat about why he had his hang ups. Their conversation always went off at tangents that had nothing to do with his obsession at all: updates on Den and Blake's health, art, travel and dreams of owning a cake shop. All they knew was that when they were in each other's company, they felt that their problems were lost in a fog of delicious amnesia.

Tess worked most Saturdays at The Blue Olive, so she could easily meet Daniel on her day off in the week, without Blake knowing. It wasn't that she was being deliberately deceitful with her secrecy. It was just that Blake would overreact to an innocent situation. He'd already grown grumpier as his court date loomed closer. She had set the boundaries of her friendship with Daniel and although her fantasies about him were very different, their friendship was platonic.

Tess was standing by The Rookery's front door saying goodbye to Daniel after their latest chat, when she asked him something.

'What are you doing on Saturday evening?'

'Don't know. Probably painting or watching a repeat of *Top Gear*. Why?'

'Now listen before you answer. Bear with me.'

Daniel closed his eyes. 'Wait a minute. Let me just hold that image.'

'Behave.' She playfully punched his biceps. 'You know how you haven't been to a bonfire party since Sean's accident? Do you think you could go to The Royal Oak's with me?'

'Bloody hell, Tess. One second you're putting naked images into my head and the next you're describing hell.'

'Could you just think about it?'

'What about Blake? Won't he want to go with you?'

'He'll be in Amsterdam for a few days. Give it some thought. I'll call you on Friday. Bye.'

'Bye.'

Back at home, Tess clicked the kettle on and checked her emails. She felt a jolt of excitement when she saw that Sean had replied to an email she'd sent him.

From: Sean Connors
Subject: Dan's exhibition
To: Tess Fenton
Hi Tess

What a thrill to receive your email. I'm sorry it's taken so long for me to reply, but I've been in Australia. Thank you for getting in touch and informing me of Dan's exhibition. I regret not keeping in touch, but we were young and wrapped up in ourselves as teenagers. It was so good to hear about Dan's work and know that he still lives at The Rookery.

I was shocked to hear about Robert and Helen. No, I didn't know about their accident and wish I could have been there for Dan and

Den. It must have been an incredibly difficult time for them both. Their parents were lovely people.

I know you asked if I could send him a good luck message but I think I can do better than that. I'm attending a conference in London on creating art using inorganic compounds in late November – sounds grand but it's just ceramics! I can't think of anything I'd rather do than come along to the exhibition and meet up again. We have a lot to talk about.

Keep in touch with dates.

Best wishes
Sean

Tess was delighted to have received a reply and overwhelmed that he would be able to attend Daniel's exhibition and not just send a message to him. Perhaps she should introduce them the day before because it would come as quite a shock for Daniel and could take his mind off his artwork on the actual day. She hoped she'd done the right thing.

Chapter Twenty-Eight

Tess and Holly were at Rose Cottage getting ready for The Royal Oak's annual bonfire and fireworks party. The house was now calm following the din of hairdryers, an Ipod blasting out through speakers and the girls' karaoke efforts while they got ready. They were adding the final touches of make-up and tweaking the last strands of hair into place.

'I hoke dey hag skarklers!' said Tess, smearing Fragile Pink lipstick onto her lips that were set in a frozen smile for ease of application.

'I'm telling you now,' shouted Holly, from Tess's bathroom, 'if they do the hokey-cokey starkers, I'm bloody coming home.'

Tess sat back and pressed her lips together to smooth the pink cream evenly. 'I said, I hope they have sparklers.'

Holly appeared at the bedroom doorway. 'Oh! Misheard you. Me too. Do you remember our bonfire nights on the beach? We'd write the names of our latest crushes in the air with our sparklers.'

'It was all right for you. You fancied Ed Holt. I had a thing for Matthew Hamilton-Bonningsby. By the time I'd finished writing his name, you'd be unwrapping your Christmas presents.'

Holly chuckled. 'I wonder where they are now.'

'Probably knee deep in nappies and mortgage repayments.'

Holly clenched her fists in excitement. 'I've told you that Doug's coming tonight and has split with his girlfriend, haven't I?'

'Only about twenty times. Are you still okay about me inviting Daniel tonight, although he might not turn up?'

Thankfully, Holly hadn't seemed to mind one bit when Tess had told her that she and Daniel occasionally had coffee together and had become good friends.

'Of course not. Anyone can see that he's gorgeous, but a girl can tell if someone likes them, and he wasn't interested in me. Doug's more my type, anyway. He's silly without being immature. I find Daniel a bit intimidating. He's artistic, he's clever, owns his own house – no, his own castle, and has travelled the world.'

Tess laughed as she checked her hair in the mirror. 'I hate to break it to you Holly, but it's being called an adult, not being intimidating.'

'Well Doug and I are going to leave becoming an adult until we're thirty. Don't you just love meeting a new man?'

'It's been a while.'

'But you must remember how it felt?'

Tess thought back to when Blake had entered her life. He'd stepped inside The Blue Olive and walked to the choose-your-own-pizza-toppings counter. Tess had noticed his good looks, athletic build and golden hair; he'd let himself go a little since then. Tess had made up his pizza while he'd pointed to the different ingredients. She'd made conversation by asking him about the book that was tucked under his arm. He'd told her that inside his book was a star ship's schematics database and that it archived every single star ship design ever conceived. Surely that should have made her distance herself light years from him from the start. But no. She'd been impressed with what she'd thought was his intellectual mind.

It seemed ridiculous now that she'd thought he was an amateur rocket enthusiast with a degree in physics, or a lecturer on space. She'd gone on a date that very night and now here she was, two years later and still dating what turned out to be a nerdy Trekkie.

Bringing her thoughts back to the present, Tess pulled on some thick socks and wrapped a scarf around her neck. 'No, it's a distant memory. A bit like our happy relationship.'

Holly threw a toy Bagpuss at her. 'Stop it before you get all maudlin.'

'You brought up the subject,' said Tess, throwing the floppy pink and white striped cat back at her.

Tess had called Daniel a couple of days previously to say that she'd be waiting at The Royal Oak's front entrance, at seven o'clock. She'd also let him know that there was no pressure to turn up if he felt he couldn't face it when the time came. However, she couldn't help wishing that he'd find the courage to meet her and face his biggest demon.

A short time later, Tess and Holly were crossing the village green, each clutching a torch. It was a cool evening with a scent of wood smoke and wet grass in the air. The girls folded their arms as a barrier against the chill, while still managing to direct the lemon beams of light ahead of them. Music boomed from the large speakers in the pub's garden and children's squeals of delight sprang from the darkness. A string of brightly coloured light bulbs danced in the breeze on the trees and the smell of caramelised onions and sausages drifted across the expanse of grass.

'Look,' shrieked Holly. 'We're just in time for the lighting of the bonfire.'

Tess shone her torch on her wrist and checked the time. Six forty-five. Her stomach lurched with anticipation and excitement.

'Quick, let's hurry.'

They both jogged over a little bridge that traversed a ditch and hurried across the tarmac parking area. They weaved through the stragglers of the crowd, both of them scanning the faces for someone special. Tess glanced towards the front entrance, but the only people in the vicinity were coming and going with drinks.

'I'm going to look over the other side for Doug,' said Holly. 'It'll be too noisy to hear you call, but I've got my mobile on vibrate.'

'Okay, so have I.'

Tess was relieved that Holly was over her short-lived crush on Daniel. Thankfully she was now preoccupied with all things Doug. When it came to men, her friend's attention span was as temporary as a bruise.

Tess watched Holly disappear into a sea of bodies surrounding the bonfire. She decided not to appear too pushy by waiting at the front door and sang along to Elton's 'Rocket Man', thumping from the speakers. After five minutes, Tess turned to see Holly waving madly and running towards her. She stopped in front of her, breathless and excited.

'Doug's phoned. He's ten minutes away.' She jumped up and down clapping her hands and grinning.

Tess smiled, sharing her enthusiasm.

'Lucky you. You know where the spare key is kept, don't you?'

'Yeah, under the little pot of pansies.'

'If we don't meet up again here, I'll see you back at mine. You're still staying the night, aren't you?'

'Yeh, of course. This is only our first date. What sort of a girl do you think I am?' Holly winked. 'I'm going to meet him by the clubhouse. See you later. I hope Daniel turns up.'

'So do I. See you later.'

She watched Holly running clumsily in her wellington boots across the cricket pitch. Tess checked her watch. Two minutes past seven. It was time to see if Daniel had arrived. Weaving her way through the burgeoning crowds, she crossed her fingers inside her pockets. The crowd thinned the further she moved away from the bonfire. Sidestepping children who were clutching hot dogs that dribbled with tomato sauce, she'd reached the car park where she had a clear view of the pub's front door. An unmistakable tall dark figure stood hunched outside the small porch. She walked towards the front door and stopped in front of him.

He was wrapped up in a coat and scarf, with his hands thrust deeply into his pockets. His smile was shy and the flames from the bonfire reflected in his eyes beneath his woollen hat, making them twinkle.

He spoke first. 'Hello.'

'You came.'

'I love hot dogs.'

'You're in luck.'

'Smell good.'

'They do.'

'I meant you.'

'Oh. Thanks.'

A few long seconds passed while they stood gazing and grinning at each other before Daniel broke the spell. 'I've got some fantastic news.'

'What?'

'Den's had the op. The lump's been removed and the surrounding tissue was clear of cancer cells.'

Tess gawped in delight before hugging him. 'I'm so happy for you both. That's wonderful.' She stood back and beamed at him. 'You see, everything's going to be okay.'

'You might just be right, you know? There'll still be chemo and check-ups for several years, but Den sounds so relieved.'

'I'm not surprised. And it's one less thing for you to worry about.'

'I hope it works out for Blake, too.'

'We'll see.'

Daniel smiled and rubbed his hands together briskly. 'Now what?'

'Now we enjoy the fireworks.'

She saw him tense. 'Let's sit on the bench beneath the tree in the middle of the green. We don't have to stand anywhere near the fireworks.'

Daniel knew which bench she meant, its seating wrapped around the trunk of a huge horse chestnut tree. It had been replaced twice in his lifetime by a local joiner. When he and Denise were younger, they'd stand on the bench trying to dislodge conkers each autumn, before soaking them in vinegar to make them harder for battle. He felt his shoulders relax at the idea of walking further away from the unpredictable explosions.

He stuck out an arm like a teapot handle for Tess to slip her arm into. She did and he squeezed it tightly against his side, enjoying the closeness of her body. She shone the torch on the rough grass and they trudged across the green towards the bench. Behind them they could hear the crowds cheer as a rocket screeched skywards.

He flinched and hoped that Tess didn't feel it.

'You okay?' she asked.

'I'm fine,' he lied.

They turned and sat beneath the skeletal canopy of the huge tree. Sitting with their arms still linked, they both looked ahead towards the distant glow of the bonfire. The navy-blue sky was bare and clear. Daniel thought how romantic this would be if they were on their own instead of sharing the village green with hundreds of people and waiting for disfiguring bombs to explode. Laughter occasionally broke free from the huddled crowd and voices cheered into the night, serenaded by crackling sparks from the fire.

Suddenly, the sky lit up with brilliant arms of cascading gold and silver stars. Bright glowing pearls rose silently into the darkness, dissolving into the heavens. Blue tracer stars crackled as they wriggled in a sparkling mesmeric dance. Gold clusters of starbursts flashed and glittered above the village green, lighting upturned faces. The whizzing and whirring echoed across the cricket pitch and far past the village.

Daniel pulled his scarf up to hide his mouth and nose. He didn't think that a soft cashmere mix, a gift from his sister, would be much protection from a wayward explosive, but it made him feel warmer and safer. He turned to look at Tess to see if she was looking at him with a pitying gaze. Fortunately, she was looking skyward with a hint of a smile on her glistening lips. Her profile was silhouetted against The Royal Oak's lights, a pale glow outlining her features. His eyes were drawn to her smooth neck as she watched another rocket explode into a chrysanthemum of stars. Her lips parted slightly as a series of whistling clusters shot into the black night. He watched her eyelashes blink with each explosion and burst of colour. From the position they were sitting in, Daniel slightly behind Tess, he could watch her in secret against a backdrop of Swarovski crystals raining down from the sky.

For the next ten minutes, while a crescendo of squeals, oohs and aahs emanated from the distant crowd, and a climax of whistles, bangs and crackles sprang from the sky, Daniel focused on Tess. He drank in the curves of her profile and the warmth of her body leaning against him. A cheer and a noisy round of applause heralded the end of the display. Tess turned towards Daniel.

'How was that?'

'Okay,' he answered, truthfully. Watching the fireworks as a background to Tess's lovely face had been the perfect way to be reintroduced to the volatile explosives. They were the colour wash to the central eye-catching subject of the painting.

He saw her face light up with relief.

'Really?'

He smiled cheekily. 'Can I have a hot dog now I've been so brave?'

'Oh, before we go...' Tess fumbled in her coat pocket and pulled out a neatly folded piece of paper. 'I found out some information that I thought you'd find interesting. Here.' She passed him the paper.

'Shall I open it now?'

'Save it until you get home. Come on, let's find those calories.'

Daniel stood up and pushed the paper into a pocket.

Tess slipped her hand through his arm. His body felt warm and safe through the fabric of his coat. They trudged in step back towards the bonfire. It was still burning brightly, but was half the size it had been.

'Will Goya and Gogh be all right with the noise?' she asked.

'You're kidding. I've shut them in a back bedroom with the television's volume turned up. At this very moment they'll be lying on their backs with their legs in the air on a memory foam mattress, watching the lads on *Top Gear* larking about.'

Tess tried but failed to stop herself from imagining what it would be like to be on Daniel's soft mattress with her legs in the air.

'You okay?' asked Daniel.

'Just a bit chilly now we've moved.'

He took his arm away from Tess's and pulled open one side of his warm winter coat. He invited her in with a nod of his head. Tess slipped inside his coat and melted into his warm body. She wrapped her arms around his waist and he closed the coat around her. They continued to walk, a little unsteadily now, towards the glorious smell of melted cheese and fried onions. As Tess walked inside Daniel's coat, she closed her eyes and let him guide the way. His jumper smelt clean with a hint of jasmine. She let her lips touch the soft wool and gave it the gentlest of secret kisses. She knew he'd never feel it through his layers of clothing. This must be the safest place in the world, she thought.

All too soon, they'd reached the bright outdoor lights that had been hung to illuminate the food tables. Disappointingly, Tess had to unwind herself from underneath Daniel's coat. After ordering hot dogs and mulled wine, they walked towards the dying bonfire. Curling tendrils of smoke spiralled upwards as yellow flames licked the air, juxtaposed against the navy-blue skies. Delicate shimmering embers flitted in the breeze like glow flies. Tess and Daniel bit deeply into hot dogs that were nestled in silver foil and tasted of happy childhood memories.

An hour later, they were walking back to Tess's cottage, her arm once again tucked inside the crook of his. They passed beneath the amber glow of a street lamp.

'You haven't mentioned the café in Padstow for a while. Are you still considering it?'

Tess shrugged. 'I feel like I'm ready for a change. Do you ever feel like you're touching life but not feeling it? I don't know if it's fate that this opportunity has arisen or if I'm running away.'

'From what?'

What *was* she running away from? Blake? She didn't need to run. She could simply say it was over.

'Perhaps not running away,' she said, 'but I want to have my own business one day and Crimpton's came up for sale.

I'm not sure I'm ready for it yet, but it's a great opportunity.'

They stopped at the gate to Rose Cottage. With the street lamp behind Daniel, she couldn't see his features clearly.

'This is just a suggestion and I don't want you to feel any obligation,' said Daniel.

'Okay.'

'If the exhibition goes well I'm going to apply for planning permission for a permanent gallery and I'll need to employ someone to run a small café at The Rookery. You could be in charge of the menu, decoration – everything.'

Tess felt conflicted. On the one hand, that thought of spending every day close to Daniel whilst running a teashop, was intoxicating. But how would she feel when he eventually met someone? She would have to watch their relationship grow while she was just the paid employee?

Before she could answer, Daniel spoke again.

'Just think about it. I don't want to pressure you for an answer.'

'Thank you for the offer,' said Tess. 'It's very kind of you.'

'Just a thought.'

'Food for thought.'

Half an hour later, after Daniel had said goodbye to Tess, he was sitting at his kitchen table staring at the piece of paper she'd given him. He'd read it and reread it several times. It was a recent copy of an interview with the author and teacher of ceramics, Sean Connors, in *The New York Tribune*. Daniel repeatedly read the middle section of the interview over and over again, as if it was a prayer of the rosary.

You teach advanced sculpture and ceramics here in
New York. Which do you have the greater passion for?
I suppose my greatest pleasure comes from making ceramics. I find glazing incredibly beautiful, and

beautiful pottery can influence social interaction. If the piece is functional and striking, I believe it makes a difference. I like to hear and see how a piece of my pottery is being used. In Japan, the pot itself represents life, as found in the tea ceremony. I like to believe that my work can change routine into ritual.

Do you find it frustrating being partially sighted in the art world?
People ask me how I design such intricate pieces with only the sight of one eye. I tell them it's all about the feel of the clay. It's so fulfilling to feel a lump of material mould and shape into anything I choose. In a strange sort of way it helps that I only have partial sight. I've been known to close my eyes when I'm creating, which my son finds hilarious.

Do you mind telling us how it happened?
It was a freak accident. I'd been invited to a bonfire party by a friend. Initially I didn't want to go, so we tossed a coin. I won the toss, but pretended that he'd won because I'd changed my mind – decided it would be fun. A rocket fell from its holding and shot into the crowd. It hit us both. I feel bad that I lied about the coin because it scarred his face. One day I'll find the courage to get in touch and own up.

Daniel laughed, having read it for the fourth time. It was the laugh of a hostage's first view of open meadows after years of captivity, heady with manic relief. Sean was happy. He had a successful career and a family. Daniel shook his head and ran his hands through his hair. His eyes glistened with tears as he laughed again with loud rasps, his head thrown back and his hands clutching handfuls of hair. He paused, open-mouthed in disbelief. Sean didn't blame him, because Sean himself had chosen to go to the bonfire that night.

Daniel stood up and paced around the table still clutching his hair. Like a demented Dickensian character, his frenzied laughter was interspersed with promises to track Sean down in the New Year. His hand slipped to cover his face as he bent forwards, his laughter slowly morphing into deep uncontrollable anguished cries. His body shuddered with violent racking sobs as he leaned on his folded arms against the kitchen wall.

He cried with relief. He cried for his parents. He cried for forbidden love.

Chapter Twenty-Nine

In Amsterdam, Blake sucked deeply on his Marlboro cigarette while he lounged on the deck of the *White Squall*. A young couple sat opposite him, searching through a plastic bag with The Dungeon Museum printed on it. The woman pulled out a set of plastic handcuffs and whispered something into her boyfriend's ear. They both giggled, foreheads touching.

Blake exhaled a stream of silver smoke when he noticed the handcuffs; yet another bloody reminder of his court date to spoil his weekend away. He turned his attention towards the tour guide and idly admired her legs. The boat navigated the canals of Amsterdam, serenely passing below numerous bridges adorned with parked bikes chained to their railings.

Scattered on nearby seats were the other six members of the stag posse, fidgeting due to their self-imposed immobility on board the boat. Despite being November, the sun shone in an azure sky but a chill breeze nipped at their cheeks and fingertips. The tour guide had started her well-rehearsed speech, but only a handful of people were listening. Blake watched her out of boredom. He wasn't particularly impressed with her looks, but she wore a very short skirt over black opaque tights and her legs were shapely. The woman continued, despite the lack of attention.

'The first pleasure cruise in the history of the Amsterdam canals took place in 1621 when Queen Elizabeth Stuart of Bohemia was welcomed into the city.'

Blake turned to the others. 'Are we pleasure cruising tonight, lads? Just looking, of course.'

Kent sniffed but didn't answer.

Blake sensed that Kent was disappointed that he'd come on the trip. His colleague had been distant and terse with him since their night out at the Llama Lounge, ever since Blake had drunkenly admitted to deceiving Tess. But Blake was determined that Kent wasn't going to spoil his weekend. He had worked damn hard to earn his commission in order to pay for this jaunt. 'C'mon, what plays in Dam, stays in Dam,' said Blake.

Kent turned to speak to another colleague, leaving Blake to flick his cigarette end into the sparkling water. He looked back at the tour guide who was still tediously reeling off facts.

'Treating visiting royals and other VIPs to a cruise on our canals became a tradition that lives on till today. From Winston Churchill, Nelson Mandela and The Beatles...'

Blake watched cyclists peddle across a double arched bridge as the boat steered beneath it. The sun momentarily disappeared, leaving the boat in the cold shadows. He listened to Kent and Jude argue amicably about who was the greatest, Elvis or The Beatles.

'Come off it,' Kent said with a laugh, 'you only prefer The Beatles because your name is in a song title.'

'You're only pissed off because the closest you've got to a famous name is Kent-ucky Fried Chicken.'

'Bwark, bwark,' teased Sam, from commercial sales, flapping his elbows to impersonate a chicken.

Blake smiled and lit another cigarette. He looked at his watch. 'Half an hour, chaps. Kick off's at three.'

Watches were checked and eyes scanned ahead to see if they were nearing the end of their trip. The tour guide had either finished or given up because she had taken a seat at the front of the boat.

The bar they were heading for was located along a narrow

alleyway, a neon Budweiser sign flashing above its doorway. The air was full of the heady sweetness of cannabis and tobacco fumes, mixed with the stale smell of beer. They twisted and turned as they made their way through a crowd of supporters. Many people were eagerly waiting for the match to start on the plasma screen that was suspended on a bracket next to the bar.

Kent's group settled into a corner on two long benches that sandwiched a long thin sticky table. Remnants of beer mats that had been previously stuck to the table and later peeled off, had left random torn shapes of paper on the top resembling countries on a map. A cloud of pale grey smoke hung in the air amidst a swelling sea of bodies. Eventually beer was ordered, the cannabis menu was perused and the match began.

With Arsenal winning 1-0 at half-time, Kent's stag group was slowly becoming inebriated with drink and drugs. As usual, Blake was drinking and smoking to excess. He drew on his spliff, squinting through a plume of smoke. He was on his fourth pint and the mixture of marijuana and alcohol were slowing down his responses. Even blinking seemed to take more time.

'What y'aving, Blake?' called Jude, wiggling an imaginary pint glass in his hand.

'Bitter.'

'And twisted,' mumbled Kent.

'And another bag of puff,' Blake yelled.

The second half of the match continued in much the same way as the first. Bawdy banter, several more rounds, more spliffs rolled and plenty of staggering towards the men's toilet. The group were generally inebriated but had their wits about them, but Blake had reached the point of no return. As the pub goers watched the players on the screen, Blake was irritating many people by swearing whenever a player tripped or yelling obscenities when the camera panned into a pretty girl in the crowd.

'Shut the fuck up,' shouted Kent. 'If we all get thrown out because of your big mouth, you're on your own.'

'Vuck off, yourshelf.'

'Get out of my face.' Kent pushed him backwards onto the bench, where he fell in a crumpled heap. Instead of retaliating, he lifted his legs onto the bench, lay on his side and closed his eyes. He was asleep in seconds.

When Blake woke, his mouth was dry and the table was empty. The match had finished, but peals of laughter and the chinking of glasses hung like a melody in the air. The bar was half-empty. He scanned around for his friends, but they were nowhere to be seen. He called to a barmaid who was collecting empty glasses from the next table.

'Hey, d'you know where the others are?'

'Others?'

'My mates.'

'No, but I don't think they left you behind by accident.'

'What?'

'The note.' She pointed to his chest. 'Pinned to your shirt.'

Blake looked down, creasing his neck into a double chin. He swayed while trying to focus on the upside down writing, making him feel sick. The girl read it for him.

'It says *"My name is Priscilla and I'm staying at The Canal Hotel. Please deliver me there if I'm still here at closing time."*'

'Bastards.' Blake sat at the table for a full ten minutes before moving. It wasn't just the nausea that kept him there, it was a growing paranoia. Whenever he looked at someone, they seemed to look away. Had his friends paid someone to kill him and dump him in the River Amstel? No, he was being ridiculous; it was just the paranoia from the spliff. He shuffled towards the end of the bench and waited a few more minutes. He'd just decided to make a dash for the exit, when a red-haired woman sidled up to him.

'You look hot,' she said.

'What do you want?'

She smoothed her palms down her tight silver outfit. It clung to her body like a layer of paint. 'I'm cheaper than the girls on Rosse Buurt. Do you like my dress?'

'What do you mean, I'm lying to Tess? Who sent you? How do you know Tess?' Blake was standing unsteadily on his feet, spittle foaming in the corners of his mouth.

The woman looked momentarily shocked, but on seeing the detritus of glasses, filters and full ashtray of rolled cigarette ends, her lips curled in disgust.

She sneered and made a sucking noise with her lips. 'If you can't handle it, don't fucking smoke it.' She narrowed her eyes in contempt, turned and sauntered towards another solitary figure sitting at a corner table.

Once outside the cold biting wind hit Blake like a punch. The narrow cobbled street was full of people wrapped up against the bitter autumn evening. As the sun had sunk into the horizon, the temperature had plummeted considerably. It was now dark and Blake had no idea what time it was. He glanced up at the sky to see if it would give him some clue as to the hour, but only star-studded black strips of sky were visible between the rooftops of the nineteenth-century architecture.

Blake strolled alongside the inky canal. The seedy world of legalised prostitution was flagrantly displayed along the length of the road. The red neon signs that tempted voyeuristic eyes to part with their euros for sexual favours, reflected in the rippling black water. Shop windows lined the edges of the leafy waterways displaying scantily-clad women sitting open-legged, their skin tinged lobster pink from the red neon bulbs. Some wore skimpy underwear with stockings, whereas others were a little more modest in hot pants and T-shirts. Some displayed their bodies sprawled on chaise longues, others sat astride a simple dining chair.

Blake noticed one woman look at her watch and yawn. She was probably counting the hours until she could pull on her dressing gown, bed socks and sip a hot cup of cocoa, he thought. He sauntered to the next window and jumped back startled when he came eye to eye with another prostitute. She was tapping on the window and beckoning to him with a curled forefinger. He took two steps backwards to regain his composure. The woman laughed at him, not unkindly he thought. He saw humour in her eyes, rather than disdain for him as a sordid observer. He chuckled. The woman winked at him and ran her tongue over her lips. He smiled at the stranger who was dressed in the smallest sequined shorts he'd ever seen. The woman turned her back, but remained looking over her shoulder at him as she wiggled her way to a single dining chair placed in the middle of the room. His eyes were drawn to her buttocks. They protruded beneath her shorts like two soft hammocks of pink flesh.

The woman looked world-weary and close to forty, but she appeared to be kind and her legs were long and lean. Her breasts swelled inside her black bra, making Blake harden at the thought of an older woman taking him in hand, so to speak. What he'd give for an uncomplicated five minutes with her. No questions asked. No compliments necessary and no boring foreplay holding up the action. Tess hadn't been forthcoming in that department recently and he needed a distraction from the relentless reminders of his court case next week. What better way to take his mind off things? The lads wouldn't know, so Tess would never find out.

He looked at the woman, no longer aware of the hustle and bustle along the busy street. He no longer heard the music, the shocked giggles from huddles of women or the drunken shouts from groups of men. As if hypnotised, Blake only had eyes for the woman in front of him. She sucked her finger and ran it across her lips and down into her cleavage, not taking her eyes off him for a second. An invisible lasso had caught him and began to reel him in.

Chapter Thirty

Tess lay curled up on the sofa watching the six o'clock news. She heard Blake let himself into Rose Cottage.

'Hiya, I'm back,' he shouted.

'Did you have a good time?'

'Good thanks. I missed you.'

Tess heaved herself up from a pile of deep cushions and they hugged.

'How was it then? Tell me all about it.'

Blake flopped into a chair and sighed. 'Nothing to tell, really. We had a boat trip on the canal, drank a lot, watched the match and hired bikes one afternoon. That's it. How about you?'

'Work, mainly. I've done some baking and Holly and I walked over to the bonfire party at the pub.' She massaged Blake's shoulders through his chunky woollen jumper. 'How're you feeling? Have you felt okay while you've been away?'

Blake shrugged. 'So-so. You know what it's like. Good days and bad days.'

'I know.' Tess patted his shoulders to signal the end to his massage. 'Do you fancy a cuppa?'

'Sounds good, thanks.'

'Stay there and watch the news and I'll put the kettle on. Are you hungry?'

'No,' he called, as Tess walked out of the lounge. 'We stopped off for a McDonald's on the way back. I've driven straight over with my bags. Thought I'd stay over tonight.'

Tess called back from the kitchen. 'That's fine.' She filled the kettle and switched it on. Blake's bags were cluttering the hall, so while the water was boiling, it made sense for Tess to throw a load of Blake's washing into the machine. She unzipped his backpack and pulled out several dark shirts, socks and a pair of jeans. She checked to see if any spare euros had been left in his pockets. The last time he'd left coins in his pockets, they'd blocked the washing machine. Tess pulled out a business card but the other pockets were empty.

With the washing machine churning, Tess pinned the card to the cork noticeboard above the microwave. No doubt Blake would ask for it in a day or two, so she'd better save it.

The following week was wet and blustery. Work had been slow and routine had become the order of the day. She'd thought about Daniel all week, reliving the wonderful evening spent at the bonfire. Her mind always lingered on the intense moment when they'd nearly kissed at The Rookery a couple of weeks earlier. He'd telephoned her to thank her for the article she'd given him about Sean, but they hadn't seen each other since firework night.

Tess lay in bed listening to the rain tapping a rhythm on the windowpane. Her bedroom felt cold even though the radiator clicked intermittently, proof that the heating had come on.

She shuddered and snuggled deeper into her warm quilt, trying to find some comfort among the feathers. Her mobile rang.

'Hello.'

'Hello, darling, it's Mum. How are you?'

'Hi, Mum.' Tess sat up, pulling her duvet to her neck. 'I'm fine, but this weather's awful, isn't it? Is it as cold and miserable down south, too?'

'It's not too bad actually. I can see some blue. Listen, darling. I don't want to sound pushy, but another party are interested in Crimpton's Tea Room. Mrs Eccles from up the lane told your dad that a middle-aged couple have set up a second viewing. I thought that I should at least let you know, so you could make a decision one way or the other. It'd be such a shame if you decided to take it on, only to find that you'd been pipped at the post.'

Tess groaned. 'I was hoping it would take a bit longer for them to get more interest. I suppose it was unrealistic to expect that they would.'

'I'm afraid so. It's a pretty café in a picturesque spot.'

'Margaret did say she could do with covering a few more shifts at work now Christmas is creeping closer. I'll ask if she can work full-time next week with Holly. I'll get back to you.'

'Okay. Just give me a buzz if you can get the time off and I'll arrange a second visit.'

Daniel turned to look at his illuminated digital clock for the fourth time. The glowing red digits read 03.41. He had fidgeted in bed for almost four hours, his mind a whirlwind of thoughts. Had he missed something important that would ruin his exhibition? How was Denise feeling? Despite speaking on the phone with her every day since her operation, he still worried about her. Was Tess sound asleep? Would she ever leave Blake? He'd call her and arrange to meet up. He missed spending time with her.

Daniel flung his duvet back and sat on the edge of the bed. It was the middle of November and the room was cold. His naked body shivered as he reached for his jeans and a sweatshirt. Walking barefoot on the soft carpet, he made his way down the curved staircase, switching on lights as he went. Maybe a mug of hot chocolate would warm him up and help him sleep.

Daniel caught sight of an envelope partly posted through

the letterbox. How did he miss that when he went to bed last night? Rubbing his eyes, he bent to pick it up. The envelope had his name written on it, in neat forward sloping handwriting. He carried it into the kitchen, presuming it was a reply to an exhibition invitation.

The kitchen greeted him with warmth from the Aga and the heady perfume from a vase of lilies. Dropping the envelope on to the kitchen table, he opened the fridge door and poured some milk into a saucepan. Goya and Gogh looked at him through sleepy half-open eyes.

While he waited for the milk to heat, he pulled out a chair and ripped open the envelope.

The first words he read were, *Love Tess*, at the bottom of the paper. He quickly unfolded the sheet.

Hi Daniel,

Mum phoned to let me know that someone else was interested in the teashop. I've managed to take some leave from work at short notice, so I'm driving to Cornwall for a few days. Tried to call you but network was down. I promise not to get behind with the menu.

Love Tess

Daniel read the note again then held it to his lips. There'd be no chance he'd sleep now. It struck him how much he looked forward to seeing Tess and how much he'd miss her. A hissing and spitting noise snapped Daniel from his thoughts. The milk was bubbling over the top of the saucepan and bouncing like white ball bearings on the surface of the Aga. He reached for the handle and moved the saucepan off the heat. As he was cleaning the Aga's surface, he burnt his finger. Cursing, he crossed to the sink and held his throbbing finger under a cold stream of water.

He watched over a second pan of milk and after switching the light off, on and off again, he walked upstairs carrying a mug of chocolate. Daniel sucked his fingertip. The pain had started to throb again.

Instead of going up a second flight of stairs to his bedroom, he stopped on the first floor and went into his studio. He sat at his desk, sipping hot chocolate. The light from the landing and the glow from his Mac were the only light source. He pressed a button that highlighted a screen full of photographs. Scrolling through photographs of his dogs, his nephews, Denise and Simon, his artwork and holiday pictures, he found the one he had been searching for. It was the photograph he'd taken of Tess in this very room, looking at his artwork. Her features were half smiling and half questioning. Her long dark hair flowed over her shoulders and shone like the surface of a conker. He touched her face on the screen with a finger, turned off the computer and looked at his watch. It was nearly four. Leaving his empty mug next to the computer, he walked towards the door, a single shard of light shining beneath it and showing him the way. The clock glowed 04.01 as Daniel stepped out of his jeans and pulled his sweatshirt over his head. He climbed into the cold sheets, shivered and closed his eyes.

Chapter Thirty-One

Tess was walking along the cliff top with Padders, the crescent of golden sand on Harlyn Bay stretching far below. Her gloved hands were pushed deep inside her pockets and the hood of her winter coat protected her from the blustery gusts. The muddy path she was following wound its way between grassy banks and thickets of brambles. Occasionally the view of the beach would be lost, only to return around the next corner. Sheep grazed silently in the field to her left and birds swooped through the air on frenetic air currents. The trees on the cliff top were bent into submission by fierce coastal winds and leaned inland. Sometimes the wind would calm to a gentle whisper and Tess could feel the weak heat of the winter sun on her face.

She'd been in Cornwall for two days and had visited the teashop for a second time. The bad news was that after reading the shop's accounts, she knew she wouldn't become rich running a little café, but nor would she earn less money than she was making now. The good news would be that she'd be baking and cooking close to where she'd grown up.

Tess looked across the peninsula to where a small fishing boat was chugging through the waves. She groaned aloud in frustration, her voice lost in a sudden gust. There was Blake to consider. He was like a closed book. Not wanting to make a fuss about your illness was one thing, but not letting your girlfriend know how things were progressing, was quite another. Tess kicked a fallen twig, aware that she needed to know because she wanted to move on. That made her think of Daniel. Did he feel as strongly about her? If he did, would he wait? She'd posted a note to him before she'd left Halston, but she hadn't heard from him. She hoped that Daniel had found it. It'd be just her luck if she'd inadvertently pushed it under the mat like her namesake, Tess of The D'Urbevilles.

Tess walked down the coastal steps and on to the pale yellow sand. It crunched beneath her boots. She waded through the soft ground until she reached firmer damp sand. The beach was furrowed in ridges, as if it were frowning at the elements. Figures in the distance were trying to fly a kite, but the wind was so strong today that the kite was flitting about wildly or crashing onto the sand.

Tess continued towards the base of the cliffs. Its steep sides would protect her from the chilly gusts. Feeling more sheltered, she climbed over fallen rocks that were scattered haphazardly onto the beach. Water trickled down the cliff face, weaving in and out of velvety lichen and barnacles that were clinging to the rock. She bent to pick up a cream shell, slipping it into her pocket; another addition to her bathroom collection.

She stood at the yawning mouth of a cave, remembering what Daniel had said about the dense bushes in his garden. He'd said that as a child he pretended the foliage was a cave to hide in. This cave was only ten meters deep, but two decades ago, it'd been a make-believe sanctuary from the sea dragon that lived in the next bay for her and Holly. Tess stepped inside the entrance. Her footsteps echoed. It was dark and damp, with hollow plops of water perpetually dripping in the gloom. Padders barked at the entrance, as if asking what she was doing in a dark cave. It didn't feel the same being there by herself, anyway. Tess turned and walked back into the winter sunshine. Shaking off the clinging chill, she pulled off her boots, rolled up her jeans and walked towards the sea. Waves crashed against huge boulders and water splashed off the rocks into splinters of light, before hushing their way up the sand. This was much more exciting for Padders and he splashed around in the shallows.

At the water's edge, strands of seaweed tickled her toes. A smooth pebble cartwheeled on a shallow wave and stopped at her feet. She picked it up and stared in disbelief. Lying in her palm was a pebble – the perfect shape of the capital letter D. Was it a sign? Tess shook her head with a smile. Now she was just being sentimental. Common sense told her that somewhere on its ocean-tossed journey, this round pebble would have smashed against rocks and split in two. She wrapped her fingers tightly around her precious rescued treasure. Glancing along the deserted beach to check that she was alone and that the kite flyers had left, she took a deep breath, closed her eyes, lifted her face to the sun and shouted out to sea.

'I love you, Daniel Cavanagh.'

His name was lost among the call of the gulls.

Tess had been walking for almost an hour when the wind's frantic gusts settled enough for her to hear her phone ringing. She rummaged in her pocket, first grasping the shell, then the pebble and finally feeling her mobile. The screen read, *Holly calling*.

'Hello, you'll never guess where I've just been?' said Tess.

'Where?'

'In our cave on the beach.'

'You're kidding. Is it just the same?'

'Exactly the same, but a bit scary on my own.'

'I presume the sea dragon didn't eat you or you wouldn't be talking to me now.'

Tess laughed. 'No, it's too windy for him today.'

'Guess what? Great news. You know the couple living above the shop?'

'Yes.'

'They've only gone and flooded the bathroom. The leak

has ruined The Blue Olive's wooden flooring and warped several shelves.'

'And that's great news?'

'Yes. The deli has closed for four days and we can go home on full pay. I'm catching a train to Bodmin tomorrow so I can spend a few days with Mum and Dad. Can we meet up?'

Tess jumped up and down in a shallow pool. 'We haven't been back here together for about three years.'

'I know. My train gets in at one tomorrow. Can you meet me because Mum and Dad will be at work?'

'I'll be there. I'll wear a carnation so you'll recognise me.'

'You're crazy, Tess Fenton. It's going to be like we were teenagers again.'

'I can't wait. See you tomorrow.'

'Bye.'

The train pulled in on time at Bodmin Station and ghostly grey figures emerged from the fog. Tess felt a bit like Roberta in *The Railway Children*. A red figure slowly appeared through the mist. Either Father Christmas had spent all year at Weight Watchers or someone was dressed festively. Tess strained her eyes to see more clearly and took a tentative few steps towards the figure. Then she grinned. Holly was wearing a red jumper with a wide black belt around her waist. She was so laden down with luggage that she carried her cream gloves between her teeth. At a distance, these had obscured her face and looked like Santa's beard.

'Mmmm mm!' mumbled Holly.

Tess hurried towards her and took her gloves out of her mouth. 'Pardon?'

'I said, help me.'

Holly dropped everything and hugged Tess. 'Any plans?'

'Not yet,' replied Tess.

'Great. Let's hit the shops in Truro then.'

Chapter Thirty-Two

Daniel was ticking items off his exhibition list at the kitchen table. Goya and Gogh were gently snoring at his feet and a glass of wine sat next to his notebook.

Marquee – Lawn and Leisure Marquees
Flowers – Thistle Do Nicely
Press – Nottingham Evening Gazette
Band – Sepia Rainbow
Catering – Tess Fenton

His pen hovered over her name. He was missing her. Maybe he should call in at The Royal Oak for an hour. Then again, the thought of noisy banter exhausted him. He needed to talk to someone who understood him, someone he could tell anything to. He looked at his watch and decided to call his sister.

'Hello, Den.'

'Hiya. How are you?'

'Not bad. I phoned last night to ask how your chemo session had gone, but Simon said you were tired and had gone to bed early.'

'Yes, I felt shattered and woke up this morning feeling a bit nauseous, but I'd been told to expect it. Anyway, how about you? How are the exhibition plans coming along?'

'I'm getting there. The invitations have gone out, I'm ticking off people on my list that need to be booked and I'm organising the canvases.'

'What about the food? Are you and Tess an item yet?'

'Behave. We're just good friends.'

'They say that all the best love stories start with friendship.'

'She's in Cornwall at her parents' house for a while.'

'Are you missing her?' Denise teased.

Daniel laughed. 'Yes, okay. I miss her company.'

'My little brother's in love.'

'Will you stop it. And less of the little brother; you're only seven minutes older than me.' Daniel paused. 'Den, can I ask you a question?'

'Of course you can.'

'When Tess came over a few weeks ago, she hinted that she wished things could be different. She says she couldn't leave her boyfriend just yet, because he's sick. I suppose it gave me a bit of hope. Now she's looking at a café that's for sale in Cornwall. You're a girl, why would she say she couldn't leave her boyfriend and then look at a business down south? And if she liked me, why would she be planning to leave? Do I keep on waiting and hoping, or am I just being a mug here?'

'She's probably keeping her options open. Have you told her how you feel about her? We girls aren't mind readers, you know?'

'Sort of.'

'What does that mean?'

'I might have tried to kiss her.'

'Tried?'

'She pulled away.'

'Good. You should be pleased.'

'Why?'

'What would you have thought of her if she'd kissed you while she was in a relationship? She'd certainly have plummeted in my estimation. Now I like her even more and I haven't met her.'

Daniel groaned. 'I'm such an idiot! I cringe whenever I think about it. Why did I put her in that position? She probably thinks I'm just an arrogant letch.'

'I'm sure she doesn't. You're just an old romantic at heart, aren't you? No more Desperate Dan, okay? Get on the phone or text her. Keep in touch. Let her know you're there for her, but not by using your lips, okay? It only needs to be a simple message, nothing flowery that will embarrass you when she gets back. Communication is at the heart of everything, whether it's married couples, parents and children or even world leaders.'

'You sound like Mum.'

'I'll take that as a compliment.'

'You should. You're coming to the exhibition, aren't you?'

'I hope so, but it depends how I'm feeling after my chemo session the day before.'

'I wish it was me and not you. You don't deserve it.'

'No one does.'

'How are Sam and Peter coping? Do they know anything?'

'We've told them I have a bad headache and need to rest now and then. When I start to lose my hair we'll have to give them a diluted version of things.'

'Children are resilient and Simon can turn his hand to anything.'

'Anything but maths homework.' She laughed. 'He's been wonderful at looking after the boys, cooking, cleaning and being the taxi for cubs and football practice. We'll be fine. I just wish...'

'You wish Mum was here.'

'You can still read my mind.'

'Look, I'll let you go. I can hear the boys calling you. What are they doing?'

'Simon's parents brought a big box over that they'd struggled to get down from their loft to take the boys' minds off things. So sweet of them. It had been up there for nearly twenty years and is full of Simon's old toys and annuals. It's right up your street. There are *Dandy* and *Beano* comics and lots of *Secret Seven* paperbacks. There's a Spirograph, Thunderbird figures, a talking Captain Scarlet figure and an Etch-A-Sketch. The boys have found an old Meccano set and have been as quiet as mice for half an hour with a couple of spanners and some instructions.'

'Tell them I'm coming down at Christmas and they're not to lose any pieces.'

'I will.'

'Seriously though, I'll be there to look after you and help with the boys. I don't want you worrying about the workload.'

'Thank you. And who knows? You might be bringing a lovely new girlfriend with you.'

'Behave.'

'Text her. *Now*!'

'I will as soon as I put the phone down.'

'I must dash before they wreck the place. Let me know what she says, won't you?'

'I will. Bye.'

Chapter Thirty-Three

Truro was a bustling cathedral city surrounded by flowing rivers. Picturesque Georgian streets mingled with eighteenth-century town houses and little bridges crossed narrow waterways. At the heart of the city's shopping centre, stood Truro Cathedral. Its gothic grey granite walls stretched two hundred and fifty feet into the pale blue sky as if reaching for the heavens. A smaller green-tipped spire added a splash of colour to its austere facade.

By mid-afternoon, the fog had cleared and a watery sun hung in the sky. Holly's parents wouldn't be home from work until gone five, so she and Tess decided to head straight into town for a couple of hours Christmas shopping. They joined the throngs of bargain hunters and began to explore the city where they'd spent many a weekend as teenagers.

Tess called Holly away from Monsoon's window display. 'Come and look at this, isn't it lovely?'

Holly joined her friend and linked arms as they gazed down into a toyshop window. On the other side of the glass was a miniature village designed as a winter wonderland. Tiny toy cottages were adorned with warm, golden lights and wreaths of holly berries hung on miniature front doors. Fir trees were decorated with glittering baubles and a choir of tiny figures sang open-mouthed at a church door. The streets and houses were covered in a blanket of snow and fairy lights twinkled through a black cloth sky. The hymn, 'O Little Town of Bethlehem' sang out of a small speaker close to the door.

'Don't you think it looks like Halston?' said Tess.

'Even nicer. No smelly cows.'

'Do you think you will ever come back here to live?'

Holly pursed her lips. 'I'd never say never, but I love city life. Perhaps when I retire in another forty years. Why do you ask?'

'I've been giving it some thought. I haven't told you this as I didn't want to upset you, but Mum's seen a teashop for sale in Padstow and has offered to help me buy it.'

Holly turned to Tess. 'You're thinking of coming back here to work? To live? What about Blake? And me? I couldn't bear to work at the deli without you.'

Tess hugged her friend and laughed kindly at her distraught face. 'I just said I'd been giving it some thought. I actually think it's come on the market at the wrong time for me. It's partly a dream I'm playing out and partly keeping Mum happy by considering it. Deep down I know I can't leave Halston. You know that Daniel and I are friends, but I *really* like him. I only hope that he'll still be single when Blake gets the all-clear.' Tess looked at her feet and kicked a small pebble. 'I feel like I've found a beautifully wrapped present but I'm not allowed to open it because I don't know if it belongs to me or not. Do you know what I mean?'

'So you're falling in love with him?'

Tess shrugged her shoulders. 'He's kind, patient, a great organiser and so talented.'

Holly snorted. 'You sound like you're giving him a job reference.'

'Yes, I'm falling in love with him, but I'm not sure how he feels. He says lovely things but I think he's relieved to have someone to talk to and to help organise the catering. He tells me he's there for me, but as what? A surrogate brother, a friend, a neighbour?'

'I'm sorry to bring it up, but have you asked Blake about how things are going? You said you were going to. He seems so much better. He rarely coughs. He's in good spirits and he has a good appetite. You said you'd stay with him until he's better, but he seems fine.'

'I know, I will talk to him but things are so hectic at the moment. We both have work, he's been away in Amsterdam, I've been busy sorting out the menu for the exhibition and liaising with Daniel. Anyway...' Tess lifted a hand as if she were stopping traffic '... no more excuses. It's his court case next week. I just need to get that over and done with and then I'll ask him to spell out to me just what's happening about his progress. If he won't tell me, I'll let him know that I can't do this any more. I'll finish with him anyway. I'm so desperate to know what's going on with his health that I've even considered going round to his mother's and asking what she knows. She'd love to fill me in on information that her precious son has omitted to tell me. Think of the power it would give her.'

'Crumbs, you *are* desperate! C'mon. Let's find a bite to eat and talk some more.'

They linked arms and sauntered up the shop-lined hill. Soon they reached an open café doorway where a hug of coffee aroma and mince pies enveloped them and beckoned them inside.

'Quick, grab that settee and I'll order,' said Tess.

Soon Holly was dipping her finger into a dollop of cream and sucking her finger. 'Good call on the mince pies, by the way. They're delicious. Now, where were we? Oh yes, so, let's say, for argument's sake, that you finish with Blake. What then?'

'I'd see how things go with Daniel. I don't want to be friends with benefits, but I'm frightened that if that's all he offers, I wouldn't be able to say no.' Tess swallowed a mouthful of pastry and brushed crumbs off her scarf. 'There's something I haven't told you.'

Holly leaned forwards. 'What?'

'I think he tried to kiss me while we were in his garden.'

'What do you mean, you *think*?'

'He sort of leaned towards me, slowly.'

'What did you do?'

Tess grimaced. 'I moved away.'

Holly's mouth was agape in disbelief. 'Daniel gorgeous Cavanagh was leaning in to kiss you and you pulled away?'

Tess stared straight at Holly. 'Hello! I still have some principles. I'm not single yet. Besides, Daniel's been disclosing some personal stuff to me, stuff I can't go in to. I've been listening, a bit like a therapist. It's quite an intimate process and it's not uncommon for people to develop feelings for their therapist. I'm also helping him out with cooking, so although we're now comfortable in each other's company, I'm wondering if any feelings he has for me are because he feels supported and accepted when he's confiding in me, especially if he's not getting that from other people in his life. I want his feelings to be real. To be about me as a person and not as someone that just offers understanding and compassion.'

'I'd have opted for just the passion, myself.'

Tess slapped Holly's hand, amicably. 'But what if he thinks I led him on by giving him so much of my time?'

'Led him on!' shouted Holly.

Tess tucked her chin against her chest. 'Shhh!'

The conversation in the room hushed and Holly buried her head deeper in her coat.

'Sorry, but that's ridiculous. You've pushed the poor man away for weeks. Honestly, you and your masochistic Florence Nightingale loyalty. I told you months ago that you could dump Blake but still support him as a friend. But no! Tess has to climb the mountain barefoot instead of catching the cable car.'

'It's not like that. If you could read my thoughts you'd

know I'm not a saint. Look, we could go round in circles forever. Time will sort things out. It always does. Let's change the subject. How's Doug?'

Holly grinned. 'He's lovely. We went to the cinema last Friday, although we spent most of the time kissing so I couldn't tell you what the film was about.'

'I'm glad it worked out for you both.'

A mobile phone beeped.

'Is that yours, or mine?' asked Holly.

'It's mine. I don't believe it. It's from Daniel.'

'Talk of the devil.' Holly grinned, rubbing her palms together with anticipation. 'Read it, then.'

A smile curled Tess's lips. 'Hi, hope you're okay. Goya and Gogh miss you and are wondering when you're coming back. Daniel. X'

'There's your proof,' said Holly. 'He says he misses you and put a kiss after his name.'

'He says the dogs miss me.'

'Argh!' Holly pretended to pull her hair out. 'I thought I was the ditzy one. He obviously means that he misses you, but he's too shy to say so. It's the oldest trick in the book to talk through a pet.'

'Is it?'

'You don't get out much, do you?'

'What shall I write back?'

'I love you and want to have your babies.'

Tess playfully slapped her again. 'Seriously, what shall I put?'

'Play him at his own game. Speak to him through his dogs.'

'Okay.' Tess grinned and shuffled her bottom to make herself comfortable before texting. 'Right, here goes.'

Hi. Tell Goya and Gogh that I'll be home soon and that I miss them too. Tess. X

Tess pressed the button and sent her message.

An hour and several Christmas present purchases later, Tess and Holly walked back to the car, laden with bags.

'I've had an idea. I'm calling in at the cathedral? Are you coming?' Tess asked.

'I'm exhausted. Give me those bags and I'll wait in the car.'

'Thanks. I won't be long.'

In front of the cathedral was a small paved area, dotted with trees and benches. Tess weaved her way through the crowds and climbed the few steps up to the front entrance. The huge arched wooden door was open, welcoming everyone into its cavernous interior.

Tess tiptoed down a side aisle, trying not to disturb the shoppers who'd called in to pray. She joined a group of people who had stopped to view the nativity scene. Tess loved Christmas and its smells of pine and cinnamon. Even at the age of twenty-six, she'd never grown out of the excitement that comes with Christmas.

Retracing her steps, she entered the small shop situated close to the front entrance. Tess chose three packets of Christmas cards with Raphael's angels on them and some gift tags. The shelves were full of prayer books, illustrated children's bible stories, rosaries and St Christopher medals. There were little statues and crucifixes hanging on the wall alongside tapestries and framed religious pictures. But Tess couldn't see what she was looking for. Then she noticed a cabinet full of wooden carvings. She crouched to study them. Nativity figures, the Virgin Mary, animals and angels had been intricately carved into beautiful gifts. Standing to look at a higher shelf, Tess gasped with delight. She spotted just what she'd hoped to find. It was a Noah's ark, the size of an egg. Out of one window stretched two long giraffes' necks and two tiny birds sat on the roof. She lifted it gently from the shelf and asked an assistant to wrap it for her.

'I was just dozing,' said Holly, when Tess reached her car.

'Sorry, I couldn't pass up the chance of one more shop.'

'I'm not sure the cathedral is the place for Christmas shopping.'

'I've found the perfect gift for Daniel's birthday. A wooden ark.'

Holly looked perplexed. 'Why?'

'You know. The day I saved him in the pouring rain and he called me Noah. Don't look at me like that, you had to be there.'

'Obviously.'

Chapter Thirty-Four

Back in Halston the following week, Tess was jolted from her sleep. A screech of brakes and loud crash dragged her from her dreams in a split second. She threw back her duvet, dived out of bed and pulled aside the curtains. Through the raindrops that were obscuring her view of the road, she could see enough to realise that a car was imbedded into the front wing of her beloved ancient Mini. Steam was rising from the engine of the other car and several neighbours had come out of their front doors to see what had happened. Tess grabbed her dressing gown and hurried downstairs.

'Please don't let it be too bad,' she mumbled aloud, knowing that she had to get into town for Blake's court case that afternoon. Blake had slept at his house in order to be closer to the Magistrates' Court.

Running to the understairs cupboard, she tugged on her boots, grappled with the key in the lock and ran down the garden and into the rain. A middle-aged man was climbing out of his car looking a little shaken.

'Are you okay? Do you need an ambulance?' asked Tess.

'Yes. I'm fine. I don't need an ambulance.'

'What happened?' There was a huge dent in her car's front wing and bonnet.

'I was on my way to work when a pheasant flew into my windscreen. I instinctively swerved. I'm so sorry.'

'Are you okay, Tess dear?' called Mrs Campbell from across the road.

Tess waved and nodded. 'Can you drive your car back a little so you're not blocking the road? Then we can swap insurance details.'

After much crunching and grinding, with broken lights

clattering onto the wet ground, the driver parked his car further down the road. One glance at her car's twisted wheel and crumpled wing told Tess that her little runaround wouldn't be running around anywhere today. She groaned with frustration. By now Tess was drenched from the rain and catching sight of her reflection in her car window, she thought she resembled a seal in her soaked pale grey dressing gown. She shivered.

'Come in and I'll put the kettle on.'

Back in the house, she filled the kettle. 'Please try to relax. Feel free to use the phone but I must get changed. I'm soaked.'

'I'll ring the AA. I'll be out of your hair in no time.'

'Don't worry. Accidents happen.'

Tess ran upstairs, her mind racing. How on earth would she get into town? How would she get to work tomorrow? Who could she ring?

Over a pot of tea, Tess and the driver exchanged car and insurance information and both put on a believable display of relaxing. The man thanked Tess for her kindness and told her that the AA was on its way to collect his car and pick him up. After fifteen minutes he left to wait in his car.

Tess wondered if Holly could spare her old car for the day. Hopefully it was still road worthy. She picked up her phone.

'Hi, Holly, it's Tess.'

'It'd better be an emergency. What time do you call this?'

'Sorry, but it is a bit of an emergency.'

'Why, what's happened?'

'Some guy's driven into my car because he was distracted by a bird.'

'The perv. Honestly, Tess, why do men see a bit of leg and turn Neanderthal? You can almost see their foreheads growing, their eyebrows getting bushier and arms swinging around their knees.'

'No, silly. This bird had feathers. It was real. Listen, my car won't go. Blake has his hearing at two and I need to get there. It's still early and I wondered if you could drive over and lend me your car? I could then drop you off at work for nine.'

'I can't, Tess. I'm sorry, but it didn't pass its MOT so it's not taxed.'

'Damn. Okay. It was worth a try.'

'What about Blake? Why isn't he there?'

'He stayed at his last night because he lives five minutes from where his case is being heard. Besides, he's got enough on his mind today.'

'Phone Daniel.'

'No!'

'Why not? You're friends and friends help each other out.'

'It doesn't seem right. He'd be helping me to support Blake. I might just book a taxi even though it'll cost a fortune into town.'

'Tess, phone Daniel. You're walking up that mountain bare foot again. Catch the bloody cable car. You'll need some support too.'

'Okay. Okay.'

'Let me know how it goes?'

'Of course. I'll ring you later.'

Tess chewed a fingernail and thought of Daniel. Would it be too cheeky to ask him for a lift? She dialled his number anyway.

'Hello, Daniel Cavanagh.'

'Hi, it's Tess.'

'Hello. This is a nice surprise.'

Tess was horrified when her voice croaked and tears

sprang to her eyes. Just the sound of his voice made her self-imposed emotional barriers fall. She inhaled several times and blinked her eyes rapidly to clear her blurred eyes.

'Are you crying? What's happened, sweetheart?'

He'd called her sweetheart. Instead of strengthening her resolve, his gentle enquiry made tears spill down her cheeks.

'I'm being silly. I'm sorry. I feel so stupid.'

'You're not being silly. Are you going to tell me what's the matter or do I have to come over there right now.'

Tess wiped her eyes and gave a chuckle at his pretence of impatience. 'I didn't know who to call. I tried Holly but her car's failed its MOT, so I can't borrow it. A man crashed into my car this morning and it's a mess.'

'Are you all right? Where were you?'

'In bed.'

'What?'

'I was in bed when the man crashed into my car, outside the house. Blake is in court at two and my car's un-roadworthy, Holly can't help and I—'

'Of course I'll take you. I'll pick you up at one, just in case the traffic's bad.'

'Really? Thank you *so* much.'

'You're welcome, Noah. It's my turn to rescue you.'

At five to one, Tess was sitting on the edge of the settee looking out of the front lounge window, waiting for Daniel. The rain was now a depressing drizzle, dimpling puddles and mirroring how she felt. Her view through the window looked like an old black and white photograph. The street scene was washed in muted grey colours with just one brave fuchsia rose, lolling by the garden gate.

The sound of a diesel engine shook her out of her gloom. Daniel's Land Rover pulled up behind her dented car. Tess stood up, grabbed her handbag and walked out of the front door, locking it behind her.

Daniel was already standing beside her car, bent double and inspecting the damage. He ran his hand over the compressed metal work and tutted.

'Nasty.' He looked up at Tess. 'Are you okay?'

'I feel better now, thanks.'

'I'm glad you rang me. Jump in or pneumonia will be added to your list of problems.'

Soon they were driving into the city centre, joining the queues of traffic. Tess was leaning against the heated leather, trying to relax. Their casual conversation had become a comfortable silence.

Daniel spoke. 'Are you going to your parents' house for Christmas?'

Tess looked across at him. He'd thrown his jacket onto the back seat and had pushed his sleeves up to his elbows. She watched the muscles in his forearms flex as his hands gripped the steering wheel and changed gear.

'I haven't really given Christmas much thought. I've bought some presents, but I haven't made any plans. What about you?'

'I usually visit Den and the family. I love to watch my nephews leave a glass of milk and a mince pie for Santa on Christmas Eve. Den puts newspaper around the hearth and when the boys are in bed, I put muddy footprints on the paper and eat the mince pie.'

Daniel turned his eyes from the road for a second and grinned at her. 'On Christmas morning the boys first thought is to look for Santa's footprints. Then I watch them unwrap presents and build Lego houses or stickle bricks monsters. I can't wait until they're old enough to make model cars and aeroplanes. And, of course, I raid their chocolate selection boxes.'

Blake usually moaned about Christmas being too expensive and said that it wasn't worth the weeks of build up. He said that lounging on the sofa having eaten a huge roast dinner felt just like every other Sunday. Tess sighed. She was pleased that Daniel seemed excited about Christmas. 'I'm sure they love having their uncle there.'

'Are you okay?'

'Sorry?'

'You just gave a huge sigh.'

'Did I? I was miles away.'

'Where were you?'

'Nowhere in particular. Just getting maudlin. Ignore me.'

The Land Rover slowed to a standstill at a set of red traffic lights. Daniel looked across at her and laid his hand on top of hers.

'That's one thing I'd find very difficult to do. I'm your friend and I'm here for you. If I can help with anything, you only have to ask me. What's your biggest worry?'

'Honestly, it's nothing really. I just feel a bit like I'm in limbo. It's difficult to make any plans at the moment.'

The lights changed and Daniel replaced his hand on the steering wheel. The warmth left by his hand gradually faded, but the electricity of his touch still tingled on Tess's skin. She looked down at her hands and absent-mindedly wound scarf tassels around her fingers.

Daniel shifted the gear stick into fourth. 'Please tell me if I'm speaking out of turn, but there comes a time when you have to stop making excuses for Blake and put yourself first. He's an adult. He has to take responsibility for his own mistakes and his own health. He chose to drink and drive. He chooses to continue to smoke. Your life shouldn't consist of living with the reverberations of someone else's choices.' After a pause he added, 'Do you love him?'

'Like a brother. I'm not in love with him.'

'You're not?'

'I've told you that I tried to finish with him a few months back. It was just bad timing. I found out that he was sick. It would have been heartless to leave him then. What if it had made him worse? They say that a positive outlook helps to heal the body, don't they?'

'They do, but you have to think of yourself as well. Life is too short to spend it with someone you're not in love with. What if he's ill for years?'

'I don't know. I hadn't thought about that. I just imagined that he'd recover over the autumn and I'd re-evaluate how our relationship had changed during that time.'

'Has it changed?'

Tess pulled at a tassel so hard that it snapped. She rolled it into a ball. 'Not really. We're friends and I care about him, but let's see how today goes and then I'll have a proper chat with him about things. I need to know how he's doing. I just need to know that he's going to be all right.'

'Of course you do.'

Daniel reversed into a parking space, adeptly negotiating the distances between the vehicles. He switched the engine off and waited until it shuddered into silence. He turned sideways to face her. 'It'll be okay, Tess. He has a good solicitor working for him and it's his first offence. You said you wrote a letter for him, didn't you? They'll all know he's suffering from stress while he's recovering from cancer.'

'You're right. Thank you for the lift.'

'Come on then. Let's go in.'

'Are you coming in?' she asked, wide-eyed.

'Only if you want me to. I'm happy to support you but if you'd rather go alone?'

'No, I'd like you to come in with me.'

The rain had stopped but the air was damp and cold. Blustery gusts made them run across the road, heads down and hands gripping their coats tightly across their chests. Daniel thrust his hands in the pockets of his chocolate-brown wool coat, inviting Tess to slip her arm into the gap he made. She did so, seeking warmth and reassurance in this welcome habit he'd developed with her. They walked arm in arm along the pavement, passing offices and a few small stores.

They turned a corner and saw the austere building of the Magistrates' Court. The building looked grimy and insipid, the colour of burnt out embers long after the fire had been extinguished. After climbing the steps to the front entrance, Daniel followed Tess through the swing doors. The lobby smelt of old books and polish and the tiled floor made their footsteps echo around the huge internal space. It was decorated with ornate wooden carvings and two sets of stairs led off at the far end. They stood reading the signs on the wall.

'He's in Court Two,' said Tess.

'This way.' Daniel took hold of her hand and led her up the stairs.

His hand enclosed her cold fingers. She loved the touch of his skin, warm and soft. She wanted to lift his hand to her mouth and gently run her lips along the back of it, inhaling his scent and feeling his soft hairs on her lips.

'Court Two,' he said, pointing. 'Nearly there.'

They pushed open a double door and came face to face with Blake, his mother and his solicitor. She realised that she and Daniel were still holding hands and let go as if she'd been burnt.

'Hello. How's everything going?' asked Tess.

'What's he doing here?' asked Blake.

'My car's broken. Another car ran into it. Daniel gave me a lift.'

Joy's lips wrinkled as she pursed them. 'Convenient.'

'He can go now. I'll drive you home,' said Blake.

His solicitor interjected. 'Mr Snipes, I'm hoping things go well today but I don't think you'll be driving for a few months.'

'A few months? I thought your job was to make sure I only get points and a fine.'

'It's not as simple as that. I'll do my best, but the decision lies with the magistrates. We have an ace up our sleeves with the letter you've written explaining your circumstances, but we don't need to go over that because it speaks for itself. Let's think positively. Right now we need to go over a few more details.'

'Wait for me afterwards,' said Blake to Tess. 'We'll go back to Mum's.'

Blake and his mother followed his legal representative into a waiting room.

Daniel pulled an apologetic face. 'I'm sorry.'

'There's nothing for you to be sorry about,' said Tess.

They pushed open the swing doors to Court Two. At the front was a small table for the court clerk who was already sitting down with a black robe draped round her shoulders. Facing the bench were two bar tables, one for the defence and one for the prosecution. She'd watched *A Few Good Men* and thought she recognised the layout. It looked just like the film set to her. She could almost imagine Tom Cruise walking in and taking over proceedings. Adjacent to these tables was the dock where the defendant had to stand. In this case, Blake.

Tess and Daniel sat at the back in an area sectioned off for families and the public. They sat in silence looking around the room for five minutes until a hush fell and Blake took his place. Next, three formidable looking magistrates sat down at the bench, before settling themselves and their paperwork. When they appeared to be ready, the court clerk stood up.

'Would the defendant, Blake Snipes, step forwards, please.'

Tess watched him stand up and walk a few steps towards the dock. The clerk addressed the magistrates.

'Your worships, Blake Snipes stands before you charged with driving without due care and attention, failure to provide a breath test at the scene, driving erratically liable to be a danger to the public, assaulting a police officer at the station and driving with excess alcohol in his blood.'

Tess was shocked to hear the list. She turned to Daniel with her mouth open in disbelief. 'I didn't know all that,' she whispered.

The magistrates nodded and scribbled down some notes. Blake shifted uncomfortably fiddling with his tie.

'Case for the prosecution.'

The clerk sat down and a woman in a navy blue suit and her hair in a tight chignon, stood up. For five minutes Tess listened while the prosecution went through the list of charges in minute detail, dissecting Blake's misdemeanours inch by inch. Blake hadn't told her that he'd pushed a police officer or fallen asleep behind the wheel. Why would he have kept that from her? Why hadn't he told her that he'd failed to give a breath test?

The prosecution lawyer continued, glancing regularly at her notes. She informed the magistrates that Blake finally agreed to a breath test at the police station, where his reading was 97mcg, the legal limit being 35mcg. She said that due to the delay in providing the sample, it had to be ascertained that at the time the defendant was stopped, he would have had an even greater reading.

Eventually, the woman sat down and Blake's defence lawyer got to his feet. He was a short, grey-haired man who shuffled his notes into order. Tess didn't think he looked as professional as his colleague who had just spoken, but she knew that he held important information that would hopefully soften the magistrates' dour expressions.

'I would like to inform your worships of the defendant's previous good name. He has never been in trouble with the police before and there are significant mitigating circumstances. What your worships can see before you is a copy of the letter that the defendant has written. It informs you of his ill health. In fact, the defendant is suffering from lung cancer.'

The public gallery buzzed into life. Tess looked over at Blake. For some reason, instead of looking relieved that everyone now knew how he was suffering, he'd sunk his head into his hands. The lawyer continued. 'Despite suffering from lung cancer and coping with treatment at hospital appointments, the defendant continues to work full-time in order to pay his mortgage. Driving is an essential element to his work. I would like to ask your worships to take this into consideration when passing sentence.'

Tess looked back at Blake. He looked pale and sweat sparkled on his forehead.

'He looks awful. Do you think he's okay?' Tess whispered.

'It must be stressful for him. It shouldn't be too much longer.'

The prosecuting lawyer stood up again. Tess thought that she might look a little defeated, but she looked pleased to be speaking again. Almost smug, Tess thought. Smirking across towards the defence team, she addressed the room.

'This is all a little confusing,' she said, sarcastically. 'According to the defendant's medical records, which have been made available to the courts, the last time the defendant saw his doctor, was on June thirtieth. He attended a consultation with Dr David Dillon. Mr Snipes was diagnosed with the common complaint of asthma. The only medication prescribed was a Salbutamol inhaler, which he uses to combat his breathing difficulties during an attack. He has never been diagnosed with cancer and has never attended hospital for any appointments.'

The public gallery was now muttering loudly and was asked to be quiet.

Tess frowned and leaned forward, as if by doing so she would understand better and her confusion would lift. What did the prosecutor mean, 'He has never been diagnosed with cancer and has never attended hospital?' Doubt slipped through Tess's mind. The 30th of June. Wasn't that the last day of the month when she'd cooked linguine as a final meal before finishing with him? Had he guessed that she was going to end their relationship? Had he blatantly lied to her? She looked at Blake. His head was bowed. He wasn't denying it. He wasn't angry at this outrageous injustice. He wasn't demanding an apology.

One of the magistrates interrupted the prosecution lawyer. 'Are you saying that Mr Snipes has lied to the court about his health in order to receive a reduced punishment?'

'It certainly appears that way, your worship.'

'May I see the defendant's medical record?'

'Lies,' shouted Joy. 'My boy is sick.'

'Silence,' the magistrate warned.

The lawyer walked across the floor, her heels click-clacking on the wood. She handed the magistrate some paperwork and took a step back while he read for a few moments. He passed it to his colleagues before handing it back.

Tess felt Daniel take her hand. She looked at him. His face was unreadable.

She felt nauseous. Her vision blurred and her ears buzzed. 'I need a glass of water.' She stood up and excused herself to the person on her left.

Daniel followed with a guiding hand on her back. People

turned their legs sideways to let them pass and they made their way to the back of the room. Seeing them leave the gallery, the public leaned forwards whispering and pointing.

Tess poured a glass of water from a jug in the waiting room. Her hands were shaking. She took a few sips and looked at Daniel. 'Do you believe them?'

'They have to check and double check their facts before presenting information in court. If they say he's only got asthma, then…'

'I can't believe it. No wonder he never spoke about his treatment. He made a deliberate choice to lie about his health. All that time pretending that he was going for hospital visits. No wonder he never wanted me to go with him. My God, he showed me an X-ray and shaved his head because he said his hair was falling out. I trusted him. How could I have been so gullible? I'm such a fool.'

Daniel gently pulled her towards him and held her in his arms. 'You're not a fool.' He gently squeezed her tighter. 'Listen to me. Don't ever say that. You were simply loyal and trusting. The blame lays one hundred per cent with Blake.'

Tess pulled away. 'I wrote the letter that's made things worse.'

'You wrote what you thought was the truth. You did it to help. It's not your fault that you didn't have the correct facts.'

'I should be glad it's only asthma. I *am* glad, but… I can't believe that he could actually do such a wicked thing.'

The usher interrupted them by poking his head around the door. 'The chief magistrate is summing up if you want to hear it.'

They just made it back into their seats as the chief magistrate started to speak.

'Mr Blake Snipes, listening to the evidence presented

before us, you were clearly intoxicated on the night in question. You were a danger to other road users and the general public. Your failure to comply with a breath test at the scene does not help your case, nor does your evident lack of remorse. You continue to blame other car drivers and your ill health. Coming to this evidence, the letter you wrote and signed categorically states that you were diagnosed with lung cancer on the day that your GP informs us that you were diagnosed with asthma. You purposefully and wilfully tried to deceive the court and, as I now understand from the usher, you also deceived people close to you. It may be your first offence, but your conduct has been contemptible. You are a weak, dishonest, manipulative and controlling individual. Considering the seriousness of trying to dupe the court with false statements, you are to return to court for sentencing in two days. Don't be surprised Mr Snipes, if a custodial sentence is passed. This court is not the place for mendacities.'

Blake looked confused. Tess saw him turn to his solicitor and mouth, 'What?'

She watched the magistrates leave through a door at the back of the room. After they'd closed the door behind them, people scuttled around in different directions. Blake's solicitor weaved his way through the bodies towards him. Tess thought that Blake looked different. She didn't recognise this pale, bald, overweight man. This wasn't the cheeky, lovable man she'd met two years ago. He wouldn't have lied to her back then. This man had grown so far away from her own beliefs and morals, that she didn't know him any more. More importantly, she didn't *want* to know him any more. As dreadful as all this was, she realised that she was free to move on without guilt.

'Would you like me to take you home?' asked Daniel.

'He lied.'

'I know. I'm sorry.'

'All this time…'

'He must have panicked.'

'Don't make excuses for him. He doesn't deserve it. So many people really do suffer from the disease every day with incredible dignity.'

'I know. What're you going to do?'

Tess buried her face in her hands and raked them up through her fringe.

'I should be pleased, shouldn't I? He doesn't have any hold on me now. I'll have to explain to him that there's no way forward from this.'

'Do you want to go with him so you can talk?'

'No. Can we leave now? I need time to think.'

Tess stood up to leave but was startled when she heard her name called across the courtroom.

'TEZZA!'

Blake sprinted across the floor and grabbed her arm.

'It's all a mistake. You'll see. Let's start again. Without any lies. I'll look after you. Let's get married.'

Tess squirmed. 'Let go. You're hurting me.'

Blake let go and stroked her arm. 'Sorry, I didn't mean to. It's just that you have to listen to me. You have to understand that I did it for you.'

Tess raised her voice. 'You told me that you were seriously ill because you thought it was better for me?'

'Yes. I heard you tell Holly that you were going to leave me. I wanted to look after you and—'

'You eavesdropped and decided to lie to me? You actually planned it and didn't make it up on the spot in desperation?'

Joy appeared behind Blake. 'You don't deserve him.'

'Keep out of this, Mum. Tezza, listen to me. I tried to make you see we could work it out. I've got a good job, a nice car, a decent salary and my own house.'

Tess gave a hollow laugh. 'Don't you know me at all, Blake? Do you think that possessions are more important to me than the person I'm in a relationship with?'

Joy interrupted. 'He's better off without you.'

Blake looked over his shoulder. 'Mum, back off.' He turned back to Tess. 'We've been through so much together. It's been great in the past and it can be great again. Can't you see I lied because I love you?'

'Stop it!' Tess shook her head and stepped backwards until her back was touching Daniel's chest. 'I'm not listening. You're just twisting everything. I don't need looking after. Go away Blake. We're finished.'

'But listen…'

Daniel put a protective arm around Tess. 'She's asked you to go away.'

'You bastard!' White spittle frothed in the corners of Blake's lips. It sprayed from his mouth. 'Get your hands off her.'

Blake lurched towards Daniel with raised fists. Tess shielded her face. Two police officers stepped forwards, one grabbing Blake's clenched hand.

'Calm down or you'll be cuffed.'

Blake twisted away from the policeman. The second officer expertly handcuffed Blake's wrists behind his back.

Joy appeared in front of Tess, a bony finger pointing inches from her face. 'You've done this. I've always said that you were wrong for him and now—'

'I think you need to calm down too, madam,' said another police officer. 'Leave now or you'll join your son in a cell to cool off for an hour.'

Blake was being escorted towards the court's exit, followed closely by his mother.

Blake repeatedly called Tess's name. His voice grew quieter the further away he was led. When she could no longer hear him, she turned and fell into Daniel's arms.

Chapter Thirty-Five

Tess stomped around Rose Cottage. She couldn't contain her anger. She'd thanked Daniel for the lift and explained that she needed time alone to take in what had happened. She muttered out loud as she strode from one room to the next, throwing Blake's possessions into a black bin liner.

Having thrown the bin liner down the stairs, unconcerned that his toiletries may break, Tess dragged the bag into the lounge. She threw in a plastic Star Fleet phaser that she found on her bookshelf, several of his CDs, a framed picture of him taken last Christmas and a jumper that he'd left hanging on the arm of the settee. Scanning the room for any further items, she noticed his car pulling up outside her house.

'No way,' she shouted, screwing up his jumper and throwing it into the bag. She ran into the hall and fumbled with her keys. She inserted the key in the lock when he pushed the door open. 'Go away.' She tried to close the door.

'I need to talk to you,' said Blake, pushing the door wider.

'I'm not listening any more. If you don't leave I'm calling the police.' The force he was pushing with, eased. With a final heave, Tess closed the door and locked it.

She strode down the hall and into the kitchen. Opening a cupboard, Tess threw Blake's Arsenal mug into the bag where it made a hollow snap as it broke. It was an amazingly satisfying sound. She pulled open the fridge, grabbed his beer cans and smelly blue cheese. Thank God she wouldn't have to put up with Blue Stilton wafting around her tidy fridge any longer.

Tess turned as Blake let himself in through the back door.

She stood still, hyperventilating at the effort of wiping him from her life. He looked sheepishly at her.

'What are you doing, Tezza?'

'What do you think I'm doing? Making you some lunch? I'm getting rid of anything that reminds me of you. And if you ever call me Tezza again, I'll be the one that needs arresting.'

'I'm sorry I made a scene earlier.'

'Is that all you're sorry for?'

'It's just that he had his arm around you. How would you feel if you saw a girl with her arm around me?'

'Sorry for her.'

'You know you don't mean that, Tez... Tess.'

'You've no idea how much I *do* mean it, Blake.' Tess looked inside a parcel of silver foil that was sitting on a shelf in the fridge. It was two slices of Blake's pizza. She rewrapped it and threw it into the bin liner. Slamming the fridge door, she turned and yanked open the cupboard that contained her wine glasses. Within seconds, a pint beer glass had been thrown into the bag and smashed.

'What are you doing?'

'I'm clearing you out of my house. Out of my life.'

'Are those my things?' Blake stepped forwards and pulled open the bin liner. 'You've broken my stuff, my Star Fleet phaser.'

'You've broken *me*. I think I'm worth a little more than a plastic gun, don't you?'

'It's not a gun, it's a—'

Tess stared at him. 'Are you serious? You're arguing the toss about whether a toy is a gun or vaporiser? You're unbelievable. God, I've been such an idiot.'

'I know you're angry now, but if you'll just listen to me, I'll explain.'

Tess stood looking directly at him with her hands on her

hips. 'There's nothing to explain. You lied to me and let me worry, cry and stress. No *wonder* you never answered any questions when I asked you about your treatment. Never once in four months did you attempt to explain things to me. What were you going to do? Pretend to suddenly get better?'

Blake opened his mouth to speak, but looked down at his feet.

Tess was becoming hysterical. 'I don't believe it. You were.' She looked around the kitchen, tears blurring her vision as she searched for anything that belonged to him. She saw the business card from Amsterdam that she'd placed on the noticeboard for safekeeping. She unpinned it and read the word *Cherry*. She paused and read the rest of the badly printed type set. Her mouth fell open when she absorbed the words, *Cherry Lips' Brothel*. She turned it over and read, *'See you again next time?'* Surely not even Blake would stoop so low?

Tess couldn't take her eyes from the words and little red logo of two shiny cherries hanging from a stalk. How had she passed it so many times without reading it? She slowly turned and stared at Blake.

'Yours, I presume?' Tess held up the receipt in front of her.

Blake shrugged his shoulders. 'I haven't put anything on your board.'

'I think I'd remember if I'd visited,' she looked down to read the name correctly, 'Cherry Lips' Brothel.'

She saw Blake swallow hard and watched the colour drain from his face. It was as much a sign of guilt as signing an admission. He took a step towards her holding out his upturned palms.

'It's not how it seems. I didn't know what I was doing.'

'Well, I can vouch for that,' Tess added, sarcastically. 'I

assume you managed something or you wouldn't have been asked back.'

'I mean I was stoned. I'd drunk too much and smoked too much weed. I didn't know what I was doing.'

'How *could* you, Blake?'

'I—'

'It was a bloody rhetorical question. I don't want to listen to your pathetic excuses. Get out. It's over. Get out!' Tess pointed towards the back door, her hand shaking with fury.

'Let me ex—'

'Get out!'

'Can we talk later?'

'About what exactly? What position you did it in with Cherry?'

'Tess, don't. Please. I'm sorry.'

'Well, that makes two of us. I'm sorry I hung around for the last few months. Get out, Blake, we're finished.' Tess ran upstairs. She stopped on the landing, turned and leaned over the banister. 'And don't forget your bloody rubbish!'

Chapter Thirty-Six

Forty-eight hours later, Tess had refused to go to Blake's sentencing. She didn't want to see him. He was on his own. A full load was churning in the washing machine. Tess was sitting down with a newspaper crossword. She was intrigued to find out what sentence Blake had received, but certainly wasn't going to ask him. Besides, she'd deleted his number from her phone. Although she'd rather face root canal treatment than call his mother, she knew that it was inevitable if she wanted to know the outcome.

Procrastination had been the order of the day so far. Hence the whirring washing machine, a gleaming bathroom, a neatly ordered letter rack and the *Telegraph*'s crossword puzzle spread out before her. Tapping her biro against her front teeth she read the first clue out loud.

'Russian monetary unit. Six letters.'

The telephone's shrill ring interrupted her thoughts. She hesitated before answering. It could be Blake trying her landline.

'Hello.'

'Hello. I thought I'd phone and see how you are.'

She felt her shoulders relax. It was Daniel.

'I'm okay, thanks.'

'I wanted to call yesterday, but you said you needed time to get your thoughts straight.'

'I'm feeling fine, honestly.'

'Have you seen him since court?'

'He came round a couple of hours after you dropped me off. Thank you so much again for taking me, by the way.'

'That's okay.'

'He caught me clearing out his things.'

'I don't suppose that went well.'

'You could say that.'

'I'm here for you if you want someone to talk to or simply need a lift somewhere.'

'You're very kind.'

'Try not to feel too down.'

'I don't. I didn't love him any more so I don't have a broken heart. I'm just mad as hell with him.'

'What did he get?'

'I don't know. I'm not going to call him, so I suppose I'll have to call his mother.'

'Sounds like a bundle of laughs.'

'It'll be as funny as a will reading, I assure you.'

'Let me try and cheer you up. How do you fancy a trip to a visiting fair?'

'A fair?' Tess hugged the receiver.

'I've heard that a fair's visiting Silbury for three days next week. It's only half an hour away. I thought it might take your mind off everything and give me a change of scenery from my canvasses.'

'I'd love to go. It's been years since I last visited a fair.'

'Great. What are you doing now?'

'I'm doing a bit of a tidy up and I've started the crossword.'

'Go on then. Ask me a question.'

Tess chuckled. 'One across. Six letters. Russian monetary unit. Blank, o, blank, blank, blank, blank.'

'Easy, I've been to Moscow. Rouble.'

'Ah ha!' Tess scribbled it down.

'Sorry, I can hear someone at the door and I'm expecting a delivery of frames. I must dash but I'll call you about making arrangements.'

'Okay, thanks again.'

'Speak to you soon. Bye.'

Would the fair be their first official date? Anticipation bubbled inside her like celebratory champagne at the thought of being alone with Daniel. The telephone rang again. She grinned and picked up the phone, thinking that he'd forgotten to ask her something.

'Hellooo,' she sang.

'Just as I thought. You sound like you're very worried about my boy.'

'Joy.'

'He's in prison thanks to you.'

'Blake's in prison?'

'Yes, with precious little support from you. Where were you?'

'I don't need to explain myself to you.'

'Probably with your fancy man.'

'What do you mean?'

'Blake told me that you'd been seeing a local artist. He gets into a bit of bother and you jump ship.'

'I know you're upset but it wasn't like that.'

'You've ruined his life.'

'I don't know what Blake has told you, but I've never been unfaithful to him. You need to look a little closer to home to find who's been unfaithful.'

'Cavorting up at the big house behind his back.'

'Listen to me, Joy, because you seem to have selective hearing. I've always been loyal to Blake and have never cavorted, as you call it. It's time to stop accusing people of things they haven't done or you'll end up very lonely in your last few years.'

'How dare you. I don't make up stories. Are you denying that you wrote the letter of lies which imprisoned Blake?'

Tess didn't answer.

'Well, are you?'

'I did write the letter, but—'

'Finally. She speaks the truth. You admit that you wrote the letter.'

'Let me finish. Blake led me to believe that he had cancer for months. He never once told me that he only had asthma. He lied to me about hospital visits and treatment. It came as a complete shock to me when I found out that he wasn't sick. And why the hell am I defending myself when it's your precious son who has been deceiving everyone. You filter out what you do hear and hear only what you want to. You and Blake have both finally pushed me too far with your lying, manipulative and selfish ways. I've left Blake, with the added bonus of never having to see you, speak to you or listen to your nasty accusations ever again.'

Tess slammed the telephone down with a crash. She waited for the tears to come, but instead of feeling sad or angry, a tsunami of relief swept through her body. She felt almost euphoric. She breathed in deeply, slowly exhaling with a smile on her lips. She was free. It felt wonderful.

A new start.

A clean page.

Chapter Thirty-Seven

It was the week before Daniel's birthday and art exhibition. Tess closed her laptop and smiled to herself. She'd just read Sean's last email before he was due to leave to catch his flight to Heathrow. They'd arranged to meet the day before the exhibition in The Royal Oak. She hoped the surprise wouldn't be emotionally too much for Daniel so close to his big party.

Within half an hour of closing her computer, her boots crunched along The Rookery's driveway until she reached the front door. She knocked and waited. After a few moments, the oak door swung open. She could feel the dogs sniffing her boots and their tails slapping her knees, but she could only focus on Daniel. He was smiling a welcome, wearing a chunky jumper and a dark olive scarf. He called Goya and Gogh into the hallway and stepped aside for her to pass.

Tess stepped inside. She fidgeted with the buttons on her coat. 'Hello.'

He took a step towards her and held her in an embrace. For a few seconds her cheek lay against his soft jumper while she hugged him back. Both dogs wanted to join in and were standing on their hind legs, jumping up and looking for attention. Tess and Daniel stepped away from each other, both laughing.

'Come on, you two, into your baskets for a couple of hours. You've had a good run on the green,' said Daniel. The dogs ran into the kitchen ahead of them.

'It's as if they can understand you,' said Tess, watching them run to their baskets.

'I speak dog. Didn't I tell you?'

They walked back through the hall and out of the front door. Tess watched Daniel lock it and check it three times. He caught her eye.

'I know, I know! I'm getting better, honestly. Didn't you notice that I didn't check the kitchen lights?'

'Then why now.' Tess pointed to the front door.

'You know. Dangerous fair rides. Scary ghost trains.' Daniel raised his arms and dangled them like a zombie. 'You can't be too careful.'

They could hear and smell the fairground before they could see it. Music boomed into the evening and the smell of roasting chestnuts wafted on the breeze. They joined a crowd, falling into step alongside parents clutching children's hands and groups of friends hurrying towards a night of rides and music.

Some earlier visitors were weaving against the flow of people in the opposite direction. They were carrying balloons, luminous bangles and trophies of soft toys. Tess and Daniel followed the procession down a pathway and across a grassy embankment. They passed a copse of trees and the fairground came into view. The cacophony of noise vibrated in their chests and lights flashed on speeding rides. Elegant horses rode up and down on an enormous carousel. People screamed with delight, as they were whisked higher and faster. Daniel reached for her hand and wound his fingers around hers.

He shouted in her ear to be heard above the music. 'Don't want to lose you in the crowd.'

Ruby red toffee apples shone as if they'd been polished and pink candyfloss frothed like old ladies' perms. Carriages rumbled past out of the green-lit ghost train and stallholders cajoled the crowds to hook a duck or test their strength. Daniel and Tess stood in front of a carousel of painted horses. Twisted poles were fixed to the horses' saddles and they rose and fell as the merry-go-round turned to the sound of a music organ playing, 'Delilah'. A wizened showman beckoned to them.

'Oh, let's,' pleaded Tess.

'Be prepared for your horse to lose.'

Daniel helped her up the roundabout's two steps. She climbed on the back of a golden cockerel and Daniel swung his leg over a horse called Dolly.

Tess hugged the barley sugar twisted pole in front of her. The ride began. It started slowly at first, rising and falling as the carousel turned. The organ played on and the ride picked up speed. Crowds and lights mingled into one as she was whisked round and round. She turned to look at Daniel. His dark hair was blowing away from his face, revealing his cheekbones and pale scar. He noticed her watching him and reached out to hold her hand. His warm fingers wound around hers as the music played on and the lights dazzled.

Eventually the carousel slowed to a stop. Daniel jumped down the two steps and turned to help Tess. He gripped her waist and she held onto his shoulders and jumped. When she landed, she realised that they were embracing. Their faces were close and their bodies touching. She felt the intensity of his gaze, oblivious of the crowds. The moment only lasted a few seconds before being jostled by bony elbows and bulging handbags.

Daniel took hold of Tess's hand again and gently pulled her away from the main walkway. He guided her to a hot dog stall where onions sizzled on a griddle.

'Are you hungry?'

She nodded. 'Smells delicious.'

Daniel ordered two hot dogs with all the trimmings. Tess bit into hers, catching dribbling tomato sauce and falling onions in her serviette. They saw teenagers scream with delight, lost balloons floating into the liquorice sky, girls fluttering eyelashes at boys, inviting them to join them on this heady aphrodisiacal evening.

'Just what I've been looking for,' said Daniel. They passed a chugging generator and he rolled up his sleeves and stood in front of a coconut shy.

'Have you done this before?' asked Tess.

'Are you kidding? I was the reigning champion for five years in my teens. That must be, oooh, a couple of years ago now!'

'A couple?'

'What are you saying?'

'Nothing, I just thought the closest you'd come to a coconut was a Bounty bar.'

'Watch and learn.' Daniel paid for three balls and lined them up as if he was about to bowl for England at Trent Bridge. The first ball missed by an inch and fell to the floor.

'Just warming up,' he said with a laugh, jogging on the spot.

The second ball caught the edge of the coconut's stringy surface, but the shell didn't fall.

'Okay, this is the one.' He rolled the soft ball between his hands and blew on it for luck. He threw it hard. It reached its target. The coconut thudded to the floor.

'Yes!' Tess clapped.

Daniel winked. 'I told you three's a lucky number.'

'Choose any of the prizes hanging on this front row, miss,' said the stallholder.

Tess chose an orange toy dog because it bore similarities to Goya. 'Thank you. I love it.' She stroked its soft ears.

Daniel dared Tess to go on the ghost train. She wasn't scared of the rubber spiders or floating ghouls, but it was fun pretending. It was a good excuse to lean on Daniel's chest and feel him put a protective arm around her shoulder.

On the cakewalk, they laughed until they couldn't move. They whirled on the waltzers and bumped on the dodgems. They shared a tub of mushy peas with mint sauce and dipped into a polythene bag containing a fluff of candyfloss.

Feeling dizzy and tired, they decided to go back to Halston and check on the dogs.

They passed the big wheel. 'One last ride,' said Daniel.

'I don't think I can take another,' groaned Tess. She clasped her stomach.

'This is a gentle one. We'll catch our breath before the walk back to the car.'

Tess looked at the twinkling lights on the wheel. It looked majestic as it rotated slowly on its axis. 'The only way is up.' Tess grinned, her words echoing the words of the song that was playing.

A man beckoned to them. They ran to the next free carriage and the bar was lowered and secured across their thighs. The cage swayed gently backwards and forwards. It moved a few feet backwards so the next couple could take a seat on the following one. A few more carriages were filled and they started to rise further from the ground. The higher they rose, the quieter the music became until it was a distant hum.

Tess looked at Daniel, half smiling and half grimacing at the rocking of the carriage. It moved up and over the top of the rotation and began to descend again, the music growing louder and the lights brightening. They sat in silence for six revolutions, each absorbing the atmosphere and looking at the lights of the fair while leaning against each other. Tess could sense sparks of electricity passing between their touching thighs. The wheel slowed as their carriage became level with the treetops. Their carriage reached the top and stopped. It swung gently.

'It's so beautiful,' whispered Tess, looking down on the glittering scene.

She felt his hand touch hers. 'You are.'

She turned to face him. Her eyes moved from his eyes to his mouth. He leaned towards her and she closed her eyes. She felt his breath on her lips and his cologne of spicy amber. He caressed her neck with his fingertips and whispered her name as his lips touched hers, hesitantly at first, gently lingering. Tess lifted her hand and slid her fingers through his hair. With a gasp, they pulled each other closer, their bodies pressing close.

They kissed passionately, gasping breathlessly into each other's mouths. His hand slid inside her coat and under her jumper, finding the warm skin of her back. His lips moved from her mouth, down her jasmine-scented neck, until he reached the soft hollow at her throat. His tongue sensually circled this sensitive area, making Tess's breath escape in shallow gasps.

Daniel steered his Land Rover through The Rookery's gates and parked it in next to the gnarled wisteria.

'A nightcap?'

'That would be lovely, thank you.'

Still clutching her soft toy, Tess climbed down from her seat and followed Daniel towards the front door. She stepped inside, wondering if a kiss meant that she was officially his girlfriend.

'I'll just let the dogs into the back garden for a minute. What can I get you?'

'A Baileys would be lovely, thanks.'

'Why don't you relax in the library? I stoked up the fire before we went out, so the room should be nice and warm.'

Tess wandered towards the door he'd pointed to. She'd never been in the library before. They usually sat at the kitchen table and a couple of times they'd carried their drinks into his studio. She pushed open the door. The room was cosy and glowing embers were still burning in the hearth. An arc of light spilled from beneath a satin lampshade that was sitting on a writing bureau. Bookcases stretched the length of two walls from floor to ceiling, crammed with hundreds of books, old vinyl records and family photographs. A thick rug lay in front of a stone fireplace opposite a soft leather settee.

Tess took off her coat and laid it on the arm of the settee alongside her stuffed toy dog. She picked up some kindling and several small logs and sat them on top of the embers. The fire crackled into yellow flames. She could hear Daniel calling Goya and Gogh back inside and hugged herself, unable to believe that she was now single and had been kissed by Daniel. Just wait until she phoned Holly.

Tess walked over to study a painting that hung on the wall near the library door. It was a watercolour of The Rookery. She wondered whether it was one of Daniel's or his mother's. Just then he came in through the door and made her jump.

'Oops! I was just admiring this picture.'

'It's an old one of mine. It's fading a bit now.'

'It's lovely.'

He paused, still looking at her.

'What's the matter?' she asked.

'I came in to ask you something, but I've completely forgotten what it was?'

'Dogs? Drink?'

Daniel stood facing her but didn't answer. He just slowly shook his head and leaned forwards until he was an inch away from her face. Although her mouth parted to speak, no words formed. She felt unable to do more than blink. Tess sensed his arm moving upwards, and still holding his gaze, she felt him cup the back of her neck with his palm. An involuntary sigh escaped her mouth as he slid the tip of his tongue along her parted lips. She closed her eyes as he pressed his lips softly against hers and kissed her.

He pulled away a fraction and Tess opened her eyes. In an instant they were clinging to each other, kissing frenziedly. They kissed deeply, their hands grasping and squeezing. Their breath was quick and audible. She cradled his head in her arms, her fingers grasping handfuls of his soft dark hair. She buried her head in his neck, smelling the warm spice on his skin.

He began to unbutton her blouse and she reached for his shirt. They kissed as they moved to the rug in front of the fire. The logs crackled and the smell of wood smoke intensified the heady atmosphere. Tess lay on her back, looking up at Daniel. His hands went to his jeans where he began to unbutton them.

Chapter Thirty-Eight

The day of Sean's arrival dawned chilly and overcast, but by the time Tess left Rose Cottage, the village green glistened beneath bursts of sunlight and racing cloud shadows. A mixture of nerves and excitement churned in her stomach as she walked towards The Royal Oak. She dug her hands deep into her pockets and glanced across the cricket pitch to the tall chimneys of The Rookery, the house itself hidden behind thick evergreen bushes and wide mature tree trunks. She tried to imagine what Daniel was doing and couldn't help but smile to herself while remembering their passionate night a few days earlier. They'd phoned and texted many times since, but had been too busy preparing for the big event to meet each other, until now. Maybe he was even looking out of his studio window and wondering what she was doing marching towards the pub an hour before they'd agreed to meet.

Tess pushed open the front door and entered the lounge area. Christmas hymns played in the background, a log fire burned in an open grate and the spicy smell of cinnamon and gingerbread filled the air with a delicious aroma.

She looked around the room, feeling a little self-conscious. Several couples sat on sofas deep in conversation but then movement from a corner table caught her attention. A tall, fair-haired man stood up and walked towards her.

'Tess?'

'Yes.'

He held out his arm and firmly shook her hand, smiling broadly. 'I'm Sean. It's so good to finally meet after all our emails.'

Tess had worried that she might find it impossible not to stare at someone without an eye, but she found herself looking more closely because he had two dark blue eyes that matched perfectly.

He gestured towards his table. 'Come and take a seat. Is Dan still unaware?'

Tess removed her coat and settled into a seat. 'He's no idea. I only hope it doesn't come as too much of a shock for him.'

'From what you tell me about his feelings of guilt, I'm hoping I can put his mind at ease. Right! Before we get chatting, what can I get you to drink?'

'I'd love a mulled wine, please.'

Sean ordered the drink and sat opposite her at the small table.

'Are you and Dan an item?' asked Sean.

'I… think so. It's very early days.'

'He must mean a lot to you if you went to the trouble of contacting me.'

'He does.' She paused. 'I'm trying to help him over a few challenges.'

Tess hadn't revealed anything about Daniel's OCD to Sean as she didn't think it was her place to share personal details, but if Daniel wanted to share his anxieties with Sean at a later date, that would be his choice.

Sean took a mouthful of beer and Tess leant back to give the barmaid space to place her glass on the table. Tess thanked her before sipping the warm, spiced wine.

'Daniel tells me you've known each other since you were both five.'

'Seems a life time away,' said Sean. 'I remember the first day we met. Dan had started school the term before me and had been given the responsibility of settling me in. I took one look at this skinny boy in grey shorts, shiny black shoes and thick-rimmed glasses and doubted that he could protect me from a fly, let alone the bigger lads.'

Tess laughed. 'Just wait until I tease him about that.'

'It turned out I needn't have worried. He was well liked and funny so he protected me with his charm rather than his fists.'

Tess sipped her wine. During their conversation she had noticed that one of his eyes moved less than the other, but it was still incredible how realistic the false one looked.

'He missed you terribly, you know? When you went to America.'

Sean nodded slowly. 'I don't really remember too much of the move. It happened so quickly after I left hospital. My family over-protected me for a long time as I came to terms with my limited vision, but when I was alone at night, I'd think about England, school and Dan.'

'I showed him the interview you'd given to the *Tribune*. You can imagine the relief he felt when he read it.'

'I had no idea he felt culpable. Nor about his parents.' He shook his head, looking into his half-empty pint glass. 'I want to see him. I can't believe he still lives here after all this time.'

Tess turned and followed Sean's gaze through the window and into the distance. The chimneystacks and top floor of The Rookery rose above towering fir trees across the cricket pitch.

Sean turned his attention back to Tess. 'How did *you* meet Dan?'

She closed her eyes momentarily, remembering her embarrassment. 'I'd gone to the local shop but had forgotten my purse. I needed pasta for a meal I was cooking. Daniel saw me floundering at the till and gave me a two pound coin.'

'Prince Charming to the rescue.'

'Something like that, but a lot's happened since then.' Tess looked at her watch. 'He should be here in half an hour. I'll go out and meet him when he reaches the green and leave you two alone to talk.'

Sean gave a tight-lipped smile and nod of his head. He ran his finger around the rim of his glass. Although he was obviously looking forward to seeing Daniel again, it seemed that he was a little anxious too.

'Have you met his twin, Den, yet?' he asked.

'No, but I'm hoping to meet the family at the exhibition.'

'It's not certain they're coming, then?'

'Den's been… ill. I think they're waiting for test results before committing.'

Sean leaned forward. 'How ill? Is it serious?'

Tess took a deep breath. 'I'll let Daniel explain. He knows more about it than me and gets frequent updates.'

'Christ! That family seems to have more than its fair share of trauma.'

Tess thought back to several weeks earlier when Daniel had opened up to her about his OCD. Almost absent-mindedly, Tess said, 'Yes. They do.'

They chatted amiably for twenty minutes about Halston, her cookery and Sean's family. Tess had bought another round and was feeling light-headed and emotional at the thought that Daniel and Sean were about to be reunited. She drained her glass and stood up.

'It's so lovely to meet you at last. I ought to go and meet Daniel on the green now. He'll need a few minutes to let the news sink in that you're here. I won't come back in with him. I'll leave you both to catch up.'

Sean stood up and helped Tess on with her coat before hugging her. 'I know I've already said it, but thank you for getting in touch. I'll see you at the exhibition tomorrow.'

'I know this will mean the world to him, after he gets over the initial shock.'

Sean nodded, tears glistening in both eyes. 'Me too.'

Tess hugged her coat tightly around her body as she left through the front door; a chill wind stinging her exposed skin. She walked across the cricket pitch but only got as far as the boundary line before she saw Daniel closing The Rookery's iron gates behind him. He walked with his hands in his coat pockets and his head bowed against the wind, only raising his head a short distance before reaching her.

He slowed his gait, then stopped. He wore a silly grin on his face. 'I've been thinking about you.'

'What a coincidence! I've been thinking about you, too.'

Daniel leaned forwards and kissed her tenderly on her mouth. His lips were warm and soft. Tess closed her eyes, not wanting to move on from this second, before reminding herself that this moment was about Daniel and Sean. She gently pulled away.

'Are we still going for a drink?'

'Yes.'

He stuck out his elbow for her to slip her arm through his.

'No, I mean you are. You have to go to the pub.'

'I'm confused.'

Tess shivered with cold. 'I've done something. I hope it was the right thing to do. I'm worried you'll be upset. I did it for the right reason.'

'Upset? What have you done? Come here.'

He reached out towards her pulled her to him, a button on his coat feeling like a cold disc against her cheek. She spoke while leaning against his chest.

'I invited Sean to the exhibition.'

'Sean?'

'*The* Sean.'

Daniel gently pushed her away from his body and looked into her eyes. The smile had disappeared from his lips and a frown line had creased his brow.

'You invited him?'

'Yes.'

'How?'

'I searched and found his email address.'

Daniel's mouth hung open in surprise. 'Did he say he'd come?'

'He's here.' Tess pointed to The Royal Oak. 'He's waiting inside for you.'

'Sean's here?' He sounded incredulous.

Tess nodded. 'I emailed him after I'd found the interview article. Remember when we talked about facing fears in order to overcome them? Well, I'm not convinced it's solely fireworks or the thought of another accident that causes your anxieties. I think it may be guilt, too. Misplaced guilt. You've read that Sean's accident wasn't your fault, but I think you need to hear it too.'

'Have you seen him? Have you spoken to him?'

'Yes, we've had a drink.'

Daniel rubbed his palm back and forth across his jaw. 'You never fail to surprise me. Are you coming too?'

Tess took his hand and spoke while absent-mindedly running her forefinger along a blue vein. 'You two should spend time together, alone. It's important. You both have years to catch up on and misunderstandings to talk about.'

'Why do I feel as nervous as my first day at school?'

She teased to ease his nerves. 'At least you're not wearing shorts or thick-rimmed glasses.'

'I see he's been giving some secrets away already. Hallelujah for contact lenses.'

Tess was relieved to see him smiling again.

'Sean and I chatted about a few things but I didn't go into any personal details about you or Den.'

'Okay.' He shook his head. 'I can't believe he's just there and I'm going to see him again.'

'I'm going to go home and do some more baking for tomorrow. Relax. He seems lovely and very laid-back. Everything will be fine.'

Daniel inhaled deeply and slowly released his breath. 'Thank you. I'll call you later.'

He leaned forwards and kissed her, before heading for a reunion.

Chapter Thirty-Nine

The morning of Daniel's birthday and exhibition had arrived. Tess stirred in her bed, consciousness pulling her from her sleep. She sat up in an instant, wide-eyed. Tonight was the night she was going to tell Daniel that she loved him. She'd almost told him last week after they'd made love in front of the fire, but Goya and Gogh had started to scratch at the closed library door. They had both laughed and leisurely dressed in the glow of the dying fire.

Everything seemed to be running smoothly. Tess's new black dress was hanging on the bedroom door. The carved ark had been wrapped to perfection in navy and silver paper. Her car had been mended, the food was all prepared and it wasn't raining.

Tess climbed out of bed and slid her feet into her slippers. Her fleecy pyjamas were warm enough to pop downstairs to put the kettle on. Tess padded out of the bedroom towards the stairs. She stopped. She felt a sense of foreboding. A cold chill swept up the stairs and she noticed the front door was slightly ajar. She knew she'd closed the door last night. She locked it every night. She crept down a few more stairs. Why could she smell such a strong aroma of food? Tess reached the bottom. She walked slowly towards the kitchen. Her hand trembled as she pushed open the door and caught her breath when she saw the devastation.

The exhibition food, that she had spent forty-eight hours preparing, was splattered around the kitchen. Mounds of cream, pastry, sponge, dough and fruit lay around the floor like a suppurating wound. Food was splashed against the paintwork and dried gelatinous liquids trailed down the side of cupboards. Thick viscous layers lay smeared across the worktops. Her tartlets, blinis, salmon en croute and spiced red cabbage were upturned on the kitchen floor. Running into the lounge, she picked up the house phone and dialled Daniel's number.

'Hello.'

'It's Tess.'

'Hi, sweetheart. Why are you whispering?'

'Someone's broken in.'

'What do you mean?'

'The front door was open and all the food in the fridge has been destroyed. It's been thrown everywhere.'

'What? Get out of the house. I'll be with you in two minutes. Have you rung the police?'

'No. I rang you first.'

'Get out, Tess. I'll ring them.'

Tess put down the phone. She opened the front door and hurried down her garden path. She didn't know what to do. A delicate frost had iced the fence. She began to shake with shock and cold. She was still wearing her pyjamas.

Daniel's Land Rover growled to a stop and he and Sean jumped down. Daniel ran to her and took her in his arms. 'Are you okay? I didn't know you weren't dressed. You must be freezing. I've rung the police and they're on their way. You'd better stand in the hall. I'll check out the house.'

'Upstairs is fine. It's just the kitchen.'

Sean joined them. 'Hi. You didn't need this, did you?'

'Morning, Sean. Sorry to have disturbed you so early.'

'No problem at all. We were up and drinking coffee.'

'Come on,' said Daniel. 'Let's take a look.'

The three of them stepped inside Rose Cottage, Daniel holding Tess's hand. 'Wait here by the radiator. Don't move.'

The men walked down the hall and into the kitchen.

'Bloody hell. What lunatic would do this? Is Blake still locked up?' asked Daniel.

'Yes. As far as I know. Anyway, it's not his style. He would try to talk to me to make me change my mind.'

Tess joined him and wrapped her arms around his waist. He stroked her hair in a daze, neither of them able to take their eyes away from the carnage.

'This is a proper British who dunnit mystery?' said Sean, scratching his head.

An authoritative voice called from the front door. 'Hello.'

'In here.'

Two police officers joined them at the kitchen door. 'What seems to be the problem, sir?'

'The house has been broken into.' Daniel pointed to the mess and let it speak for itself.

The policeman whistled in disbelief and shook his head. 'Have you any ideas who could have done this?'

'Tess's ex-boyfriend was sentenced several weeks ago. His name's Blake Snipes. Are you able to check if he's still locked up?'

The policeman spoke into his radio relaying the information. Within minutes the answer came back that Blake was still in prison. The officers inspected the rest of the house, before they all sat at the surprisingly clean kitchen table. Notes were made as Tess answered questions. What time had she gone to bed? What time did she notice the destruction? Did any neighbours hold grudges?

'I find one thing very confusing,' said the officer who was taking the statement. 'There doesn't appear to have been a break in. No force has been used and there's no damage to windows or doors. Does anyone else have a key?'

'Only me and Blake. No wait! I gave Mrs Campbell a key to let the gasman in to check the oven some months ago. But she's a lovely old lady.'

'We'll need to speak to her anyway. There's nothing we can do at the moment. As nothing seems to be missing, I'd say someone has a grudge. Are you sure you locked the door?'

'Yes, I think so. I mean, I always do, but...'

'Coo-ee!'

'That's Mrs Campbell. She's probably seen the police car,' said Tess.

'We might as well have a chat with her now, if it's okay with you?'

Tess nodded before shouting, 'Mrs Campbell, in here.'

'Oh my, what a to-do,' flustered the elderly lady as she shuffled into the kitchen.

'Hello, Mrs Campbell, I believe?' said the senior officer.

The old lady lifted her head up to the policeman's face with some difficulty. 'Goodness me. Policemen get younger and taller, don't they?'

The officer smiled. 'Mrs Campbell?'

'Yes, I'm Eileen Campbell.'

Tess hadn't known that her neighbour was called Eileen. How strange to find out while being interviewed by a policeman.

'Do you mind if I ask you a few questions?' asked the officer.

'How exciting. Not at all. I've seen people being asked that on television.'

'Come and sit down, Eileen,' said Daniel. He pulled out a dining chair for her that she accepted gratefully.

She looked around at the mess on the kitchen floor. 'Oh my goodness. Whatever happened?'

'Someone's destroyed the food for tonight's art exhibition,' replied Tess, her voice breaking. Daniel moved to stand behind Tess's chair and rubbed her shoulders.

The officer who had been taking notes, sat down next to the old lady. 'Did you see or hear anything unusual during the night, Eileen?'

'I knew it seemed odd when I saw someone. You know I don't sleep much these days? Actually, I don't eat much either. I'm getting old, you know? I used to be able to sleep for ten hours, straight. Now my hips hurt and I can't get comfortable. I was saying to my doctor the other day, I said, doctor I'd be better off on a perch with a blanket over my head, like Chippy. You know my little Chippy, don't you, dear? Oh, where was I?'

'I asked if you'd heard anything strange or seen anyone hanging around last night. You said you'd seen someone.'

'Yes, dear, I did.'

They all looked at her.

'Who, Mrs Campbell?'

'I don't know.'

'But I thought you said you did.'

'That's right.'

The officer sighed. Daniel moved across to her and knelt down beside her.

'Hello, Eileen.' The old lady looked at Daniel with her pale blue eyes and beamed in recognition. Her set of beige teeth, set slightly apart, resembled a line of dominoes waiting to tumble.

'Daniel, my dear boy. It's you. I saw two handsome strapping men behind Tess, but I didn't recognise you. My eyes, you know?'

'I think you're doing just fine. You said you'd seen someone. Can you tell us what you saw?'

'I couldn't sleep. Have I already told you that? I went to check on Chippy and he was being a good boy, as usual. I had a peep out of the front curtains. Habit really. I never usually see anything. But last night, I saw someone walking up Tess's garden path.'

'Did you recognise them?'

'No.'

'Did you see how they got in, Eileen?' interrupted the policeman.

'They unlocked the door with a key.'

Everyone shifted in their seats. Tess began to feel very sick.

'It was dark. How do you know it was a key?' asked the policeman.

'Well, obviously I couldn't *see* it. But a streetlight is outside the cottage and I saw the person put their hand in their pocket and pull something out. They touched the door with it and it opened straight away. I'm not Sherlock, but I guess it was a key.'

Daniel smiled and rubbed the thin skin on the back of her crooked hand.

'Can you recognise the person?' asked the policeman.

'No.'

Everyone's shoulders dropped in disappointment.

'But I took a photograph with my new camera as they left.'

'This is just like *Miss Marple*. We watch it in the States,' said Sean.

'Do you have your camera on you?' asked the officer.

'It's here in my handbag. That's what I came over to tell you but you kept asking me questions.' She opened her bag and rustled about inside. 'Can you get it, Daniel, dear. My joints aren't what they used to be.'

Daniel opened the bag wider and moved aside a bag of Mint Imperials, a case containing her glasses and a packet of tissues. A little leather case was nestled in the corner under her purse. He pulled it out.

'May I?'

'Of course. It's my dignified camera and it's so easy to use. I just press a button. My son sent it for my birthday.'

Daniel didn't correct her. He scrolled through

photographs. Chippy eating. Chippy sleeping. Chippy standing on his perch. Chippy sitting on furniture. There were a few pictures of houseplants and then the picture in question. It was dark and grainy and the figure was off centre, but it clearly showed a face he recognised. Daniel handed it to the officer who'd been asking the questions. He looked at the photograph and passed it on to Tess.

'Do you recognise this person?'

Tess covered her mouth with her hand. 'It's Blake's mother. Joy Snipes.'

The room began to bustle with activity. The policeman stood up and spoke into his radio. He asked Tess for Joy's address and a car was dispatched to pick her up. Daniel and Tess both thanked Mrs Campbell and told her how wonderful she had been.

Twenty minutes later, the police had left and Sean was helping Mrs Campbell across the road and back home. Daniel and Tess stood with their arms wrapped round each other, rocking gently. Tess felt Daniel kiss her hair and rest his mouth there as he breathed. She felt his breath on her skin and sunk deeper into his chest before suddenly remembering something. She jumped backwards.

'Happy birthday. I'm so sorry I forgot. What a terrible way to start your birthday.'

'Thank you. Personally I think having you in my arms wearing just your Winnie the Pooh pyjamas is the best possible start. It's only half past nine and as long as you're okay, that's all that matters. We took a lot of the party food to my fridge and there's plenty more in the two fridges in The Rookery's garage.'

Daniel and Sean spent an hour at Rose Cottage helping Tess to clean up the mess but left at eleven as Daniel had some last minute preparations to sort out and Sean had offered to shop for some more food. Thistle Do Nicely had delivered and decorated a huge Christmas tree, which had been placed at the foot of The Rookery's staircase. Garlands had been tied with red tartan bows and draped along the length of the first staircase, and flowers had been arranged into huge glass vases.

In order to prevent the food from being out of the fridge for too long, it wasn't being put out until the last moment. A couple of girls who worked behind the bar at The Royal Oak, plus the publicans' two daughters, had said they'd be happy to help for the evening. They were going to arrange Tess's food on the long dining table and help to clear away afterwards. Flash Bang Wallop Pyrotechnics had been hired for the firework display. This was a secret Daniel was keeping from Tess. He wanted to surprise her. He hoped she'd be proud of his progress, although he knew that he couldn't have improved so much without her help. If Sean could fight and beat adversity, then he had no excuse.

After a hectic day of organising and hanging paintings, Daniel looked at his watch. He had an hour for a quick shower and to get ready before the first of his guests arrived.

Tess was relieved that the destroyed food was only about a third of the buffet and they had probably over-estimated the amount they would need, anyway. Thank goodness The Rookery had three huge fridges and Sean had bought more desserts. The police had phoned to say that they were questioning Joy and she had admitted emptying the fridge; but only after she'd been shown the photograph. Apparently, it had been the first time she'd been speechless during the whole interview. They rang again an hour later to say that they'd be keeping her in a cell for the night because she'd become aggressive towards the interviewing policewoman. They were now awaiting the arrival of a psychiatrist to assess her mental health.

Chapter Forty

Tess lowered herself into a hot bath. She lay back and closed her eyes. Bubbles tickled her back as they ran along her spine and up to the surface. Nothing was going to spoil this evening now. She imagined spending the night with Daniel and repeating the scene in front of the fire. She soaked for twenty minutes, leaving a conditioning mask on her hair, rubbing Sanctuary sea salt into her skin and shaving her legs until they were as smooth as sugared almonds. She applied her make-up with the precision of an artist and curled her hair until it fell in soft spiralling tendrils. The two hours she'd set aside to pamper herself had flown by.

Tess arrived at The Rookery for seven thirty. She wore a black sleeveless dress with a fitted bodice, showing just a hint of cleavage. Its waist was nipped with delicate pleats, from which flowed layers of soft silk that swayed and flowed down to her calves. Accentuating her waist was a wide silk sash in chartreuse-green, the colour of the French liqueur. Adorning her neck and ears were her grandmother's pearls and on her feet, bead-encrusted stilettos.

Before she'd left Rose Cottage, she'd twirled in circles in front of the mirror, feeling the layers lift and flow around her thighs. Here, standing in front of the Hall, she felt out of place. It didn't feel like the fairy-tale place where she and Daniel had grown to know each other. It was full of strangers and looked different with Christmas decorations. She fiddled nervously with her clutch bag, inside which, was safely nestled Daniel's ark.

The band began to play as Tess walked to the back of the hallway and through the long dining room. Goosebumps prickled her arms. Huge church candles had been lit and the lights had been dimmed to give a comforting and inviting atmosphere. The dining table was laden with her carefully and lovingly prepared recipes, the food already having attracted numerous guests. The buzz of conversation was occasionally interrupted by high-pitched laughter, or glasses chinking as people toasted the festive season.

Tess passed through the dining room and into the exhibition room. It was full of people studying Daniel's work. Murmurs of appreciation buzzed around the exhibition. Where was Daniel? Tess turned to the huge bay window and French doors and gasped audibly at the magical sight in the garden.

In the darkness, the marquee had turned from the enormous white tent, into a world of make-believe. The pathway leading from the gallery to the marquee was lined with dozens of silver lanterns, showering yellow beams along the coconut matting. An arch of fairy lights spanned the pathway, twinkling a warm welcome at the marquee's entrance. The band was now singing Sade's 'Diamond Life', the singer's voice flowing like warm treacle around the enclosure.

Tess followed a small group of people through the fairy lit arch into the marquee. She stood entranced at the stunning beauty of the ceiling. It was draped in a midnight black star cloth, lit from behind and looking like a galaxy of stars. A huge black painted backdrop reinforced the night sky theme and the sides of the marquee were hung with long black pleated drapes. The band played on a raised platform and to the left was a bar area.

Staff served guests sitting on plush sofas. She spotted Sean talking with a small group of men while sharing a bottle of wine. It looked more like a hotel lobby than a glorified tent. The black and white chequer board flooring spanned a large area for dancing and the corner peaks of the marquee were lit up in midnight blue and azure. Upright poles were adorned with winter flowers of poinsettias, evergreen euphorbias and blood red holly berries, all interwoven with a plethora of long waxy green leaves. A scattering of tables and chairs gave refuge for tired dancers, or diners who were eating her recipes. In the middle of each table stood a sculpture of cinnamon sticks, dried fruit, pinecones and mistletoe, wrapped in a shawl of dark shiny green leaves. Powerful but quiet heaters, made the huge area as warm as toast on this frosty December evening.

Tess was now desperate to find Daniel and tell him how amazing everything looked. She walked back through the gallery and into the dining room. People were now crowding around her table of food, groaning with pleasure at the tastes and textures. She crossed the hallway dodging a gathering of people and poked her head into the kitchen. It was empty.

She was about to return to the gallery to look at Daniel's art and wait for him there, when a movement on the stairs made her look up. Daniel was walking down the sweeping staircase. He was wearing a black suit and white shirt, undone at the collar. His dark hair was swept back away from his face. His handsome face softened when he saw her. He reached the bottom step, stood in front of her and lifted her hands in his.

'You look beautiful.'

'Thank you.'

He gave a small bow and winked. 'The food is amazing. Thank you so much. I couldn't have done it without you and all your hard work.'

'But you've done an amazing job. It looks like a land of make-believe outside. It's so beautiful.'

'They've done a great job, haven't they? All I did was tell them what I wanted and where to put it.'

'Yes, but that's where the artistry lies. It could have looked like Santa's grotto under someone else's direction.'

'That's not a bad idea for Christmas. My nephews would love it. They're coming tonight. I can't wait for you to meet Den.'

'What time are they coming?'

'Later. Den had an afternoon check up at the hospital that couldn't be changed. Then they have to drive up from London. I've just phoned them from my studio and they've set off.'

Tess opened her clutch bag and felt for the ark. 'I can't believe that I'll be meeting your twin tonight.'

'Sorry. I'm being beckoned from the gallery.' He kissed her cheek. 'Save a dance for me,' he called over his shoulder.

Tess let go of the ark and let it drop back into her bag. She knew she had all night to give him his gift, so decided to take some food into the marquee and people watch for a while. She balanced some blinis on her plate and walked through the gallery. She saw Daniel explaining a piece of work to an elegant couple, the woman's diamonds glittering on her ear lobes. As Daniel pointed at the picture in question, the gentleman's gaze followed his arm, but the woman's eyes lingered on Daniel's face. Tess frowned. She was feeling a new and unwanted emotion. She felt a nervous twinge in the pit of her stomach. Could it be jealousy? It wasn't something she'd experienced very often.

Tess walked under the twinkling archway and sat close to the band in order to watch the dancing, wishing that Holly and Doug would hurry up. She ordered a glass of mulled wine and watched the guests, their hair swinging while laughter punctuated dance moves and perfume lingered in the air.

Tess's drink arrived. She took a sip of the warm ruby liquid and began to relax. The band started to play a beautiful piece of music, so she leant back and listened to the gentle strains of 'Come Away With Me'. The female singer had a wonderful voice. Tess felt tears prickle her eyes, which made the artificial starry sky in the canopy of the marquee streak with misty sunbursts. The romantic words and her relief that tonight had actually arrived, was making her emotional.

Thankfully, the tempo picked up for the next song and Tess found herself tapping her foot to the music. She saw Daniel shaking hands and ordering a whiskey for an elderly gentleman at the bar. They were both smiling broadly, so perhaps he'd sold a painting.

The band stopped for a break and the DJ seamlessly took over the music. He introduced himself and congratulated Daniel on his art exhibition, the beautiful marquee and wished him a happy birthday. Everyone cheered and clapped, and in turn, Daniel raised his glass in the air to thank them. Tess sipped her warm, spiced wine and shivered in anticipation of spending the night with him.

Hozier's 'Take Me To Church' started playing. The main lights dimmed and muted disco lights reflected off the rotating glitter ball. Tess loved the emotive track and with a little mulled wine bravado, she joined several small groups dancing in the soft shadows of the dance floor. The heat had brought out the scent of cinnamon and pine from the Christmas table displays and fairy lights twinkled in the swathes of material draped above them. The atmosphere was intoxicating. Tess could feel the silk from her dress sliding against her thighs and calves as she swayed to the music.

Arms enclosed her from behind, sure and firm. She could smell faint bergamot and sandlewood from Daniel's seductive cologne. He kissed the nape of her neck while moving in time to the music, his soft lips sending a frisson of tingles down her spine. She yielded to his touch, sinking back against his taut body.

'You're a delicious temptation, Tess Fenton,' he whispered. 'How could I watch you dance without holding you?'

Tess swayed to the music, leaning her head back against his chest. She felt his lips move up from her shoulder towards her chin. Her head tilted backwards. Slowly. Powerlessly. All the more sensual because he was still behind her, still out of sight in the shadows. They swayed in unison, his arms draped around her waist, running a finger along the pattern of her lace underwear beneath her silk dress. Tess was breathless. Dizzy. Trembling.

All too soon the track came to an end.

She turned to him and took hold of his hands. 'Is Den here yet? I can't wait to see how strong the resemblance is.'

'I got a call and they're running late. Bloody road works on the motorway.'

'That's a shame.'

'At least I've been able to talk to several buyers without feeling guilty for ignoring the family. I'm sorry, I feel like I'm neglecting you but I have to dash again.'

'I understand. It's your big night. Go.'

He squeezed her hands and left while she watched his silhouette leave the dance floor and disappear into the crowd once again.

Chapter Forty-One

Tess had spent some time chatting to Sean but he was entranced by Daniel's paintings and had left her to take another look round the exhibition. It was nearly nine by the time Holly and Doug arrived. Tess saw Holly first, standing at the doorway scanning the interior of the marquee. She stood up and waved. Holly spotted her and waved back excitedly, beckoning to Doug, who was behind her. Holly grabbed his arm and half dragged him over towards Tess's table.

'Tess, you look amazing, you remind me of Audrey Hepburn in that dress.'

'Thank you. I love yours,' replied Tess, feeling the gold, sequinned mini dress.

She turned to Doug. He was tall and wiry with short dark hair. 'Hi, Doug. I'm glad you could make it.'

'I couldn't turn down my favourite shop assistant, could I?' he said, winking at Holly.

Holly grinned, then spoke in a voice that sounded distinctly like Minnie Mouse's. 'Doug, be an angel and get me a vodka and orange.' She squeezed his cheek with her thumb and forefinger and gave his skin a small shake.

'Do you want one?' Doug asked Tess, seemingly unfazed by Holly's actions.

'No thanks. I need to keep a clear head so I can keep an eye on the buffet.'

He disappeared towards the bar area.

'What was all that about?' asked Tess.

'What?'

'The voice and the cheek wobbling thing.'

'It's just *our* thing.'

Tess sat back down and wondered if she and Daniel would have a *thing*. She gestured for Holly to sit down and spoke more quietly.

'There was a bit of a hiccup with the food this morning.'

'What sort of hiccup?'

'Someone came in and ruined a lot of it.'

'No!'

Tess nodded.

'Did they smash a window?'

'No, there wasn't any damage to my house. She used a key.'

'She?'

'Blake's mother.'

Holly leaned forwards. 'You're kidding me!'

Tess pursed her lips and shook her head.

'How do you know it was her? Did you catch her at it?'

'My neighbour saw her unlock my door in the early hours. She must have used Blake's keys. Thank goodness for Mrs Campbell's insomnia or we'd have no proof.'

'What an evil woman. Has she been arrested? God, I'd love to have seen her with handcuffs behind her back.' Holly sniggered. 'Good riddance to both of them, I say. You can move on now. How are you feeling?'

'Now this evening's finally arrived, I feel like my emotions are all over the place. I nearly bawled at a beautiful song earlier.'

'You're supposed to dance to them, not cry at them. Why are you so stressed? You've finished with Blake, your food turned out fabulously and you're free to be with the man of yours and most other women's dreams.'

'I know. The madness will be over tomorrow and we can look forward to Christmas.'

'You never know,' whispered Holly, 'you might be staying the night here, if you know what I mean.' She nudged Tess playfully.

Tess hadn't told Holly that they'd already had unforgettable sex. She'd wanted to keep it private and hug that evening's memories to herself for a while. It had been so wonderful that she didn't want to spoil the memory by being asked probing questions about the mechanics of the deed. Thankfully, before she could reply, Doug returned to the table with their drinks. They talked for twenty minutes, discussing Joy's earlier antics, The Blue Olive and Christmas. During a lull in the conversation, Tess realised she hadn't seen Daniel for nearly an hour. She didn't want to interrupt him, but thought she would wander back into the house just to catch a glimpse of him.

'I think I'll pop inside and get some dessert. I'll be back in ten minutes.' Tess left the marquee and walked along the archway of fairy lights, back into the exhibition room. There were sticky dots on several canvasses and framed paintings that indicated they'd been sold. Fantastic, she thought. He must be having a successful evening. She couldn't see Daniel in the gallery, so she walked through to the dining room. There were lots of empty plates on the table; in fact all the savoury dishes had gone. She looked at the remaining desserts trying to decide what to have. There was the exotic fruit platter that had a selection of prepared fruit, chopped and ready to eat on skewers. The peach schnapps cake was disappearing fast and so was the chocolate truffle torte. Tess helped herself to a skewer of pineapple, mango and strawberries.

'Hello. I'm told you're the cook.'

Tess turned to face a large lady of indeterminate years. She could have been an old looking fifty-something or a young looking seventy-something. She smelled strongly of musky perfume and wore thick make-up beneath a bouffant hair do. Expensive jewellery dangled from her neck and ears and she had the aura of titled gentry.

'I did much of the catering, yes.'

'How do you do,' she replied, shaking Tess's hand. It was an infuriating handshake where only her fingertips were offered. 'Lovely food.'

'Thank you.' Tess hoped that that was the end of the conversation. She really wanted to find Daniel.

'Do you cook for a living, or is it a little sideline business?'

'This is the first time I've catered for so many. I usually help out at charity functions at The Royal Oak, but I work in town.'

'Oh. What do you do?'

'I work in a deli in Maddox Square.'

'Hmm.'

Tess felt the whoosh as she plummeted in estimation in the woman's eyes.

'How do you know Daniel?' continued the lady. She snapped off a piece of icing from a cup cake and popped it into her mouth.

'I haven't known him long but we've become friends.'

'Yes, it's so easy to get along with Daniel, isn't it? What a lovely man. If I was a few years younger...'

More like a few decades, Tess thought ungallantly.

'I bumped into him five minutes ago but he was in a bit of a tizz.'

'Was he? Is he all right?' asked Tess.

'He will be when his lovely Dee Dee gets here. He's been clock watching all evening waiting for her to arrive.'

Tess swallowed hard. That same twisted knot of jealousy tightened in her stomach. Who was Dee Dee?

The woman continued. 'Yes. It's lovely to see two people who are so close. They're always on the telephone. They love each other so much and have been through such a lot together over the years.'

'Years?' Tess felt like she had lost the power of conversation and the ability to breathe.

'Don't look so worried, dear,' said the woman, patting her hand. 'He'll be fine when she arrives and he can give her a big hug.' She waved at an elderly man. 'There you are, Cyril.' She turned and left.

Tess felt nauseous. She put her fruit back down. She *was* the cook. She was a helpful neighbour. She was a friend with benefits; something she'd hoped she wouldn't become. Why had he never mentioned a woman called Dee Dee? Had he just been flirting over the last few months before things had got out of hand on the night of the fair? She felt her throat tighten as she fought back tears. She walked in a daze into the hall, stopping dead when she saw Daniel talking to another man at the bottom of the stairs. She edged a little closer and hid behind the Christmas tree in order to listen. Tess caught the tail end of Daniel's answer.

'Okay, Mike. I'll get in touch next week. Excuse me but I've left my mobile in my study and as I said, she's not here and I'm worried. She's my guest of honour.'

'Sorry to have missed her. Give her my love,' the man said.

It seemed that everyone knew that Daniel and this Dee Dee woman were an item, except her. Tess heard Daniel running upstairs and with her heart racing so much that she felt dizzy, she followed him. She remembered the last time she'd climbed this staircase. They'd been together and the whole magical day was imprinted in her memory as a day to be treasured. It had been a sham. Tess stood outside his studio and listened.

'Hi, where are you? It's not the same without you here. Twenty minutes, that's great. Yes of course you're staying here the night. You'd be staying the week if I had my way. I'm looking forward to spending the day together tomorrow. Hurry up.'

Tess felt bile rise into her throat and ran silently down

the carpeted stairs into the toilet in the hall. She sat on the lid of the toilet for ten minutes. A few knocks on the door had disturbed her, but the guests had gone away. She stood up and looked in the mirror. Her make-up was ruined. Her mascara was smudged around her red swollen eyes and her nose was full of tears and mucous. She'd gone over a lot in her mind sitting in this little room. The friendship had only seemed so special to her, because as the woman had said, 'it's so easy to get along with Daniel'. He was nice to *everyone*. She'd misread the signs because she was vulnerable having been lied to and cheated on by Blake. As for having sex last week, they'd had fun at the fair, the opportunity had arisen and they'd taken it.

She took her powder compact out of her bag and patched up her face as best she could. Taking a deep breath, she slowly opened the door and peeped outside. A few strangers wandered through the hall. She sidled out of the door, hurried through the house and back into the marquee, never looking up once. Tess looked for Holly. Her friend was sitting back at the table rubbing her feet and complaining.

'Honestly, Doug, you've got two left feet, you clumsy oaf. Tess where have you been? Whatever's the matter?'

Tess felt the tears stinging her eyes again.

'Doug, can you make yourself scarce for five minutes,' asked Holly.

Doug got up without a word and walked in the direction of the bar. Holly put her arm around Tess's shoulders.

'Tell me what's happened?'

'I've been such a fool. Again. I've just found out that Daniel's in love with someone called Dee Dee.' Tess searched for a tissue in her bag, wiped her eyes and blew her nose. 'They've been seeing each other for years. He's waiting for her to arrive and she's staying the night.'

Holly reached out and held her hands. 'You're kidding. Are you sure?'

'I heard him with my own ears. They're going to spend the day together tomorrow too.' Tess sobbed into her soggy tissue and blew her nose again. 'I'm leaving. I'm driving back to Mum's for a few days. I'll ring work on Monday. I've got a couple of days owed to me. I can't stay and see them together, Holly. I've fallen in love with him and I can't bear it.'

Holly hugged her. 'I'm so sorry. I'm going to give him a piece of my mind, leading you on like that.'

'Not tonight. Let him enjoy his birthday and exhibition.'

'You're too nice, that's your problem.'

'Bye. I'll ring you tomorrow.'

'I can't promise I won't read him the riot act. This woman should know that he's been leading you on.'

Tess kissed Holly's cheek. She had told her friend about the kiss that she and Daniel had shared on the big wheel, but was glad she'd kept their passionate evening a secret.

'Bye.'

'Bye. Please drive carefully.'

Tess walked out of the marquee and turned to the right, away from the main path that led into the gallery. She trudged through muddy grass, her heels sinking into the soft wet ground. One shoe got stuck in the soggy lawn, making her step into the brown sticky mud with her bare foot. She picked up her shoe and continued to walk around the side of the huge building, limping with one shoe on and one shoe in her hand. A handful of security lights lit her way until she found herself at the front of the house. A few people mingled around the front door, smoking and laughing. The drive was full of sharp gravel, but Tess couldn't wear her ruined shoe, so she painfully hobbled across the width of the path and hid among the trees in the front garden.

Just as she was about to make her way through the trees and towards the gate, she saw Daniel run out of the front door. He'd taken off his jacket and he was grinning as he ran down the drive, his white shirt billowing in the breeze. A figure ran towards him from the opposite direction.

A woman.

Tess watched as they ran into each other's arms and Daniel twirled her around in his embrace. So, Dee Dee had arrived and Daniel was happy on his birthday.

A burst of fireworks lit up the navy sky. Tess looked up to where a chrysanthemum of vibrant colours flashed and crackled above her head. Anger at Daniel's double standards and pride at his achievements, fought each other for space in her thoughts. At least something positive had come out of this friendship, she thought, bitterly. At least he was over his firework phobia.

Tess noticed that the woman and Daniel were now holding hands and looking skywards. Daniel leaned towards her and whispered something in her ear before they both ran in through the front door. The last of the smokers also made their way round to the back garden, in order to get a better view of the magnificent display.

A man ran down the drive holding hands with two small boys, all three of them laughing and looking into the exploding sky. Tess could hear the distant 'oohs' and 'aahs' from the guests as she disappeared out of the front gates.

Chapter Forty-Two

Daniel was looking for Tess. He'd waited so long to introduce her to his sister, and now he couldn't find her. He scanned the upturned faces of the crowd having searched the rooms inside. He'd really wanted to watch the fireworks with the two most important women in his life. His arm was loosely draped around his sister's shoulders. She looked so happy. He looked among the crowd for Tess once again, and caught sight of Holly. She was staring at him, unsmiling. He waved but she looked away instead of returning his wave. Perhaps she hadn't seen him in the shadows. When he looked back, she was pushing her way through the crowd towards him. She walked up to him with her arms folded.

'Hi, Holly. I've been looking for Tess. Have you seen her?' he asked.

'You can stop pretending.'

Daniel frowned. 'Is everything all right?'

'Don't give me that routine. Tess knows what's going on and thankfully she found out before she got in too deep.'

'I'm sorry?'

'You should be.'

'Seriously, Holly. I don't know what you're talking about.'

'I just wanted to tell you that I think you're a fake opportunist,' she said. 'Look at you with your arm around her.' She looked at Denise then back to Daniel. 'You know what they call men like you? Players. You should be ashamed of yourself and I think it's only fair to tell you,' she said, turning back to Denise, 'that your boyfriend has been flirting with and kissing my best friend. She's fallen in love with him and now he's broken her heart.'

'My boyfriend?' Denise laughed.

'Not if you had any sense,' said Holly.

Daniel felt confused, but kept replaying in his mind what Holly had said about Tess having fallen in love with him.

'Hailey—' said Denise.

'Holly,' corrected Holly.

'Sorry, Holly. I think you've got your wires mixed up.'

'Is your name Dee Dee?' asked Holly.

'Yes, some people call me that.'

At that moment, Sean, Daniel's brother-in-law and nephews joined them.

'There you are, Den,' said Simon, kissing Denise's cheek. He extended his arm to Daniel. 'It's so good to see you. I've just been chatting with Sean who tells me you went to school together. It's great to finally get here. Den has been crossing off the days, haven't you, darling?'

Daniel shook his brother-in-law's proffered hand. 'It's good to see you too. I'll get you a drink but we're just sorting out a little problem first.'

'What problem?'

Daniel scratched his temple. Holly was now staring at Simon.

'Is your best friend called Tess, by the way?' Denise asked Holly.

'Y–es.'

'Good. We're getting somewhere. Simon here,' she turned to him, 'is my husband. These are our sons and Daniel here, is my twin brother.'

Daniel watched Holly stand paralysed for a few seconds while she absorbed these facts. He saw her look from Simon to the boys, then from Denise and finally to him.

'Oh shit! Sorry. I feel *so* stupid. We thought you had a twin brother called Den. I'm really sorry, but Tess came crying to me and said she'd overheard you asking someone called Dee Dee to stay the night. When I saw you with a woman I'd never seen, I'm… God, I'm sorry.'

'Is it true? Tess really told you she loved me?'

'Yes.'

'She actually said that?'

'Yes.'

Daniel turned to Denise with a wide grin. 'She loves me.' He hugged his sister and swung her round in a circle. He turned to Holly, grabbed her shoulders and kissed both her cheeks before standing back. 'You're a wonderful, slightly crazy, loyal friend to Tess and I hope that when I find her and tell her I love her too, that I'll see a lot more of you. Now where is she?'

'Ah!'

'What?'

'She's left.'

'Gone home?'

'Yes.'

'I'll run and get her to come back. I'll explain.'

'Her parents' home.'

Daniel's grin evaporated. 'She's driving back to Cornwall? Now?' He raked his fingers through his hair. 'I can't leave yet because purchasers have asked to see me later. She can't have gone far. Where's my mobile?' he asked no one in particular, as he searched his suit pockets. 'Damn, it must be in my studio.'

He turned to Denise. 'Do you mind if I disappear for five minutes and fetch it?'

'What're you waiting for? Run and get it. Quickly.'

Daniel ran through the gallery, past the dining table and skirted the huge Christmas tree.

'Hey, Daniel,' someone called.

'Can't stop. Something very important has come up,' he shouted, taking the stairs two at a time.

He pushed open his studio door and ran to his desk. Papers fell on the floor as he searched manically for his phone. He opened drawers, rummaged inside and slammed them shut again. He lifted paperwork, rifled through sketches and opened boxes of paints. He turned his head left and right, looking around the room helplessly. He had an idea. He dialled his own number from the landline on his desk. He could hear his mobile ringing. Damn, it was in his suit trousers after all. He must have missed it in the panic.

'Come on, Tess. Come on, Tess,' he chanted, as he tapped out her number.

'You have reached the Orange answer phone...'

'Fuck!'

Chapter Forty-Three

It had been the worst journey south Tess had ever experienced. Still wearing her party dress, she'd only taken the bare essentials from Rose Cottage before leaving. Her emotions were fragile, fuelled by impossible fantasies. She'd only been driving for ten minutes when she'd had to pull over. Her vision had glazed as if the windscreen had been smeared with Vaseline. Her tears weighed heavy, quivering on her eyelashes until they'd spilled down her cheeks. No amount of cheek wiping and sniffing had stopped them. Tess had pulled into a farm entrance where she'd fallen forwards onto the steering wheel, her whole body shuddering with uncontrollable sobs.

She could mend a broken pastry case and nurture a soufflé to dizzying heights. Why couldn't she sort her own life out? Why couldn't she see past the surface of a man's character? Perhaps she expected too much. Maybe she should buy that little teashop in Padstow and start again. Life would be simpler and free from heartbreak and deceitful men. But even that was impossible now. Her mother had informed her there was now a sold sign stuck to the agent's board.

The grey smudge of Nottingham with its pavements covered in a rash of gum could go to hell. And so could Blake and Daniel.

Tess had called her parents to say that she would be driving through the night and not to wait up. Naturally, hearing how upset she had sounded, they had re-stoked the fire and waited for her until the early hours of the morning. When Tess had arrived, she'd cried bitterly, explaining that a man had broken her heart.

At four in the morning, Tess lay on her bed in her parents' house listening to the relentless waves hushing up the beach. Rain tapped against her window like irritated fingers as she turned her pillow over in order to find a dry patch that hadn't been dampened by tears.

Exhaustion eventually lulled her tormented mind to sleep. She dreamed of her little cottage flooding, turning everything she valued into soggy flotsam. Her dream then moved to the beach at Watergate Bay, where she and Daniel were walking along the water's edge. A huge wave had knocked them off their feet, but when Tess had recovered and stood up, Daniel had disappeared.

As Tess slowly drifted back into consciousness, she experienced a few glorious sleep-dazed seconds, when her thoughts were filled with Daniel and the exhibition. Slowly, the sound of waves drifted into her senses and reality stung her. She opened her eyes, reliving the shock while staring at the ceiling.

Sunshine spilled in through a gap in the curtains and once again tears pricked at her swollen eyes. She flung herself on to her stomach and buried her face into her pillow, trying to erase the vision of another woman in Daniel's arms. It didn't help. The image still taunted her. She turned to look at the clock. It was nearly noon.

Tess plodded wearily to the bathroom, for once ignoring the view behind the curtains. She turned the thermostat up a little in the shower, peeled off her nightclothes and stepped under the spray. She stood still and let the hot water sting her body. Maybe a little physical pain would cancel out her emotional chaos. When Tess's body was lobster-pink, she wrapped herself in a comforting towel and perched on the edge of the toilet. As she sat there, she could hear voices in the kitchen below her and the sound of the cups chinking.

Her parents must have heard her get up and were making a pot of tea. She felt bad that she'd bought her anguish to her parents' peaceful house and decided to try hard to be strong for them today. She dried herself and dusted her body with her mother's freesia talcum powder. Back in her bedroom she pulled on some jeans and a warm polo neck sweater. Switching on her hair dryer, she blasted the dampness out of her hair and tied it back into a loose ponytail. Some rouge helped to brighten her pale face, but her eyes still looked sad and swollen.

Tess trudged downstairs, breathing deeply and forcing a smile for her parents before opening the kitchen door. Inside, her mother and father shifted guiltily at the table. Had they been talking about her?

'Morning, darling.' Her mother smiled.

'Hello, Tessie,' echoed her father.

'Morning. Is everything all right?'

'Everything will be fine, you'll see,' said her father, taking a sip from his mug.

Tess noticed a third mug and presumed it was for her. She reached to pick it up but it was lukewarm and half empty.

'Oh,' said Tess. 'Have you had a visitor?'

'I've had two cups,' said her father.

'A neighbour popped round,' said her mother at the same time. Flustered, Celia looked at her watch and then at her husband.

Her father clarified the situation. 'I've had two cups *and* Mrs Tulley popped round.'

Tess looked from one to the other of them. They were fidgeting uncomfortably. She hoped they weren't planning some neighbourly get together in order to cheer her up. That would be the last straw.

'How are you feeling this morning?' asked her mother.

'Numb, but okay, thanks.' Tess saw her mother look at her watch again.

'Are you going out, Mum? I'll keep you company. It'll keep my mind occupied.'

'No, darling, no plans.'

They really were acting very strangely this morning, thought Tess. She walked over to switch the kettle on. Perhaps she'd been selfish coming down here and spilling out her troubles. She'd upset their peaceful weekend and orderly routine.

Tess poured boiling water into her mug and dunked her tea bag up and down a few times before dropping it in the bin. She cradled her cup between her hands and sipped the hot liquid. She noticed her father whispering to her mother. Before she could ask them if they were expecting visitors, her father turned to her.

'Tess, would you pop upstairs to your bedroom window and tell me what you think of the new garden layout?'

'What. Now?'

'I really would appreciate your opinion.'

So that was it. They were going to keep her mind occupied with gardening. At least it was better than a neighbourly gathering.

'I will, Dad. Can I get some toast first?'

'If you could just pop up now, because I'm just off to the garden centre.'

I really have disturbed their peaceful existence here, thought Tess. She trudged back upstairs. They were acting so strangely. She walked towards her large bedroom window, pulled open the curtains and looked down into the garden. Strange. It didn't look any different. What did he mean by a new garden layout? The lawn, the line of white stones defining the boundary to next door, the washing line, the shed and the picket fence with the little gate. It all looked the same. Feeling confused, she glanced up to look out to sea for the first time that morning. It was blustery, but sunny. The beach was empty, except a few dog walkers and a handful of hardy surfers. She was looking forward to taking Padders for a walk on the beach later.

She spotted a dog bouncing over the waves. It looked just like Goya. Her heartache stabbed her again and tears threatened at the thought of Daniel's lovely dogs. They'd be with their mistress now. She pressed her nose against the cold glass. That's funny, she thought. That other dog looks like Gogh. Her breath misted the window, so she wiped the glass with her sleeve.

Her eyes focused on the middle of the beach. The two dogs had now stopped next to a man who was bending to pick something up. She screwed up her eyes to see clearer. No, the man wasn't picking something up. He was drawing in the sand with a stick and the brown dog was trying to take the stick off him. Tess surprised herself by smiling at the scene. The man was trying to complete a circle.

By now she was totally engrossed and opened the window to see without hazy glass obstructing her view. She could see now that it wasn't a circle; it was a heart. A giant heart. Her stomach lurched when she read the words written inside it.

Daniel loves Tess.

The man stood up and waved in her direction. She recognised the dark hair blowing around his handsome face.

How? When? She started to shake. Why was he here? What about Dee Dee? She waved back then dropped her hand quickly. She was mad at him. He'd lied. What should she do? She turned to her cupboard, turned to her handbag and turned back to the window. She didn't know whether to find a coat, find her shoes or cry. A scream of excitement escaped her mouth then she grabbed something from her handbag and ran downstairs. Her parents were standing arm in arm at the kitchen doorway, smiling indulgently.

'I knew you were up to something, I just knew it.' Tess laughed, pointing at them.

She ran to the front door, opened it and disappeared into the winter sunshine. Padders ran after her as her mother shouted, 'You haven't got any shoes on.'

Tess ran the length of the lawn, tore open the gate and sprinted down the steps onto the beach. She continued to run, slowing down as she got closer to Daniel. She stopped a short distance away from him, suddenly feeling wary. Why was he here?

'Hello.'

'Hello, Cinderella. You fled the ball.'

Tess looked at her bare feet and dug her toes into the cold damp sand.

'I missed you,' he said.

She spoke quietly. 'I went upstairs. I heard you tell Dee Dee that you loved her.'

'I do.'

Tess's head jerked upwards and looked into his eyes. She raised her voice. 'Then why are you here?'

'Because I'm *in love* with you.'

Tess frowned. 'I don't understand. I saw you both together. In each other's arms.'

'You saw me hugging my sister. You heard me talking to her on the phone.'

'Your sister? I didn't know you *had* a sister.'

'I've spoken of her often. My twin. I told you Den lived in London and was ill.'

Tess slowly raised her hands to her mouth in disbelief. 'Den is your sister? I thought Den was your twin brother.'

Daniel smiled and took a step closer to her. 'Sorry. She's always been called Den by family members, and friends call her Dee Dee. If you'd waited and listened to the rest of the phone call, I told her that I couldn't wait for her to meet you.'

Tess covered her face with her palms.

'I wish you'd waited and spoken to me first.' He took another step closer.

She lowered her hands. Her heart was racing. Her mind was spinning with this new information. They were now four steps apart.

'How is she?'

'She's doing great.'

'That's wonderful.'

'It is. It was a wonderful evening until you disappeared. I wanted to dance with you.' He took a step closer. 'Touch you.' Another step. 'Make love to you all night.'

Tess wondered how she was standing, how she was breathing.

'I love you,' he continued. 'Ever since the moment I saw you looking so vulnerable in The Royal Oak. I think about you when I wake up, throughout the day and last thing at night. I have a fantasy that one day, when you're ready, you'll live with me at The Rookery. We'll wake up every morning together, I'll open a permanent gallery and you'll run a teashop there. I know you've always wanted to bake... and I just want to make you happy.'

Tess felt dazed. She was standing on Harlyn Bay. The sun was shining. Three dogs were playing together and running around them in circles. Daniel was standing in front of her declaring his love and asking her to live with him.

'Tess? You're very quiet. I'm not frightening you away, am I?'

Tess made a noise that was half laugh and half sob. 'I love you too, and I don't think I've ever felt this happy in all my life.'

With one last step, he wrapped one arm around her waist and kissed her. Tess felt his warm lips cover hers as she pulled him closer. They clung to each other, their bodies pressed tightly together. He tasted of sea salt and coffee. His jumper was soft, his body was hard and he smelt of fresh air. She could hear his breath, fast and urgent as they stood on the tip of the heart drawn in the sand. Eventually, they slowly pulled apart.

'I feel so stupid. I'm sorry,' said Tess.

'It was just a misunderstanding. I wouldn't have met your lovely parents or got to see where you grew up, if I hadn't followed you.'

'I suppose. Oh, I've got something for you.' Tess pulled a silver and blue package from her waistband. She handed it to Daniel. 'Happy birthday, for yesterday.'

Daniel unwrapped his gift and smiled when he saw the little carved wooden ark. 'Thank you, Noah. It's perfect.'

A froth of bubbles and cold water trickled over her toes and Daniel's shoes as the tide came in.

'What is it with us and floods?' said Daniel, lifting her into his arms.

Thank You

Dear Readers

Thank you for choosing to read *You've Got My Number* out of the numerous wonderful books currently on the market today. I loved creating all my characters but Tess and Daniel were my first couple, so they're very special to me. I'm still in love with Daniel and miss visiting The Rookery!

If you loved *You've Got My Number* and have a minute to spare, I would be so grateful for a short review on the page or site where you bought my book. Your help in spreading the word is hugely appreciated. Reviews from readers like you are invaluable and make a huge difference in raising a book's profile. It makes authors very happy to see that you've enjoyed their books.

Thank you
Love Angela x

About the Author

Angela Barton was born in London and grew up in Nottingham. She has three wonderful children who are now grown up but still live close by. Angela's Springer spaniel lived a long, happy life and is remembered on the cover of *You've Got My Number*. Passionate about writing both contemporary and historical fiction, Angela has won and also been shortlisted for several writing competitions. She reads avidly, makes jewellery and embroidered pictures, always with a cup of tea to hand.

Angela is a member of the Romantic Novelists' Association and Nottingham Writers' Studio.

For more on Angela visit:
www.angelabarton.net
www.twitter.com/angebarton
www.facebook.com/angela.bartonauthor

More Choc Lit

From Angela Barton

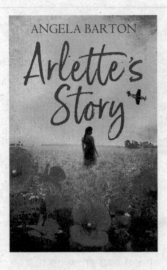

Arlette's Story

One woman's struggle to fight back against the enemy in order to protect the ones she loves.

When Arlette Blaise sees a German plane fly over the family farm in 1940, she's comforted by the fact that the occupying forces are far away in the north of the country. Surely the war will not reach her family in the idyllic French countryside near to the small town of Oradour-sur-Glane?

But then Saul Epstein, a young Jewish man driven from his home by the Nazis, arrives at the farm and Arlette begins to realise that her peaceful existence might be gone for good …

Visit www.rubyfiction.com for details.

ANGELA BARTON

Magnolia House

When you open up your home and your heart …

Rowan Forrester has it all – the happy marriage, the adorable dog, the good friends, the promising business and even the dream home after she and her husband Tom win a stunning but slightly dilapidated Georgian townhouse in London at auction.

But in the blink of an eye, Rowan's picture-perfect life comes crashing down around her and she is faced with the prospect of having to start again.

To make ends meet she begins a search for housemates, and in doing so opens the door to new friends and new beginnings. But could she be opening the door to new heartbreak too?

Visit www.choc-lit.com for details.

More from Choc Lit

Why not try something else from the Choc Lit selection?

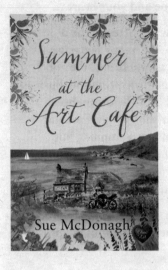

Summer at the Art Café
Sue McDonagh

From watercolours and cupcakes to leather jackets and freedom …

If you won a gorgeous purple motorbike, and your domineering husband said you were too fat for leathers and should sell it, would you do as you were told – or learn to ride it in secret?

Artist and café owner Lucy Daumier intends to do just that – but learning to ride is far from easy, especially under the critical eye of prickly motorcycle instructor, Ash Connor.

But gradually she gets the hang of it, and in the process re-discovers the girl she used to be. So starts an exciting summer of new friendship and fun – as well as a realisation that there is more to Ash than meets the eye when she is introduced to his seven-year-old daughter, Daisy.

But can Lucy's new-found happiness last when a spiteful family member wants to see her fail?

Visit www.choc-lit.com for details.

One Summer in Little Penhaven

Angela Britnell

**Could one summer
change your life?**

When high-flying American
lawyer Samantha Muir finds
out she's lost her partnership
whilst on an assignment in
London, she has a dramatic
reaction.

Rather than returning home,
she resigns, leaves her business suits behind and jumps on
the first train to Cornwall at the encouragement of a friendly
stranger.

The village of Little Penhaven, where Samantha eventually
ends up, is a world away from her life in Knoxville,
Tennessee – and local farmer Cadan Day is certainly a
world away from any man she has met before. But could
the Cornish village and Cadan play a part in Samantha's
summer of self-discovery?

Visit www.choc-lit.com for details.

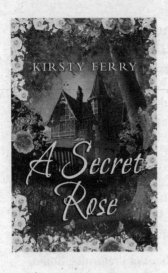

A Secret Rose

Kirsty Ferry

Book 1 in the Cornish Secrets series

"Wherever you go, I will follow ..."

Merryn Burton is excited to travel down to Cornwall to start her first big job for the London art dealers she works for. But as soon as she arrives at Pencradoc, a beautiful old mansion, she realises this will be no ordinary commission.

Not only is Pencradoc filled with fascinating, and possibly valuable artwork, it is also owned by the Penhaligon brothers – and Merryn's instant connection with Kit Penhaligon could be another reason why her trip suddenly becomes a whole lot more interesting.

But the longer Merryn stays at Pencradoc the more obvious it is that the house has a secret, and a long-forgotten Rose might just hold the key ...

Visit www.choc-lit.com for details.

Just a Boy Friend
Lucy Keeling

Book 1 – Friends

What do mascara wands and gardening shears have in common?

Absolutely nothing! At least that's what wannabe beauty influencer Sophie Timney thinks when her friend Polly suggests involving her brother Marcus in Sophie's make-up tutorials. She needs more views, Marcus needs promotion for his gardening business – in Polly's mind joining forces will help them both. Sophie isn't so sure.

Because Marcus Bowman has a habit of getting under her skin in a way that no exfoliating face scrub ever could. But, as the views and comments on her videos begin creeping up, it becomes increasingly obvious that Sophie's subscribers like Marcus, and what's even worse is that Sophie might be starting to feel the same way …

Visit www.choc-lit.com for details.

Introducing Choc Lit

We're an independent publisher creating
a delicious selection of fiction.
Where heroes are like chocolate – irresistible!
Quality stories with a romance at the heart.

See our selection here:
www.choc-lit.com

We'd love to hear how you enjoyed *You've Got My Number*.
Please visit **www.choc-lit.com** and give your feedback
or leave a review where you purchased this novel.

Choc Lit novels are selected by genuine readers like yourself.
We only publish stories our Choc Lit Tasting Panel want to
see in print. Our reviews and awards speak for themselves.

Could you be a Star Selector and join our Tasting Panel?
Would you like to play a role in choosing which novels
we decide to publish? Do you enjoy reading women's
fiction? Then you could be perfect for our Tasting Panel.

Visit here for more details…
www.choc-lit.com/join-the-choc-lit-tasting-panel

Keep in touch:
Sign up for our monthly newsletter Spread for all the latest
news and offers: www.spread.choc-lit.com. Follow us
on Twitter: @ChocLituk and Facebook: Choc Lit.

Where heroes are like chocolate – irresistible!